THE LAST OF THE WHAMPOA BREED

. . .

Modern Chinese Literature from Taiwan

Modern Chinese Literature from Taiwan

Wang Chen-ho, *Rose, Rose, I Love You*

Cheng Ch'ing-wen, *Three-Legged Horse*

Chu T'ien-wen, *Notes of a Desolate Man*

Hsiao Li-hung, *A Thousand Moons on a Thousand Rivers*

Chang Ta-chun, *Wild Kids: Two Novels About Growing Up*

Michelle Yeh and N.G.D. Malmqvist, editors,
Frontier Taiwan: An Anthology of Modern Chinese Poetry

Li Qiao, *Wintry Night*

Huang Chun-ming, *The Taste of Apples*

Chang Hsi-kuo, *The City Trilogy: Five Jade Disks,*
Defenders of the Dragon City, Tale of a Feather

Li Yung-p'ing, *Retribution: The Jiling Chronicles*

THE LAST OF THE WHAMPOA BREED

Stories of the Chinese Diaspora

Edited by PANG-YUAN CHI

and DAVID DER-WEI WANG

COLUMBIA UNIVERSITY PRESS *New York*

Columbia University Press wishes to express its appreciation for assistance given by the Chiang Ching-kuo Foundation for International Scholarly Exchange and Council for Cultural Affairs in the preparation of the translation and in the publication of this series.

COLUMBIA UNIVERSITY PRESS
Publishers Since 1893
New York Chichester, West Sussex

Library of Congress Cataloging-in-Publication Data
The Last of the Whampoa breed / Edited by Pang-yuan Chi and David Der-wei Wang
p. cm.
ISBN 0–231–13002–3
1. Chinese literature—Taiwan—20th century. I. Qi, Bangyuan. II. Wang, Dewei. III. Series.
PL3031.T32L29 2003
895.1'080951249—dc21 2003046165

Columbia University Press books are printed on permanent and durable acid-free paper.

Printed in the United States of America

c 10 9 8 7 6 5 4 3 2 1

Contents

. . .

Foreword

. . .

IN THE YEAR 1924 WHEN THE NEW REPUBLIC WAS still in a chaotic state and warlords were fighting one another for power, Dr. Sun Yat-sen established the Whampoa Military Academy near Canton to train officers with a modern concept of honor and loyalty to a unified China. Its early graduates did become the backbone of resistance against the Japanese during World War II. The "Whampoa Spirit" became synonymous with unrelenting prowess and the promise of protection that the new nation greatly needed.

The scene, however, changed at the end of the bloody Sino-Japanese War that lasted for eight years. Exhausted and homesick, the soldiers found themselves facing an even more formidable foe at home—the Communist insurgents from within. In 1949, without enough warning, the vast motherland they had defended so valiantly was snatched from beneath their feet. Many were exiled and had to live the rest of their lives in Taiwan, an island $^{1}/_{350}$th the size of the mainland. For 40 years, communications between Taiwan and mainland China were entirely cut off by the 160-mile-wide Taiwan Strait.

When the defection of some generals to the Communists was made public after 1988, the "Whampoa Spirit" became a source of jokes, of betrayal, surrender, and shame. In less than thirty years, the once popular anthem of the Whampoa Academy dissolved into obscurity.

With the arrival of more than a million soldiers and their dependents, the government built about 800 military compounds all over Taiwan. (The population of Taiwan was about five million then; currently it is 22 million.) The ones that had families were allotted housing in these compounds according to their military rank. Each compound evolved into an independent community. The children there grew up listening to stories of the good old days in mainland China. Some of the more talented, starting in the 1970s, have written down their unique childhood and coming-of-age stories. Included here are mainly their stories of exile in Taiwan. The only exceptions are the "uncle" in "The Last of the Whampoa Breed," who was left behind on the mainland after his general's defection to the Communists, and the 131 soldiers who starved to death on a tiny isle called the Cove of the Loving Mother.

"Faces, Bronze Faces" as the prologue presents a most vivid portrayal of these he-men, aged and fading away after long years of waiting, longing, and disillusionment. From the sadly ineffectual, even comic attempts to "recapture the mainland" as narrated in "I Wanted to Go to War" to the real return in "1,230 Spots," forty years have passed, and nothing is the same. Many veterans no longer have homes to return to, and many return to find their homes as the young wives they left behind—aged and coarsened beyond recognition. The sharp contrast between the *homeland remembered* and the *homeland in reality* shatters their lifelong dreams. As a result, many "return" to Taiwan. Some died earlier; the old soldier in "Tale of Two Strangers" asks to have one half of his ashes sent back to the land of his dreams, and the other half scattered over the island that has sheltered him for forty years.

Some, like Old Man Yang and the painter in "The Valley of Hesitation," have formed new attachments, settled down, and made peace with life in Taiwan. Their second generation, after some adjustments, has also managed to find a place in the native island world, such as the boys in "The Vanishing Ball" and the girls in "In Remembrance of My Buddies from the Military Compound."

All of a sudden, in 1988, the ban on travel to the mainland was lifted. People in Taiwan were permitted to visit. This was followed by an avalanche of essays and stories depicting gut-wrenching, bittersweet reunions. The quantity was comparable to the literary output of nostalgia in the 1950s. We have here, in this collection, two stories ("My Relatives in Hong Kong" and "Spring Hope") written a little before that time, when families could only meet in Hong Kong. They were chosen because they are genuine in feelings and natural as a link between the separation and subsequent reunion.

These stories are worth telling to a western audience because there is nothing like this in North American and European experiences. These soldiers were not moved around and stationed at regular military bases, they were severed from a traditional past and burdened with unfulfilled promises and uncertain futures. Many of them were doomed to live and die homeless and loveless. Yet, manifested in the life stories of many is a magnanimous and natural dignity, a voiceless, noble pride that has transcended prolonged mental suffering. These feelings make us believe, as the stalwarts on the general's staff in "State Funeral" do, that we shall not let history be burned to mere ashes.

Pang-yuan Chi

Acknowledgments

. . .

"Faces, Bronze Faces" was published in Sun Wei-mang's *Youyu yu kuangre* (Melancholy and fanaticism) (Taipei: Sanmin Bookstore, 1992).

"Shore to Shore" appears in a collection by that name by Pin-zai Sang (Taipei: Elite Publishing Company, 2001).

"I Wanted to Go to War" also appears in the collection *Shore to Shore* by Pin-zai Sang (Taipei: Elite Publishing Company, 2001).

"The Stone Tablet at the Cove of the Loving Mother" was published in the Literary Supplement of the *Independent Evening Post*, March 30, 1993.

"Old Man Yang and His Woman" was first published in *I Want to Be a King* (Taipei: Unitas, 1993).

"1,230 Spots" was published in the Literary Supplement of the *United Daily News*, Taipei, April 14–15, 1996.

"Valley of Hesitation" was published in the Literary Supplement of the *United Daily News*, Taipei, August 9–11, 1995.

"State Funeral" is from Bai Xianyong's *Taipei People*, edited by George Kao (Hong Kong: Hong Kong Chinese University, 1999).

"Tale of Two Strangers" won first prize in the 15th China Times Daily Literary Contest. It is included in the collection of prize-winning works, *Tale of Two Strangers*, edited by Yang Tse (Taipei: China Times Daily Publishing Company, 1992), pp. 38–62.

"The Last of the Whampoa Breed" was published in Dai Wencai's *Tiancai shu* (The book of geniuses) (Taipei: Chiuko Publishing, 1994).

"My Relatives in Hong Kong" was published in the Literary Supplement of the *United Daily News*, Taipei, June 6–15, 1986.

"Spring Hope" was published in *The Last Night Train* (Taipei: Hong-fan Publishing Company, 1986).

"The Vanishing Ball" won first prize in the Best Stories Contest held by *Central Daily News*, Taipei, January 1992.

"In Remembrance of My Buddies from the Military Compound" was published in *In Remembrance of My Buddies from the Military Compound* (Taipei: Ryefield Publishing Company, 1992).

Timeline

. . .

1924	Founding of the Whampoa Military Academy near Canton by Chiang Kai-shek (1887–1975).
1937–1945	The Second Sino-Japanese War.
1946–1949	Civil war between the Chinese Nationalist Government and the Communist revolutionaries.
1949	The Chinese Communist forces, headed by Mao Zedong (1893–1976), defeat the Nationalist government army and take over mainland China. The Nationalist government retreats to Taiwan, followed by more than a million soldiers and civilians.
1950	Chiang Kai-shek is elected President of the Republic of China in Taiwan.
1950–1953	The Korean War.
1958	Chinese Communist forces launch a massive attack on Kinmen Island, a Nationalist base in the Taiwan Strait; the battle lasts for forty-four days and ends with a cease-fire.
1966	The Great Cultural Revolution begins in mainland China.
1972	United States President Richard Nixon visits China.

1975	Chiang Kai-shek dies in Taiwan. Chiang's son Chiang Ching-kuo (1910–1988) is later elected president.
1976	Mao Zedong dies; the Great Cultural Revolution ends in mainland China.
1979	The U.S. government establishes formal diplomatic ties with China.
1987	Taiwan lifts martial law.
1988	Chiang Ching-ko dies. Taiwan residents are allowed to visit their families on the mainland for the first time in forty years.
1989	On the mainland, after a period of greater freedom of expression, the government cracks down: student protesters are gunned down during the Tiananmen Square Incident (June Fourth Incident).
1997	Great Britain returns Hong Kong to China.
1999	Taiwan's opposition Democratic Progressive Party wins the presidential election.

THE LAST OF THE

WHAMPOA BREED

. . .

*Prologue: Faces, Bronze Faces**

. . .

by SUN Wei-mang

translated by Nicholas KOSS

You have probably noticed those he-men who shout "Steamed rolls! Dumplings!" through the back lanes. Those who drive taxis late at night. Those who have opened a noodle stand by the side of the road. Those who have orchards in the mountains. Everywhere, in every city and town, their bronze faces appear, spouting southern drawls or northern twangs. To your father and his generation, because they too have gone through the loss of home and the ravages of war, these men are as common as sunrise or sunset. But to you who were born and raised in Taiwan, these men are like old volumes calling to be opened and read.

If you consider a meeting with them just a matter of chance, or contact with them simply ordinary business, these bronze faces will float by quietly like logs in the river. But if you have an innocent curiosity about what has happened in our stormy past, and if your young eyes want to look back on the dusty roads traveled, you will like these men. After you've joked around and become friendly with the man selling steamed rolls on the corner, he'll stop his bike by your door and tell you about his baptism of

*From Sun Wei-mang's collection of essays, *Melancholia and Ecstasy* (Youyu yu kangjo) (Taipei: Sanmin Bookstore, 1992).

fire on the battlefield. When late at night you get into a taxi to go home to Muzha, you can tell from the erect posture of the driver beside you that this man once wore a military uniform. He will tell you about the Battle of Guningtou that saved Taiwan from the Communists.[1] In the midst of your talk, you will seem to see ferocious armies go to smoke, and ashes scatter. When you go hiking along the Cross Island Highway, the men living by the orchards will recount to you stories about battle trenches filled with bodies. With your various experiences of the battlefield from the movies, at the moment the veins tighten on the faces of those men as they spit out their words, your imagination will carry you back in the flow of time to that begonia leaf–shaped mass of land called China. Bullets will whistle past your ears and cannons flash before you. Looking up, you will see waves of men rushing past. It will be just like the Han dynasty poem: "smoke of beacons slant on the plains; lean horses neighing in empty moats." And you will be taking it all in, looking at everything around you. You will be like Chunyu Fen from the Tang dynasty, who dreamed of the loss of love and power.[2]

Those men are an old bronze mirror on the past. You are outside the mirror and want to extend your hand to touch what is within, but you are unable to reach any of the thousands of things there. Maybe it is all fabrication, but you have seen the flow of kaleidoscopic events in the mirror as it passes by. Time greedily swallows all, but from recollection, from search through memory, these men, as if snatching fish from the mouths of cats, can recov-

[1] The Battle of Kuningtou was fought in October 1949. The National Army had won a great victory over the Communist invaders. Guningtou is a fortress on Jinmen Island shielding Taiwan.

[2] Chunyu Fen is the main character in "Prefect of South Bough" (Nanke Taishou zhuan) by Li Kung-tso (770–848).

er the past. Serious tomes of history and catchall records cannot contain the lived experiences of these men.

If you carefully size up these he-men, you will discover the wheel marks of time on their bodies. Often you will see the stark contrast of their bronze skin with your own soft skin that has not been through the biting rigors of cold and snow. The furrows on their faces are not the wrinkles brought on by old age but the scratches etched by years of sweat. Each line and each wrinkle marks one of the vicissitudes in their lives. Running through the fires of the battlefield was for them a marvelous combination of bitterness and honor. But they do not depend on the return of their memories to live. Their sturdy shoulders carry the burdens of today's life. Compared with their ragged, hungry wanderings of the past, their present simplicity in food and drink is of no concern to them. They cannot understand the desire of the new generation for fancy clothes and fine food or the shivering of this generation on a winter day in Taiwan's subtropical weather. Their local accents have been eroded by Mandarin Chinese and no longer have the distinctive sounds of their home provinces. Nevertheless, you can still catch the flavor of a dialect in a word oddly pronounced, a special cadence in their speech, or an occasional regional slang term.

When you young people meet these he-men, listen. Listen carefully. You may want to be receptive to the waves they send out, and be responsive, be generous in compassion while sharing their sorrow and happiness. You too will want to enter their stirring and tense, flesh-and-blood former lives. You will come away with only admiration and respect. Is yours a generation that has only listened to stories and has only watched? Probably you will start to see your own inadequacy.

These bronze faces will continue to pass in and out of your life. And so, you might still enjoy reading something about them.

Shore to Shore

. . .

by SANG Pin-zai

translated by Michelle WU

Outside the Keelung Cultural Center there is a grassy hill. The hill descends into a narrow strip of harbor. Instead of boats, the harbor is full of giant logs, half immersed in the sea. Periodically, trucks come and load up with the logs, and then new logs are lowered into the water. When the logs reach a certain number, it is possible to walk on them across to the shore on the other side. There lies an empty lot that leads to the post office.

Benches have been placed on the grassy slopes so passersby can rest their tired feet. Because of the slope's incline, all the benches slant forward, and people sitting on them have to bend forward a bit, too. The benches resemble third-class seats on trains. They have backs and can accommodate three adults if they all squeeze a little. The benches, however, are not made from wood; they are made from cement.

In 1950, from May 20 to the beginning of July, I slept on those cement benches every night.

At that time, the Keelung Cultural Center wasn't a cultural center yet. It was called the Chiang Kai-shek Hall. It is the same building, though.

On May 18, 1950, late at night, a navy ship left Zhoushan's Olive Harbor. It was filled with Nationalist soldiers retreating to

Taiwan. I was on the ship, not as a soldier but as a stowaway. I was only eleven years old.

I was on the ship because of my sister.

My sister was nineteen years old then, and everyone commented on her beauty. A whole company of soldiers was staying at our house at the time. A company commander who was in his twenties had spotted our house and decided to station his troops there. When he gave the order, he was sitting astride a brown horse. The wide leather belt around his bulging belly was the same color as his horse. A handgun was attached to his right side, and the holster was also brown. Two tassels hung from the holster and jostled together in the wind. Two soldiers stood by the horse. The one in front was in charge of taking care of the horse, and the other was the messenger; of course, I didn't know this at the time.

In front of our house stood a very big water basin that was used to collect rainwater from the eaves. I hid behind it, poking my head out. I watched him ordering his soldiers to do this and that. I couldn't understand his words, so I had no idea that he wanted our house.

There were seven or eight men in his company. Some were soldiers and some were officers. The officers stayed in rooms and the soldiers slept on the floor in the hallway. The company commander demanded a room for himself. He chose the room that my brother and I shared. My brother was away at school in the city, so it was really my room. Since he wanted my room, I moved in with my sister, and my mother set up an extra cot for me.

There were eight of us in all: my grandma, my parents, my elder sister, my elder brother, and two younger sisters. My father was away at sea fishing most of the time. Even when he came home, it was to unload fish. He would stay for two or three days at the most, and head off to sea again. Grandma was a strict vegetarian, and would chant Buddhist mantras in her room all morning. She rarely left her room. So Mother ran the household.

We had never seen soldiers before, and no one knew for sure how much power a company commander actually wielded. Nevertheless, he was the highest-ranking military officer around, because the soldiers in the village were all under his command, and he was saluted wherever he went.

Our village had a strange name: Siqian Village. There were some thirty families, and all made a living fishing. Since our grandfather's time, our family was considered to be quite influential, because we had four fishing boats—two big ones and two small ones. The big boats fished, and the two small boats netted jellyfish. Several families had depended on us for their livelihood for several generations.

Commander Xiao seemed to enjoy horseback riding. He rode his horse everywhere, even short distances that we kids could run, stopping for breath only twice. The country roads were narrow, and horses could go no faster than goats. But he didn't seem to mind. He rode all over the place, exploring everywhere. He had a whip that resembled a little snake. He flung it about from left to right all the time, even when he wasn't on horseback. I saw him whip a soldier once. The soldier had done something that displeased him. He was standing before him, and with a lash of his whip, a red welt rose on the soldier's cheek. Later, though he always smiled when he spoke to us, I would steer clear of him because of the whip in his hand.

He never did hit civilians, and he was actually quite courteous to members of my family. He even addressed my grandma as "Mom" in our local dialect, and ordered the soldiers to keep quiet when Grandma was chanting Buddhist mantras. But we were still afraid of him. Grandma smiled at him when they met in the hallway and called him Commander Xiao. Her smile would immediately disappear, however, once his back was turned. I knew that she did not like the soldiers at all.

When the soldiers were not around, she told us again and again not to talk to them. Her words were especially meant for Elder Sister. She was already engaged to the son of a factory owner in Shanghai. Grandma was in charge of the arrangements. With a group of men unrelated to us hanging around the house—what rumors might get started!

The retreat from Zhoushan was a secret military maneuver. It was said that even the soldiers were kept in the dark. Three or four days earlier the company of men had left. On May 17, at dinnertime, Commander Xiao suddenly appeared on horseback.

He was alone. Grandma was away at Auntie's. Father was at sea, and Mother was the only adult at home. Since the commander had lived with us for a month, Mother invited him to come in.

After exchanging pleasantries, he told us that the troops stationed in Zhoushan were about to retreat secretly to Taiwan. He wasn't confiding in us; he was telling us this because he wanted my sister to go with him.

I have no idea what my mother's feelings toward Commander Xiao were, but she must have liked him. More importantly, my mother was not happy with my sister's marital arrangements. She wasn't happy because my sister wasn't happy. At my sister's age, it was understandable that she would feel an aversion to prearranged marriages. So Commander Xiao's proposal touched a chord in my mother's heart.

After dinner, my mother consented to his proposal. But under one condition—they had to take me with them.

My mother had not received any schooling, and she seldom decided important matters at home. But she actually made this momentous decision on her own. In the fifty years to follow, I had a hard time figuring out what she'd been thinking and what gave her that kind of courage. But because of her boldness, my life took a drastic turn!

Commander Xiao gladly agreed and told us to get ready, saying that he would come for us in a while.

After he left, Mother put down her bowl and chopsticks and summoned my sister and me into her room. By the lamp on her dresser were two stacks of silver dollars and some gold rings. She rolled out a piece of sturdy cloth, measured it, and sewed it into a sack for the silver dollars and rings.

As she sewed, tears streamed down her cheeks. She wiped them with the back of her hand and did not say anything to us for a long time. We stood before her, and Elder Sister was sobbing as well. I didn't feel like crying; I was actually feeling quite happy.

Mother finally opened her mouth. She spoke to Elder Sister, asking her to take good care of me. Stammering, she said Commander Xiao was not a bad person, and that it was an achievement for him to have been appointed commander at such a young age.

Her hands did not stop even while she was talking. The sack was ready in no time. She put the silver dollars in one by one. I counted fifty-four in all. I knew paper money was practically worthless. Only silver dollars and gold were accepted. If the fishing was good, Father's two boats were able to earn a dozen silver dollars after two or three months at sea. Mother had hidden the coins from us. Those fifty-four silver dollars must have taken them years to save.

With the sack tightly sewn, she weighed it in her hands. Still not satisfied, she opened the drawer, took out a piece of flowered cloth, and wrapped the sack several times, finally stitching the bundle securely with thick, strong thread. She lifted her head and looked straight at me. My sister gave me a tap on my shoulder, and I moved toward Mother.

"Boys' ambitions should extend to all corners of the world," she said. This was a much quoted line in opera performances.

She beckoned me to move closer.

"When you get to Taiwan, be obedient to your sister, and to Commander Xiao. Don't be afraid of hardship. Come back when you can. Will you remember my words?"

I nodded. Mother kept looking at me. Suddenly she leaned against me, placed her head on my shoulder, and burst out crying. I panicked, not knowing what to do. I just stood there, not knowing whether or not I was supposed to cry.

In a while, two soldiers came to fetch us. They were both familiar faces.

Mother had already packed two bags for us. The big one was for Elder Sister and the small one was for me. My two younger sisters, three and six years old, stood at the door watching us leave. My youngest sister stood by the water basin crying, "I want to go, too!"

"I am going to Taiwan. It is too far for you. Dragon Boat Festival is almost here; I will buy you a big rice dumpling wrapped in bamboo leaves when I get back." Dragon Boat Festival was a month away, and I sincerely believed that I would return within a month's time.

The soldiers told us to hurry, because the troops waited for no one. Mother told my younger sisters to go in. The doors were shut, and we were on our way.

The moon had just risen in the sky, and it was very dark. Mother walked between my sister and me. She kept hold of my hand. Her hand was shaking so much that mine almost slipped out of her grasp. She kept turning to look at me, using her other hand to tidy my hair. Her tears never stopped.

"Be obedient to your sister, and to Commander Xiao. Be ambitious. . . ." She kept mumbling these words.

As we left our village, the soldiers ordered her to turn back. She pretended not to hear and walked a bit farther. When we reached a steep slope, the soldiers became impatient. They stood at the top of the hill scolding us. Mother stopped and let go of my hand.

"Mom, go home, we will be back soon anyway," I consoled her.

The soldiers wouldn't let us speak. They slapped our backs and pushed us on like prisoners. We weren't even allowed to turn around.

"Come home soon!"

"Be obedient!"

In the night sky, Mother's voice became fainter as the distance grew. I quietly turned around once but could no longer see her.

Commander Xiao had to command his company, so he merely looked at us, told us to follow the troops, and left without saying anything else. The troops took off soon. We were the responsibility of the two soldiers who accompanied us, and they stayed with us all the time.

We followed the troops. Olive Harbor was in Olive County, a place I had never heard of before. We walked on and on for what seemed like forever. I got sleepier and sleepier. My feet never stopped moving, but my head fell asleep. If Elder Sister hadn't held my hand, I would have fallen over and never wanted to get up again.

I have no idea when we arrived. It had to have been sometime after midnight. The troops had received orders to rest by the side of the road. I fell asleep on Elder Sister.

The sun woke me. I saw the harbor before me, and five or six navy ships docked at sea. More troops arrived and looked for places to sit down. A cavalry troop arrived with more than a hundred horses. Some soldiers were on horseback and some were walking. They couldn't find a place to settle in, and there was bickering.

It was close to noon, and we had not yet boarded the ship. The harbor was jam-packed with people, and the troops that arrived later had to find a spot farther away from the harbor. There seemed to be no end to them.

We did not have any breakfast. At noon, food was passed out, and we were given some.

To the right of us someone suddenly stood up and started talking excitedly. I stood up, too. I thought the general or magistrate must have arrived, but I couldn't see anything.

"They are going to kill the horses!" said a soldier beside us.

"Why kill the horses?" I asked.

"Because we can't take them with us. Can't leave them for the Commies, can we?" I knew "Commies" referred to the Communists.

I remembered Commander Xiao's horse. Were they going to kill it, too? I ran toward him, but before I got to him, I saw a soldier lead the horse toward the beach, where countless horses had already been gathered. Wooden stakes were nailed into the ground, and the horses were tied to the stakes to prevent them from running away.

Later, a dozen soldiers arrived with machine guns. Five machine guns were lined up in a row. At the order of an officer, shots were fired. The horses whinnied and fell. In a few minutes, no horses were left standing. Rivers of blood ran into the ocean, dyeing it red.

I was stunned. Elder Sister pulled me back, scolded me, and told me that we should get ready to board.

I had never boarded a large ship. It was the first time I had seen so many people aboard any vessel, all of them soldiers. We were directed to a corner in a large cabin (I later learned it was called the “tank cabin”). I was a little scared, and I sat close to my sister. She seemed to be scared, too. She never let go of my hand.

In a while, the commander came over to us with a smile on his face. “Everything is set now; for a while I was quite worried.”

“Worried about what?” my sister asked.

“Too many civilians. I was told that civilians might not be allowed on board.”

“And then what happened?”

“I don’t know for sure. Could have just been rumors. Now that you’re on board, everything should be fine.” He chatted with us for a while and then left when someone called him.

The troops came on board, and before long, the tank cabin was full. I looked out and discovered that the decks were full of people, too. Most had guns in their hands and square backpacks on their backs. While everyone was standing still it was okay, but if they started moving they would bump into each other. The weather was hot, and everyone was sweating. The impatient ones started to curse and swear, causing a commotion.

Hours had gone by, and the ship still hadn’t moved. I slept for a while, leaning against my sister. I woke up in a sweat and discovered that my sister had fallen asleep, too.

I snuck out onto the deck. The deck had been separated into different compartments, with boxes of ammunition and pots of food to divide them. I saw a lot of women among the troops as well as some strong men bound by rope. They were not in uniform. They’d been abducted to serve in the military.

Suddenly, some of them got loose and tried to run away. There was great commotion, and soldiers with guns were set upon them, swearing all the while.

Some of the men jumped into the sea. The soldiers did not jump into the sea to pursue them. They merely fired into the water. Some men were hit, but they continued to swim. Some died from exhaustion. But some did manage to escape.

This happened many times, sometimes at the stem of the ship, sometimes at the stern. Some of the men were shot with rifles, some with submachine guns, and some with machine guns. The corpses tossed in the waves like dead cats or dogs, trailing a pool of blood beside them.

Days before the troops started to retreat from Zhoushan, men and boys had been abducted. Some were abducted on the road and some from their homes. My cousin next door was getting married when soldiers stopped the marriage procession and abducted the groom as well as the four men who were carrying the bride's sedan chair. The poor bride was left there in despair. I also heard that returning fishermen were abducted on their way home. They were right beside wheat fields, and the wheat was taller than they were, so they ducked in, trying to escape. The soldiers fired on them. None was captured because they were all shot dead.

Suddenly a hand grabbed me from behind. It was my sister.

"Why have you run off on you own?!" She was very angry as she pulled me into the cabin. "Something's gone wrong!"

"What?"

She didn't answer. We were already inside. Two officers stood beside Commander Xiao; both were higher in rank. They had a blue file and were writing something in it with fountain pens. Both wore poker-face expressions and looked very impatient.

Commander Xiao kept smiling. He was pleading for something. I gradually made sense of what he was saying, and my insides twisted into a knot—they were ordering my sister off the ship.

"Orders from above. We're just following orders. We can't help you even if we want to," an officer said.

I looked back. A long line of women had already formed behind the two officers. They were about the same age as my sister. They all looked pale, and some were crying.

"There are troops on the docks who cannot get aboard because the ship is full already. General Shih is very upset. He has ordered that, apart from military dependents, all women must leave!" the other officer said.

Commander Xiao was only a low-ranking officer. He couldn't disobey and had no choice but to consent.

My sister and I stood six feet away from them. My sister kept her head bent, and her hand in mine was icy cold.

If she couldn't stay on board, then I wouldn't be able to either. I was so disappointed. An officer came toward us and asked her for her name. She responded honestly. He was just about to leave when my sister said suddenly, "Can my brother stay? He is a boy. The superior officer just said that women cannot stay on board, but he is a boy!"

Her words took both officers and Commander Xiao by surprise; I was stunned.

My sister turned to remove her bundle and took out the little sack. She asked the two officers to go to a corner with her, and all three of them stood with their backs to the crowd. I saw her gesturing, but I couldn't hear what she was saying. In a while, the three of them returned, and the two officers were smiling.

"Okay, little boy, you can go to Taiwan," one of them said, and they went off to round up other women.

As they left, my sister cried. She took my hand and led me to Commander Xiao. As she sobbed, she said, "Please take good care of my brother. If he is disobedient, you can scold him or hit him, but please don't let him let him go astray."

Commander Xiao had a smile on his face, but he did not look pleased at all. My sister said lots of things to him, and he finally nodded.

"Hurry and thank Commander Xiao," my sister said, patting me on the back. She continued, "From now on, you are alone in the world, and Commander Xiao will be like family to you. If you're not good, if you are disobedient to Commander Xiao, we will be very upset at home, okay?"

I nodded my head in confusion. Actually, after all the dramatic twists and turns I was no longer interested in going to Taiwan. If my sister wanted me to go home with her, I would be happy to oblige. But she was determined that I go to Taiwan with Commander Xiao, and she didn't seem to care whether or not she made the trip herself.

The women who had to leave were clustered in a group. Several soldiers armed with rifles were standing guard over them. They ordered my sister to join them. My sister said yes, but hurriedly pulled me aside to where we had been sitting. She unfastened her bundle and removed the sack with the silver dollars. She quickly stuffed it into my bundle.

She removed two gold earrings from her ears. They were given to her by her fiancé as an engagement present. She stuffed them in, too. She refastened my bundle, weighed it in her hands, and gave it back to me.

"Little brother, I will be leaving you. When you get to Taiwan, remember to write home often. And remember to be good and obedient."

She hugged me, and I felt something itchy on my neck. It was her tears. The soldiers barked at her, saying really nasty things. She gently pushed me away and wiped her eyes, joining the other women.

I ran up to the deck and leaned over the rail. I saw a little boat filled with women moving toward the harbor. My sister was among them. I looked for her but couldn't find her.

At dusk the anchors were pulled up and the ships left. I changed places and sat with Commander Xiao. He walked up and down watching over his company but rarely talked to me.

I used to climb around on my father's boats and had been out to sea to catch jellyfish, so I was not seasick. We had bread for dinner. I ate my share and even had others', because they were too seasick to eat.

The next morning, Commander Xiao spoke to me. Most importantly, he wanted me to hand my silver dollars and gold over to him, "because," he said, "you are a child, and it is not safe to carry so much money on you."

But in the afternoon, he gave me three silver dollars and said it was some pocket money for me. There was a small shop on the ship, but everything was very expensive. I didn't spend a cent.

Commander Xiao didn't pay much attention to me. I couldn't stay in one spot, and I ran around all over the place. It was very stuffy in the cabin, and many people were smoking. I coughed incessantly, so I spent most of my time on the deck, leaning against the rail, looking at the sea. My home was out of sight, and I had lost all sense of direction. What was Mother doing? Had Grandma and Father gotten home yet? Since my sister wasn't able to come with us to Taiwan, would she be married off in Shanghai?

Two days later, the ship arrived in Jilong. It was still dark, and the ship was docked in the outer harbor. The engines had stopped, and the quiet was soothing to the ears. People crowded up to the rails, and everyone was talking and feeling excited. As it grew brighter, the houses in the distance became clearer. More people gathered in the harbor, as if to welcome us.

Around seven o'clock, hundreds and thousands of young girls in uniform, led by their teachers, arrived at the harbor. They all had small flags in their hands. They came from different schools, and they lined up in groups. Each group held up a red banner with the name of their school written on it. From my position, I could read clearly KEELUNG GIRLS' HIGH SCHOOL.

Next, a band of thirty people arrived. Four or five people followed with a red banner and two bamboo poles. They moved to the front and unfurled the red banner, propping it up on the bamboo poles. The gold characters read, ZHOUSHAN TROOPS, WELCOME TO TAIWAN.

Our ship moved into the harbor, and the band started to play, and the students started to cheer. The waving red flags filled the harbor with an air of festivity.

Finally, Taiwan! I was so excited I started to wave along with all the adults.

My eyes glued to the harbor, I was captivated by the festivities. I did not notice that the troops had begun to move. When I saw the first group of soldiers setting foot on shore I suddenly woke up. In a panic, I ran for the cabin.

But the deck was so crowded I could hardly move. Those who had been sitting were now standing, and the troops inside the cabin had lined up and were ready to debark. I tried to make my way back in, but I was moving against the tide, and I was so small. No one budged to let me by.

After much pushing and shoving I finally made my way back into the cabin. There were still people in there, but not Commander Xiao's company. I ran back onto the deck, and it was still jam-packed with people. I dived in and out of the crowd, looking for Commander Xiao, but to no avail.

A soldier asked me, "Who are you looking for?"

"I am looking for Commander Xiao."

"What is his name?"

"I don't know."

"Which unit?"

"I don't know."

The troops moved into two lines, and military vehicles picked them up. From the deck, I saw military trucks carrying loads of soldiers. Few people remained on board. I still couldn't find Commander Xiao.

I was probably the last to leave the ship. I don't know which company I was following. I just debarked with them. Two lines of students stood on the embankment, and we were given a welcome pack that contained a piece of bread, a piece of cake, and a very big banana.

The troops had left, and the students, too. I was alone on the deserted docks.

I did not leave the docks. I clung to the hope that Commander Xiao would come back for me. But I waited till it got dark, but he did not show up.

I was afraid that someone would shoo me away, so I hid behind the back door of a warehouse. There was nothing in the warehouse, so the doors were left ajar. From a slit in the door I had a full view of the docks. If Commander Xiao came looking for me, if he called my name, I would be able to hear him.

But he did not show up. Apparently he did not plan on coming back for me.

I ate the bread and the cake for lunch. I took two tiny bites of the banana and decided to save the rest for later. But by night I was so hungry, and there was nothing else to eat. I ate the rest of the banana for dinner.

From where I sat, I was only three or four steps away from the ocean. I watched the tide rise and recede. As time went by my panic increased. It dawned on me that I was facing the danger of starving to death.

I cried and cried. The tears never stopped. Whether my eyes were open or shut, images of my family flickered before me. If they only knew the predicament that I was in!

In the darkness, my panic grew wings and started to fly all over the place. What's worse, I was discovered by the guard watching over the docks. He was a soldier. He pointed his rifle at me, stared at me maliciously, and pretended that he was going to execute me. I was so scared that no words came out of my mouth. All I could do was cry.

He kicked me twice and, grabbing my arm, yanked me all the way to the dock entrance and threw me out.

It must have been eight o'clock, and there were many people on the streets. Men and women wore wooden clogs that made clapping sounds. The streets were filled with the sounds of clogs clapping against the pavement. I roamed about, feeling like a thief. I didn't even dare to lift my head.

After an hour or so, I passed a small cement bridge and saw a building that was taller that the civilian houses and shops. A wooden plaque inscribed with THE CHIANG KAI-SHEK HALL hung across the door. Before it was a small square paved with cement, and before the square was a hill that sloped down to a harbor filled with floating logs.

There were many people on the square and the hillside. Some were sitting and some were standing. Some had fans in their hands. It was hot, so they were probably there to get some fresh air.

I walked toward them slowly and found a corner on the hill where I could sit down. In crowds, I was less afraid. Then I realized that this was a public place, and no one would shoo me away.

There were kids my age there. They were laughing and playing, chasing each other, reminding me of myself two days ago. They were so happy because their homes were nearby and they had adults to protect them. It was a freedom that was lost to me.

Some kids ran up close to me and looked at me in wonder. Some even smiled at me. But I dared not greet them. I was afraid of them finding out I had no parents and no home.

A middle-aged man pushing a cart was selling boiled eggs steeped in tea. He hollered, "Tea-leaf eggs, come buy tea-leaf eggs!" The aroma of eggs filled the air, but he wasn't doing good business. I had had half a banana for dinner and was already famished. The aroma of eggs made my stomach rumble.

"I want to buy some," I said when he passed by me.

He stopped and looked at me with disbelief. "Do you have money?" he asked.

"Yes." I had the three silver dollars that Commander Xiao had given back to me. I gave him one and asked, "How many eggs can I get for one silver dollar?"

He took the silver dollar, blew at it, and put it by his ear. I knew he was checking to see if it was real. Grown-ups at home did that all the time.

"Three!" He took the silver dollar and wrapped up three eggs for me. The New Taiwan Dollar had just been issued. One silver dollar could have gotten me three New Taiwan Dollars, and I could have bought all his eggs. But of course, I didn't know that at the time.

It grew late, and the people dispersed. I walked around, staying in the vicinity, and saw the benches that were fixed to the ground. Under the dim lamplight they looked wooden, but up close I discovered that they were made of cement. All the benches had been occupied before. Now that the crowds had thinned, they were vacant. I was so tired that I flopped down on one of them.

I was only eleven years old, and I was small, so the bench could be my bed. I lay on the bench with my hands cradling my head and looked up into the sky. The stars glittered, just like the stars at home. The sky was the same, but on the ground, my life was no longer the same!

The next day, the sun woke me up. In a moment of delirium, I thought I was at home in my own bed. When I came to my senses, I ached all over. It must have been from sleeping on the cement bench all night. There were also red spots all over my body, mosquito bites, no doubt.

Out of habit, I searched for water to wash my face. There was water right in front of me. I tried it, and then remembered it was seawater. It was salty. But there was no other water to be found. I grew up by the sea, and I knew that you shouldn't bathe in salt water, because it would only make the itching of dirty skin worse. Since I couldn't find any fresh water, I had to go without washing.

Soon I was hungry again, but I didn't know where to go for food. I only had two silver dollars left. If one silver dollar could only buy three eggs, then two would only buy six eggs, and I would go hungry again the next day.

I tried to go without breakfast. It was summer, and once the sun came out, it was hot. By noontime the cement benches were scorching. I left the hill and circled the Chiang Kai-shek Hall. In an alley behind the hall I saw vendors selling food. Round stools were placed beside their food carts. Some sold noodles; some sold dumplings wrapped in bamboo leaves. The smell of the food wafted into my nostrils; my stomach rumbled and my mouth watered.

For lunch I had a bowl of noodles. I also wanted to have a dumpling wrapped in bamboo leaves, but I stopped myself. The vendor was probably Taiwanese, and I couldn't understand his words. But he was kind. I gave him a silver dollar, and he gave me back a lot of change.

I ate at his food stall again at dinnertime. This time I had two dumplings wrapped in bamboo leaves. I gave him the change that he'd given me at noon. He looked at me, didn't say anything, and threw it all into a metal plate.

My last silver dollar saw me through another day. From the third day on, I was penniless. I had nothing to eat all day long.

By nighttime, I was bent over from hunger. The hill was still crowded with people. I couldn't get a bench. I squatted in a little corner hugging my knees, my head bent, weeping in the dark.

Hunger brought on a deeper fear—I was afraid I was going to die anytime. The fear resembled a bottomless pit. I was floating in it, a lonely and desolate soul. Any situation could have obliterated me.

For those three days, apart from the few words I'd exchanged with the vendors when buying the eggs, noodles, and dumplings, I had spoken to no one. When Commander Xiao was staying with us, I had learned to speak Mandarin. Quite a few people on the hill and in the square spoke Mandarin, but I dared not speak to them, even if they were kids, too. I was very scared. I felt as if I was a secret, and the moment I opened my mouth the secret would be revealed. So I hid myself in a corner, and if anyone approached me or looked my way, I would look down or walk away.

I starved for another day. By night, I had no strength left, not even to turn my body over to lie on my other side.

On the morning of the fifth day, I lay on the bench, exposed to the sun, and did not get up for a long, long time. At noon, I finally entered the Chiang Kai-shek Hall and found a water faucet in the toilet. I washed my face and drank some water. Leaning against the wall, I seriously contemplated my desperate situation.

I told myself that I couldn't die like that, but I didn't know what to do to stay alive.

Leaving the Chiang Kai-shek Hall, I walked along the streets. I found a place where crowds gathered. I walked over and discovered the marketplace. Discarded vegetable roots and stalks were rotting on the ground. I picked them up, filled a bag, and went back to the Chiang Kai-shek Hall.

I washed the vegetables under the faucet, and when no one was around, I started to eat. I had no idea what the vegetables were. Some tasted bitter, some tasted sour, and some tasted acrid. I puckered my lips and kept chewing, swallowing everything before my stomach reacted.

But my stomach was on the alert. Sometimes it started objecting when the food was still in my mouth, so that much of the food never made it to my stomach.

I threw up practically everything that I swallowed. But after rinsing my mouth I continued to eat—out of defiance. I kept saying to my stomach: how can you say no to this food, what else do you expect?

This went on for a few days. I did not starve to death, even though the vomiting never stopped. But one day, a strange thing happened—my belly started to swell, and my belly button protruded like a pregnant woman's. My whole belly was extended and taut.

My belly swelled terribly, but I was very constipated. Once I labored for an hour over the toilet, to expel only a few drops of putrid green water with a dead roundworm.

And so miraculously I survived without getting sick.

I soon lost track of my days. One afternoon, I roamed the streets, trying to venture a bit farther. At the entrance to an alley I smelled the fragrance of cooking rice. I followed it. At the end of the alley was an old man with a head of white hair. He was squatting before a water faucet scrubbing dishes. The dishes were piled high. When he was done with a pile he would enter the door and come out with another pile to wash.

I moved closer, and stopped five footsteps away from him. He did not notice me at first, but when he did, he merely glanced at me and continued with his work. I stood there for a long time and finally caught his attention. As he carried out a new pile of dishes to be washed, he looked at me and asked suddenly, "Are you hungry?"

I nodded.

He put the dishes down and went back in, his back hunched. Soon he came out with a bowl of rice. On top of the rice was a slab of meat and half a fish. He put the food before me.

I was shivering all over, and could barely extend my hand. I took the bowl in both hands and started to eat with my head bowed. He handed me a pair of chopsticks, but I had already devoured half the bowl of rice.

"Take your time, I can give you more when you've finished. This is a restaurant; there's no lack of leftover food and rice."

He gave me another bowl. I devoured it in no time.

"Not full yet?"

I shook my head.

"You must not eat any more or you'll get sick." He asked, "Where are your parents? Why aren't they taking care of you?"

His question produced torrents of tears from me. I kept shaking my head, because the louder I cried the harder it was for me to stop. I wanted to answer him, but I couldn't say anything.

After a while, I finally answered his question. He sighed and said, "You're to be pitied. But I'm not much better off. I'm almost seventy, and I'm alone in Taiwan, too. I know the owner of this restaurant. I wash dishes for him. He gives me food during the day, and at night, I watch his restaurant for him. From now on, you can help me wash dishes, and I'll ask the kitchen to set aside leftovers for you. As for sleeping arrangements, you'll have to continue sleeping where you have been. Is that okay with you?"

Of course it was okay. It was great! I was so grateful that I was ready to kneel down and pound my head on the ground to thank him.

From then on, I had food to eat and was no longer hungry. The old man's name was Zou, and the restaurant was Lao-zheng-xing. Fifty years later, the restaurant was still there, and another one had opened in Gaoxiong.

In early July, I met another savior. He was a soldier named Yi. His company was stationed in Jilong. He often passed the Chiang Kai-shek Hall and had seen me many times. Though I was no longer starving, I still had a swollen belly. My peculiar circumstances made him curious. He stopped to talk with me, and after assessing my situation, he asked, "Do you want to become a soldier?"

"I'm so young, can I?"

"Some of the kids in my company are younger than you!"

He brought me to meet his company commander. There was a vacancy for a private soldier, and I filled it. That marked the beginning of my military career, starting as a child soldier.

I Wanted to Go to War

. . .

by SANG Pin-zai

translated by Nicholas KOSS

About an inch below my ring finger, on the back of my right hand, there's a scar that extends to the right, to where the back and palm of my hand meet. When I make a fist, the scar swells up as if a little white worm has been sleeping there. This scar is a mark of war. And it is also the only reminder of my one time in battle during my fifteen years in the service.

I should not have been allowed to become a soldier when I did. I was eleven years old. But I should not have been discharged when I was either, at twenty-six. During those fifteen years I went from a child soldier to a captain, and I spent two years serving with the troops of what was called the "Anti-Communist, Save-the-Nation Army." This unit did not have "noncombatants." It was very similar in nature to the special units in Hollywood war films. It wasn't a spy outfit, but its missions were often related to spying. When these soldiers had nothing to do, they just stood around looking tough. But, once they were in battle, their brains weren't in their heads but in their hands. And when necessary, these troops could be thrown like hand grenades.

In the military class on political training, the superiors often gave this exhortation: "The revolutionary soldier does not fear death." But they did not say "fear death"; they said, "does not know death." "Do not fear death" is, of course, a slogan, like "a good death is better than a bad life." But who is not afraid to die? So no matter how loudly it's proclaimed, as soon as the shooting starts, you find excuses to disappear or you're scared shitless. "Not knowing death" is also a slogan, but compared to "not fearing death," it is much more applicable. Because for twenty-odd years, from the 1940s to the 1960s, only this unit was in constant battle with the Communists. Whether it was being attacked or attacking, there were deaths involved. And, after experiencing so many deaths, the nerves get used to it. Death becomes just another mundane event; it is masked by the familiarity that makes it ordinary. Even sadness and grief begin to seem excessive.

Among those troops continually engaged in combat, the section that fought the most was the "Success Team." The so-called "Success Team" was similar to the navy's "Frogmen Team" in nature and mission. The members of that team were known as the "water devils." After the famous battle over Quemoy on August 23, 1953, the opposite sides of the straits engaged in a "war of propaganda" rather than continuing "military provocation." The navy's frogmen fell to the status of tourist attraction for the military. When distinguished foreign visitors came, the frogmen performed calisthenics, showing off their bronzed, muscular bodies and their animal-like ferocity. However, by that time, I'm afraid that not even all their officers had experienced battle. But such was not the case for the Success Team of the Anti-Communist, Save-the-Nation Army, determined to save our country. These soldiers continued to make their way across the Taiwan Strait. Whatever was "inconvenient" for the regular armed forces, these soldiers were sent to do. I have no way of knowing if their actions were recorded in our military history, but they did prove that we were still very much engaged in military conflict with the Chinese Communists. It was not simply a war on paper, not just a shouting match over loudspeakers.

At that time I was a reporter for the military news service, so definitely not combat personnel. Nevertheless I still was a soldier, eating the same food and getting the same pay. Although my rank was low, for better or worse, I was still an officer, a first lieutenant. Often I would hear soldiers telling their combat stories or see them rolling up a shirt sleeve or a trouser leg to reveal bullet wounds or knife scars. I couldn't help feeling secretly guilty, knowing that I was probably the only one in this army who had never seen battle.

The good thing about being a reporter was that I met a lot of people and could go places off limits to others. Our news office was about a ten-minute walk from the Success Team's camp. I often went there to shoot the breeze with them and knew all thirty-plus officers and soldiers in the unit by name. And they never forgot to give me a call when they were planning a good meal and an evening of entertainment.

The best time I had with these soldiers was swimming. Swimming was their basic training. Of course they swam when the weather was hot, but when there was ice and snow, they jumped into the water, too. Like frogmen, they wore only red trunks, which, I heard, was to keep the sharks away.

I liked swimming and could swim pretty well. Before joining the news agency, I had worked at odd jobs for the section of this army dealing with the sea. Its code name was "On the Water." Swimming was required, of course. The Anti-Communist, Save-the-Nation Army had developed out of guerrilla troops. Ninety percent of the On the Water troops had previously been sailors. Once they became soldiers, they still lived on boats, and like the soldiers in the Success Team, they were "amphibious."

About six months before I reported to the military news agency, the On the Water troops were still training together with the army's Fifth Battalion at a naval station at Zouying. One of our classes was swimming. At the completion of this training, we swam, class by class, for more than four hours from Zouying to Chengging Lake near Gaohxiong. This gives you some idea of my swimming skills.

The Success Team's camp opened onto the ocean. On both sides of the beach were large reefs that protected the bay. The water was so clear you could count the fish swimming there. There weren't any waves to speak of. This was the most beautiful beach I'd ever seen in my life.

The team leader was Cantonese. He had reached the rank of major. His name was Zheng Guichuan. He was about thirty-five years old and still a bachelor. He was not only the team's top officer but also the top drinker. He drank away about half his salary, yet I never heard of him actually being drunk. One time at a party for the team, he went from table to table challenging others to drink: you had to keep refilling your tin bowl (which was required equipment for officers and soldiers) until you'd downed a whole bottle. After Zheng finished doing this and returned to his seat, he continued to drink.

A soldier's salary is low, so expensive liquors were out of the question. At that time the Alcoholic Beverage Monopoly sold a liquor called "Luck and Long Life." One bottle cost NT$6. This was the drink used in the mess hall. The soldiers called it "suicide liquor" because of its high alcoholic content. If you drank too much you got a headache, and if you became drunk, the pain was so bad that suicide was your only thought.

I knew very well that hanging out with the Success Team provided a kind of psychological compensation for me. I longed to participate in battle. This desire was probably completely unrealistic; therefore, I could at least experience war through them.

Then the unforeseeable occurred. One afternoon, I was sipping tea with Team Leader Zheng in his room. All of a sudden he asked me, "You want to fight just for the fun of it?"

The question was so unexpected that for a moment I didn't know how to respond. Was he serious? Or was he just making fun of me?

"Do you have another mission?" I asked to avoid answering.

"I can't tell you that. Just say if you're up for it or not."

Judging from the tone of his voice, he was serious. My heart was already pounding.

"When?" I asked.

"You're just like a little girl," he said, laughing. "You're afraid, aren't you?"

"Who's afraid?"

"If you're afraid, just say so. If not, I can figure out a way for you to come. I don't have enough authority to do it on my own, though. I'll have to check with the commanding officer."

"Okay. I'll go."

I really don't know if I was afraid. But I know I was excited. This was the day I'd been waiting for.

That was in October 1962. It was the evening of October 9, a little after nine o'clock, when Team Leader Zheng called me on the phone. The army newspaper had just come off the press. All he said was: "Come over when you're finished."

Half an hour later, I arrived at their camp, all the time thinking the chances were very good that the time had come. Team Leader Zheng pulled me into his room, dragging me as if I were a kid. Laughing, he said, "You're a lucky little shit. The commanding officer has approved."

"You mean it's tonight?"

"You got it. Now since I've told you, from this moment on, you can't leave the camp. You'll sleep here tonight."

For the sake of secrecy, when the team had a mission, no one could have any outside contact. Even though I hadn't fought before, this much I understood.

He spread some blankets on the floor in his room and told me to sleep there. That way he could keep an eye on me.

The team had already gone to sleep; soon the barracks resonated with loud and soft snoring. But I couldn't even shut my eyes. Was I going to fight? What sort of fighting? What would my assignment be? And most important, would I come back alive?

For so long I had been yearning to fight, and now I would. But like a coward, I was growing frightened. I had only been alive for twenty-three years. My girlfriend was in Taipei. Her father said that if I didn't get out of the army he wouldn't let her marry me. If I died in battle, would she really not marry for the rest of her life as she had promised? If so, her father would surely regret his words.

It was near midnight and I still had no desire to sleep. Feeling cold, I covered myself with a blanket.

Team Leader Zheng was sitting by his bed, smoking. The light from the desk lamp reflected off his determined and serious face. He was definitely thinking about the mission. He was in charge. The outcome was on his shoulders.

"Don't sleep if you can't," he said abruptly. Since only the two of us were in the room, he must have been talking to me.

"You can't sleep either?" I said, turning to one side.

"We'll sleep when we get back. In fact, there's not much time for sleep."

"When do we leave?"

"Listen for the whistle. I'll explain the mission after everyone is up. Before that I can't say anything."

He threw me a cigarette. Even though I didn't smoke, I lit it and started to inhale madly, realizing I was getting more and more tense.

"You're afraid the first time you go to battle. But after you've been under fire a few times, there's no fear. It's like the first time you're with a woman. You somehow muddle through. Later there's no more desire for it!" Pointing his cigarette at me, he said, "You must know what it's like with a woman."

How could I talk to him about that kind of thing?

"The mission this time is very simple. And absolutely safe. Otherwise, I wouldn't bring you. If everyone moves quickly, we might be back in time for breakfast," he explained.

Would it really be so simple? He had often been on the battlefield, so of course he was relaxed. But there was no way for me to relax.

"For God's sake, fill me in. I'm sleeping in your room. It's impossible for me to give away any secrets." I really couldn't restrain myself anymore.

"Orders are orders. I must do everything by the book. Fighting must follow the regulations. One mistake and it could cost someone's head."

"Are you like this every time you're on a mission?"

"Every time." Still holding his cigarette butt, he came over and patted me on the head as if I were a toy or something. "It's good that you're with me. If there's any trouble, I'll protect you."

After he said that, I felt even more uncomfortable. Trying to save face, I said, "I'm fine. I don't need your protection."

"You're right. At any rate, stay calm. Relax. We'll have a good talk when we get back. It'll be interesting."

"Tell me about one of your battles," I said. "I don't feel like sleeping."

"Okay. I'll tell you a good story," he said, returning to his place. He lit another cigarette and leaned toward me. "This wasn't even six months ago. Our orders were to take someone over and pick someone up. It was still a few hours before the scheduled pick-up time, and we would have attracted attention if we'd stayed in a group. I told everyone to split up. I walked up and down the streets and looked around, but that got boring, so I went to a movie. There was a girl sitting next to me who kept laughing at me. After the movie, I teased her a bit and invited her for ice cream. To my shock she wrote her address on a slip of paper for me."

"Really? She must have fallen for you."

"She must have. But it could also have been a trap."

"What happened next?"

"There wasn't any 'next.' An hour later, we'd picked up the person and brought him back."

"Do you still have the address?"

"What the hell for? I tossed it ages ago."

It was already past one. He went out for a long time. At exactly two, I heard two blasts of the whistle, followed by Team Leader Zheng's "Get up."

Immediately, the barracks were flooded with light. It was clear the time had come.

A supply sergeant came in and threw a bundle of things at me.

"What are these?"

"Red shorts. A handgun. A navy knife. An army belt. And a packet of propaganda," he answered.

I opened it and took a look. The supply sergeant told me to put on the red trunks first and then the belt. Next I was to fasten the handgun to my left side. On the right went the navy knife and the plastic bag with the propaganda.

He inspected everything, checking to see if I had fastened it all tight enough. "The bullets have already been loaded," he added. "You have twenty-four shots. But the safety lock has been closed. Only open it when you need to shoot."

Another whistle sounded outside. Immediately the air grew tense with footsteps hurrying to the field. The supply sergeant gently patted me on the back. I was the first to leave the room.

Everyone's equipment was the same. Everyone was bare-chested and clad in red shorts. I wasn't part of the regular formation, so I tactfully stood in the rear.

There was still some talking going on in the ranks. But as soon as Team Leader Zheng appeared, there was immediate silence. He walked into the middle of the formation and flashed a look at each face from the head of the formation to the rear. Then he said, "I will now announce our mission. Everyone has a plastic bag with propaganda sheets. They are our mission. Has anyone forgotten what day this is?"

"October tenth," someone shouted.

"Right. October tenth. Our national holiday. We want to help our fellow countrymen on the mainland remember this day." He continued, "This mission is very simple. Once we've landed, everyone is to split up. We'll have an hour to find places to post the propaganda. Walls and trestles are fine. But try to find spots where a lot of people will see them in the daylight. Don't put them too close together. Do you understand?"

"Yes," the team shouted in unison, myself included.

"I have a large flag here," he said, patting a big plastic bag attached to his right side. "I want to find a place to raise it! Let's coordinate our watches; it's 2:26." Left hands were extended and watches set to the same time. Waving his hand, Team Leader Zheng then gave the order: "Depart!"

And so thirty-some men started jogging to the beach. The sky was dark but filled with stars. There was no moonlight. The sound of sixty-some feet running along the beach prompted a primitive feeling of tribal resolve.

My heart still felt tense. Our mission really wasn't difficult. But wouldn't our enemy discover it? And if so, were we to fight or flee?

And then, the team leader hadn't said exactly where we were going.

As we ran up to the edge of the water, we saw a Together-class landing craft moored there. Before the sound of running feet had stopped, soldiers were entering the water and swimming toward the craft.

This H-class boat was nicknamed the "Sea Duck." Based on their weight, landing crafts were divided into four classes: "China," "America," "Unite," and "Together." The "Sea Duck" was the smallest. Light in weight, it was the most maneuverable. After everyone had gotten on, the assistant team leader ordered roll call for each group. This was my chance to count the number present. Including myself, it was thirty-seven.

The landing craft headed out, its motors shattering the night's silence. We were all gathered on the firing deck. Since there was not much room, everyone had to stand. The entire deck had only a single mercury light. I saw some of the soldiers covering their mouths and yawning.

Team Leader Zheng moved next to me and tapped me on the shoulder. With his mouth almost against my ear, he said, "Still nervous?" Smiling ironically, I nodded and then asked, "For God's sake, where are we going?"

"The place is called 'P'," he said, making a face at me.

"'P'? As in 'P' in the alphabet?"

"You got it."

This, of course, was code. "P" must have been the abbreviation for "place," just as "D" is for "day." But why did we still have to use code, if we were almost there?

"Fighting is not the same as writing an article. You don't have to know too much." He continued, "A place is just a place."

"Do you use this each time you go on a mission?"

"You got it. Each time the place is called 'P'."

It seemed as if he didn't want to tell me. If I didn't believe him, I could always find out more later.

"Soon we'll have to start swimming. For about two miles. That shouldn't be any problem for you. I'm telling you first so you can prepare yourself."

"Why do we have to swim so far?"

"Because the landing craft has to remain in international waters. Otherwise, we'd be attacking the mainland, wouldn't we? The boat will wait for us and then take us back."

After half an hour, the twin engines of the boat were reduced to a single one. The noise of the motors was cut in half. This was much easier on my ears. Ten minutes later, the remaining engine was shut off. The boat came to a standstill, rocking left and right as it was struck by waves. I still hadn't figured out what was going on. I only saw that those below were starting up the metal steps on both sides and getting on deck.

Team Leader Zheng remained beside me. He gave me a little nudge and said, "We're here." He and I were the last ones on deck. Everyone else had started swimming toward a murky destination.

Once in the water, what had originally been a squad of thirty-seven soldiers crowded together now became a scattering of little dots tossed up and down by the waves. The weather wasn't bad and stars filled the sky. Once it was light, there would be a bright sun.

Because the water was deep, it was cold. First I swam freestyle to allow my body to warm up. Zheng stayed with me. At the same time he kept his eye on all those swimming around us. Most were ahead of us, so he swam faster, wanting to be in front, and I lost sight of him.

After swimming about a quarter mile, I switched to the breaststroke, which saved my energy. Although I could swim over three miles, my problem was that I swam slowly. Especially compared with those on the Success Team, my speed was not up to par. My sense of pride, however, would not allow me to fall behind, so I swam with great effort and didn't slack off. In this way, I managed to reduce the distance between us. I was only slightly behind.

It must have been with the team leader's permission that we stopped for a couple of minutes to rest before swimming on. Almost everyone else had already reached shore. I and two or three other slow swimmers emerged from the water soon afterward.

But just as I took a couple of steps out of the water, two lights shone from either side of the beach. They were searchlights the size of automobile tires. Each was a thousand watts. They lit up the arc of the beach brighter than midday.

The searchlights illuminated the beach and the men on the beach. By now all thirty-seven men were out of the water, and each was bathed in light.

"Fall flat!" Team Leader Zheng shouted the command once and then repeatedly.

Some heard and fell flat, but others continued to charge ahead. And still others, probably because this was all happening so suddenly, froze in fear and just stood there motionless.

All of this took less than two minutes. Then from both lights came the sound of machine-gun fire. From the whizz of the bullets, I knew they were 50-mm machine guns.

The crossfire from the machine guns formed a sheet of bullets and cut the beach in half horizontally. Three-fourths of the Success Team's officers and men were under fire. Only a small percentage escaped it. Obviously the Communist troops wanted to block our access to the sea and planned to capture us alive.

Immediately, the roar of a loudspeaker sounded from the Communist camp: "My brothers in the army of Chiang Kai-shek. Your movements are under our control. Not a single one of you can get away. Put down your weapons and surrender. The People's Liberation Army will treat you fairly."

Behind the searchlights the grass was about waist high. The Communist troops were hidden in the nearby shrubs. We didn't know how many there were. But the number of men was not the key factor; rather, it was the two searchlights and the two machine guns. The Communists were blanketed by darkness and we by light. We had become easy marks.

Our only weapons were handguns and navy knives. With machine guns, or even mortars or hand grenades, we would have been able to fight. But we could only watch helplessly as we became target practice for the enemy.

The loudspeaker repeated the same message again and again. The two machine guns never stopped firing and increased intensity, it seemed. Squiggling bullets blazed through the darkness. Wave after wave of smoke thick with a nitric smell billowed in all directions.

Some of our troops had already fallen. Sounds of death were rising. Under fire, our men surged forward and shot into the shrubs. The Communists manning the machine guns immediately returned fire. More of our troops fell.

"Retreat! All-out retreat!" Team Leader Zheng's shouts sounded again.

But how could we retreat? The way back was blocked by machine-gun fire.

Only a few of our men had any luck, and I was among them. We were the ones who had lagged behind because we swam so slowly.

I had been lying near the water. As soon as I heard Zheng's command, I immediately turned and dove back into the sea.

Once in, I swam underwater, trying to stay as close as possible to the ocean floor, because as soon as Zheng had ordered the retreat, the machine guns turned their sights on those of us heading back into the sea. They were wildly blasting the water's edge.

Many bullets fell down through the water onto my head. Because I was below the surface, they were not deadly but more like raindrops. Alternating between the surface and the depths, I thought of the "Sea Duck" awaiting us.

I wasn't an expert at swimming underwater. But the bullets skimming the surface whizzed after me like hornets. Facing death, I didn't dare lift my head above the water. Spurred by an intense desire to survive, I was able to swim about 1,000 feet underwater, coming up only when I figured the bullets were no longer flying over me.

Once above water, I just had one thought: to swim my fastest toward the landing craft. I swam freestyle because I could make time that way. Even though it took everything out of me, I never thought of resting. I never swam so fast in my life and I passed a number of soldiers. Somewhere along the line, the ones I'd been swimming next to fell far behind me.

I was the third one to reach the landing craft. The first one on helped me up. Once aboard, I helped the others who were arriving. By this time, the boat was warming up and I heard the sound of the motor. It was time to head back.

But there were still soldiers in the water swimming toward us. Because of the high waves and dark night I couldn't make out how many, but there were definitely some. I could clearly see them waving to us.

"We can't wait!" said the captain angrily. "If we wait, we won't make it out of here!"

Pointing to the men still in the water, I said, "Just a couple more minutes and they'll be here."

The captain paid no attention to me and gave the order to his subordinates to start off. Two soldiers from the Success Team rushed over to stop him. The captain forced them back, angrily pointing across the water. "Are you blind? The gunboats have already come out."

Looking in the direction he was pointing, I saw two gunboats racing toward us. They were only about half a mile away. First the gunboats raced side by side, but then they fanned out. It was clear they wanted to outflank us and force us back to their port.

One gunboat fired first and then, four or five seconds later, the other one fired, too. Two flaming bombs landed in the water, one in front of us and the other behind, creating waves as high as a three-story building. They hit about a quarter mile from our boat. Like two huge hands coming together, the gigantic waves collided and lifted our boat high in the air.

"Full speed ahead!" The captain was standing on the steering deck. Columns of water drenched him from top to bottom at though clothing him in a liquid suit.

From the two gunboats came one bomb after another, each shooting into the air before falling into the water. Under this intense fire, our boat surged forward against the waves. Gradually, the sound of the cannons grew more distant and the waves no longer engulfed us. We had finally escaped.

The boat came level. The silvery light of morning appeared in the east. A new day was about to begin.

Once aboard, I'd sat down on the walkway at the front of the boat. I'd been through such danger, and now I could hardly move. In my mind, I kept seeing those deadly bullets crisscrossing the beach, and my ears were full of the desperate shouts of dying soldiers.

Now that the danger was past, I felt exhausted to the point of paralysis. I had used up all my reserves of energy and I couldn't move a muscle. One by one, the other soldiers who had survived the disaster appeared on the deck. I counted them to myself: there were seven of us.

Everyone gathered around me, either standing or sitting. For a long while, no one said anything.

The captain had already changed into his snow-white navy officer's uniform. Smiling, he came over and congratulated us.

"Congratulations for what?" interrupted an angry soldier standing to my right. "What the fuck? God damn it! What the fuck?"

Who was he cursing? He probably didn't even know himself.

"You shouldn't blame me," the captain said indignantly. "If I could have waited, I would have."

I turned to look out, as if I could still see those soldiers swimming toward us.

Unperturbed, the captain walked away, leaving just the seven of us.

Pointing to my right hand, one of the soldiers suddenly asked, "Why are you bleeding so much?"

Only when he pointed did I realized that my right hand was covered with clotted blood. I nervously cleaned it away with my left hand, discovering an inch-long gash that ran to my fingers. That was where the blood had been coming from.

Only because he had mentioned it did I begin to feel pain.

"You really didn't feel anything?" asked the soldier who had pointed it out.

"If you hadn't said something, I wouldn't have known."

"And you probably don't know when you were hit, do you?" asked another soldier.

"I don't," I said, inspecting my wound. "I don't know if I was hit by a bullet, or if one just skinned me."

Of the seven survivors, I was the only one wounded. Even though it wasn't serious, it became a big thing. Immediately someone called for the medic to dress my wound and bandage it. Sitting on the walkway, I extended my right hand.

"Only seven of the thirty-seven coming back," I muttered. "How could this happen? How did they know?"

"That's no mystery; it was a spy," said the soldier behind me.

"What will happen to them?"

"It's better to die. If they're captured, what kind of life would they have?"

Suddenly I thought of Team Leader Zheng, and my heart tightened. "Did anyone see the team leader?"

"Dead!" answered a voice hard as steel. "I saw him fall."

"Are you sure?"

"Absolutely! A bullet got him in the chest. I was about three steps away from him."

The boat was gliding smoothly through the water, the waves beating time against its sides.

It was morning now. The sun had risen slowly above the horizon and the water reflected a blushing red. Already the little island of Dongyin had come into view.

The Stone Tablet at the Cove of the Loving Mother

. . .

by WANG Yo-hua

translated by Michelle WU

Aboard the fishing boat *Full Lucky Star*, I cruised the islands of the South China Sea. My mission was to write a series of travel articles for a geography magazine.

I recorded the navigation routes that the fishermen took, their methods of fishing, their catch, and their way of life. I also visited several islands in search of good stories.

One day, the *Full Lucky Star* had engine trouble and was forced to change its course. That's how we came to land at the Cove of the Loving Mother. There was a primitive, tumbledown jetty on the tiny island, and it took the *Full Lucky Star* some time to drop anchor and tie up. The repairs would take some time, too, so I grabbed my camera and press folder and decided to explore the sandy island with the cook, whom we called Old Man Jiang, and a young sailor named A-chang.

According to Old Man Jiang, the island was called the Cove of the Loving Mother because of a stretch of rocky shoreline lined with strangely shaped rocks. When the wind wove through the numerous cracks and holes in the rocks, its howling sounded like someone calling, "Mama, mama." That howling wind reminded many wandering fishermen of their mothers back home.

I harbored no illusions about this little island, nor did I expect to dig up any worthwhile material for my articles. It was only a tiny atoll covered with white sand and craggy rocks. Various kinds of seagulls circled in the sky above, filling the air with their shrill cries and scattering the ground with their droppings. The entire area of the island wasn't more than two square miles, and it was shaped like a crescent. We found ourselves facing a row of collapsing wooden shacks. They had once been occupied. To the right of the shacks was a dried-up pond. Even though the structures were in ruins, we could still tell where the outhouse and the kitchen had once stood.

Old Man Jiang seemed to be no stranger to the place. He looked around, kicked the dusty boards, then made his way to a mound of sand in front of the compound. Squatting down on his haunches, he started to dig.

I walked up to him. Old Man Jiang knew his way around these waters, and he had had many extraordinary and amazing experiences. He had a good grasp of the events that had taken place on the various atolls and sand shoals. Some of his stories were so bizarre they verged on the incredible, and his heavy accent made it rather difficult for me to understand him at times. Still, he had been a great help to me, providing much material for stories.

"Old Man Jiang, what are you up to now?"

The withered old sailor slowly exposed a stone tablet that had been buried in the sand.

I squatted down to examine it.

"Can you see it? Can you see it?"

Quickly, I brushed away the sand. The stone tablet was about six feet wide and ten feet high. There was a dark brown inscription on it. Judging from the appearance of the stone and the inscription, I could tell that it hadn't been erected very long ago. I had already come across two dozen stone tablets like this on nearby islands.

I helped clean off the sand and snapped a few photos. The inscription read: IN MEMORY OF THE 131 COURAGEOUS SOLDIERS WHO STOOD FAST AT THEIR POST AND GAVE THEIR LIVES FOR THEIR NATION. It had been erected by a navy commander on a certain date.

"The men are buried up there, more than one hundred of them." Old Man Jiang stood up and pointed.

I got to my feet, too, and gazed in the direction he indicated. A dark gray stretch of rocky reef lined the horizon; seagulls hovered over the rocks. A-chang was out there, too, climbing about, probably searching for seagull eggs. He was a young and always looking for adventure.

"Old Man Jiang, how did all these men lose their lives here?"

I tried very hard to recall the name of the navy commander. Of all the monuments I'd seen, this tablet was the plainest, the least ornate.

"Um. . . ." Sitting down on the unearthed tablet, Old Man Jiang lit a cigarette. There was a faraway look in his eyes.

"Was there any fighting? I don't see any signs of fighting at all—there's nothing here. How did the troops survive with nothing to live on? And this little island has no strategic significance. . . ."

I flipped through the data in my press folder. There was no record of the Cove of the Loving Mother. It was just a tiny nub of an island. I found it hard to imagine how so many people could have died there.

"There was no fighting. Back then, the government sent more than a hundred men because they said that Vietnam, the Philippines, and Malaysia all wanted a presence here. We were sent to occupy this island."

"First come, first served."

"They all came to hoist their flags. So our government decided to send men over. We came in two ships filled with guns and gunpowder. We fired at anyone trying to approach the island. That scared the other countries off, and no one dared to land."

I noticed a cement pole standing in front of the compound. That must have been a flagpole.

"What about food and water? What did the men live on?"

"Military supplies. Nothing grows on the island, and the wind really blows hard. The military supplies arrived once a month by boat. That was all that sustained us."

"Then how did the men die? Was it some disease?"

"The military supplies didn't arrive. They all starved to death. Do you know what it's like to starve to death?" Old Man Jiang asked.

"You must be kidding. How is that possible?"

I suddenly felt sick, trying to imagine what it was like for those men to stand on the beach every day waiting for the supply boat.

"Hey, hey, those were tumultuous times. There was still a power struggle going on, the navy was a mess, and no one was in charge. A revolt here, desertion there. People killing each other. No one was at the helm, and they just forgot about us."

"Oh." I recalled that period of political chaos.

"The boat didn't arrive until a year later. Finally someone remembered that we were still here."

"Then, then . . ." I was so overcome with emotion I stuttered.

"All the men had starved to death, 131 of them, with the exception of one man. He was half deranged. Every day he hoisted the national flag and fired at approaching boats."

"So one man survived. Why on earth did he still hoist the flag every day? Wait a minute, Old Man Jiang, how come you know all these details? Did you just say 'we'? What do you mean 'we'?"

"Hey, hey . . ."

Old Man Jiang threw his cigarette butt into the sand and stood up.

"Hey, you guys—"

Over by the rocky shoreline, A-chang started to shout frantically. The seagulls flapped into the air with a sudden whoosh. A-chang came scrambling back toward us—running, tripping, crawling. The startled seagulls burst into a shrill chatter.

"A pile of dead men's bones, a pile of skeletons—"

Old Man Jiang looked at me with a grim smile and headed for the *Full Lucky Star* without saying a word.

A-chang ran up to me and tugged at my arm. Breathlessly, he gasped, "A pile of skeletons. There're even bones in the bird nests. What the hell is going on here?"

"Go ask Old Man Jiang. He knows the whole story. I'm going over there to check it out."

Pushing past A-chang, I took out pen and paper.

"Fuck, what lousy luck!" A-chang spat and cursed as he made his way back.

I walked toward the pile of bones, the skeletons of men who had starved to death. After all the commotion, the seagulls had returned to the rocky shoreline, and now their cries sounded frantic and wretched.

Many of the corpses hadn't been buried deeply enough, and in time, the bones were exposed. Pecking out fragments of the more delicate bones, the seagulls had used them to build their nests.

Slowly I circled the little sand-covered island. I found no other monument or remains.

This was a desolate spot. It had no strategic significance, and there was nothing here but seagull droppings. Who gave the order to send men to it? What were those men like?

The men had lost their names and their identification numbers. Would I be able to find out who they were? Maybe. Did their families know they had starved to death here? Maybe not.

The wind picked up, whirling flecks of sand. The rocky shoreline reverberated with cries of "Mama, mama. . . ." They tugged at my heart.

And if I were to identify these men, what then?

Men like to erect monuments. But monuments teach us nothing. Monuments are erected in every dynasty and every age. And men repeat the same crimes over and over again.

"Well, well, how are you going to fight in a war if you get so scared?" jeered the captain. Back on the boat, everyone was making fun of A-chang.

"You don't know for sure. When the time comes, I'll kill if I have to. It'll be different when I go into the service. Then I'll show you what I'm made of. . . ." Red in the face, A-chang defended himself.

As the boat left the Cove of the Loving Mother, the wind was blowing hard. I thought to myself how, in a couple of days, Old Man Jiang's stone tablet would be buried in sand again.

Old Man Yang and His Woman

. . .

by LU Chiang

translated by Nancy DU

No leading by them by the nose, no pulling them with a rope—with only the swift, rapid flicks of a dried reed, Old Man Yang and his wife herded their cattle and sheep.

At the edge of the island where the lofty Manongwang and Mudanbi mountains merged to form a range, smoothly extending to the Pacific coast, enclosing green fields and grassy valleys, the hills rose majestic and luminous. Sometimes the land appeared cold, barren, and desolate, stretching away without a soul in sight. Sometimes it was lost in fog and the rain and mist would roll in, turning it gloomy and lonesome. Amid all this, Old Man Yang and his wife, and the cattle and the sheep that followed them, lived without any desire for hustle and bustle. They wandered noiselessly along the wooded paths, green slopes, and coastal windbreak forests, stopping now and then to look for food. My friends and I considered Old Man Yang the rightful ruler of these coasts and plains. And his wife, a woman who babbled, expressing every emotion in her gestures and her grin, reigned as his carefree queen. As for the cattle and sheep that marched forever beside them, they were his invincible troops. Occasionally these soldiers had to watch out for the reed in their master's hand, but most of the time they wandered enviably free, avoiding the jaws of the lions, tigers, and other wild beasts that had long since disappeared or retired behind bars in city zoos.

Old Man Yang was a man of distressingly few words. For over ten years, his wife had relayed her needs through simple expressions and gestures. He understood completely. The language of the cows and sheep was even simpler, so he never had to waste words. Sheep and cattle buyers from plains and cities alike both enjoyed and dreaded doing business with Old Man Yang. They liked him because he never dwelled on trivial details; he ignored current market prices and set his own rules. To him, cows and sheep were to be sold individually, priced according to their size. Once a price was fixed, he stubbornly stuck with it. But buyers feared him for the very same reason. If he didn't like trading with you, it was impossible to find him. Still the fact remained that his livestock was sought after by gourmets and pleased even the most discriminating palate.

I had also heard that Old Man Yang killed many enemies in that "foreign land" near his hometown in the north. Back in the days when he was a robust farmer, he was sent off to war from the countryside where he had labored and sweat. He left with the cries of loud, abstract slogans ringing in his ears. Time and again, he fought in desperate battles, killing both the tall American GIs and the South Korean soldiers. Later he was captured; he longed to return home but didn't want to be drawn back into the frenzy of those movements. He went to an unknown island and put on his uniform once again. Then in another battle, shrapnel caught him in the shoulder and the leg. Afterward, he always stood and walked a little stooped. He saw this as his greatest shame. The injury had robbed him of his height, and he was plagued by dreams of a strong, upright body. Sweeping his palm upward, he liked to show how tall he was in the old days. Back then, he could grab onto a twenty-foot pear tree "with one easy hook of my hand."

It was said that when Yang left the army, he refused all offers of assistance from his superiors and friends. He arrived on this stretch of land alone. It was just a spot like many others where, as a soldier, he had camped after long marches, a place without any of the grandeur and beauty of the savage, wild fields of home. But somehow it conjured up for him the place he had come from. He settled on a strip of land beside the mountain and tended his vegetable garden. He logged enough timber and bamboo to build himself a cabin, even though he ran the risk of being caught by the mountain patrol. On the day his cabin was finished, Old Man Yang drank himself into a stupor. The evening was shrouded in darkness and mist; Yang's unsteady steps led him toward the jet-black mountains. His legs gave out and he collapsed, passing out in an abandoned house in the tribal village. Demons were said to inhabit this house; few dared cross the threshold. It was also the sparring ground for wild rats and snarling mountain cats. He lay there groaning, retching, and bleeding. As it was not uncommon in those parts to see a drunkard sprawled on the ground, no one paid any attention to him. Yang woke up cradled in the arms of the woman who would later become his wife. She had covered him with a coarse linen sack and used the heat of her own body to warm him. With her mouth, she sucked clean the wounds where jagged rocks and thorny bushes had cut him.

People said Old Man Yang's wife used to be the most beautiful girl in the village. When she left home, she headed north to the city. There, she worked in factories; she was a waitress, a coffee girl. . . . Later, a small article appeared in the newspapers about a girl who was brutally raped by a gang of thugs. Her brothers sent her back home to the mountains where she was free to wander. But she had lost her ability to speak. She could only stare wide-eyed, mouth gaping as if she were calling out, pleading for help, though no words ever left her mouth. This perplexed the village shamans and gradually, one by one, the villagers forgot her. But the raping did not cease, especially by drunkards and workers from out of town. The news of Old Man Yang's marrying her became the talk of the village and he became the local laughingstock.

We had never considered finding out if there was much truth to these rumors. The fact remained that Old Man Yang truly warranted our interest. But he kept very much to himself. Whenever I encountered him, he would greet me with "Ah!" as if the sound alone was sufficient answer to all our questions.

Once, driving, I noticed him lift his reed to shoo the cows from the side of the road as I approached. His wife and sheep seemed somewhat startled by the commotion. Stopping the car, I climbed out to tell him to take his time. Our conversation then drifted to how one of his cows would soon go into labor—I had just read a manual on livestock. I offered him water from my mountain spring, but he insisted on drinking his own homemade wine, and offered me a sip. This encounter was the start of our friendship. Afterward, I would occasionally drop by to give them rice or some clothes.

Through our conversations, I learned that he had once been a shepherd on a vast plain. Gesturing, he described to me the vastness, the richness of his plain; how the edge of the grassy horizon merged with the blue sky; how, as far as the eye could see, grazing cattle and sheep were scattered over the field. His description recalled to me television images of ancient China; that distant dream was as vivid as if it had been only yesterday.

Usually, after Old Man Yang and his wife had herded the cattle and sheep into the grassy fields, they would sit side by side, either sipping wine or staring wordlessly into each other's eyes. Sometimes, they would just lean against a tree trunk and close their eyes as if taking a little nap. I'd heard rumors about what

Old Man Yang did to his woman in their little cabin by the mountain. But the fact remained that no one had ever seen him lay a hand on his wife or treat her harshly. I'd seen Old Man Yang delivering calves and lambs. He would be drenched in sweat, his hands covered in calf's blood or lamb's amniotic fluid, and utterly absorbed, as if performing a sacred task. Later, he told me that when it came to delivering calves and lambs, no one had his experience.

Old Man Yang draped a string of beads around his wife's wrist. Whenever she had time, she would hold it in her palms, gently caressing the beads one by one. She would murmur to herself as she turned each bead around slowly. He told me it was for redemption, for himself as well as for her. His eyes glistened as he spoke these words, and in a low voice, he told me he had received a letter from home. His father had passed away two years before; his mother was sick in bed. I urged him to return home for a brief visit. My words seemed to encourage him. His mouth twitching, he pulled a gray, crumpled letter out of his jacket. The letter told of happenings back home. Some people had moved, others had separated, and a yearning for dreams long gone was tangible between the lines. What interested me was the picture in the envelope and the signature at the bottom of the letter. The picture showed a tall, aging woman surrounded by several middle-aged men and women and a bunch of children. On the back of the picture, someone had written from left to right the names Ta Niu, Er Niu, and Niu Junior; grandchildren stood in the front row, and on either side were the daughters-in-law. . . .

"These are my children and their wives," Old Man Yang said, rubbing his hands together and looking lost. His reed was still clamped tightly under his armpit.

"Is this your wife on the mainland?" My suspicion was quickly confirmed.

"I was planning to return," he said under his breath.

"And her. . . ." I pointed to "her," who was still murmuring in a low voice to the sheep.

Old Man Yang sighed deeply.

After the Lunar Festival I no longer saw Old Man Yang and his "family" wandering in the hills. I guessed he had gone home. Then, one drizzly morning in the middle of winter, I heard the sound of unruly hooves outside. Soon after, my fellow workers, all covered in mud, scrambled into the house. I dashed outdoors with a stick in my hand.

Completely out of control, a herd of cattle stampeded wildly in every direction on the plain. All around, trees shook and the pastures were trodden into sludge. I jumped out of the way.

It was her. Old Man Yang's woman came sprinting up the path toward me. Whip in hand, she lashed and struck viciously at the cattle in front of her. Her face, a mask of anger, was flooded with rain or tears. It was the first time I'd seen her cry.

She raised the whip, lashing at my face as I tried to stop her. I managed to block her way. She stood there, babbling and screaming wildly. She did not appear to be frightened, though she kept pointing at herself.

"Where's Yang?" I asked her.

In the past when I'd asked her this question, her face would break into a smile. She would stretch her neck in Old Man Yang's direction. But today she just kept howling; the rain and tears on her face made her features all a blur. Suddenly, she ripped open the buttons on her raincoat. She had nothing on underneath except a man's vest, a vest that had obviously belonged to Old Man Yang. I took a deep breath. Her beautiful, full breasts filled my eyes. I stepped back, wondering if this time she had been pushed too far.

"Where's Yang?" I asked her again. "Ah Tsun, go home, go home!" I motioned to her with my hands and tried to signal her to button up her raincoat again.

She ignored me and continued to take her coat off, still muttering incoherently. She lifted her vest and took out a letter. I took the letter in my hands; it was from Old Man Yang. The envelope burned with the heat of her skin and the smell of her sweat. Old Man Yang was still back home in Liaoning. He had to attend to his mother's funeral and did not mention the date of his return.

I asked my friends to help chase the cattle that had scattered everywhere, in the hills and valleys, over the meadows, across the marshlands, and along the coast. The cows remained oblivious to our hollering and lashing. With her up front, we managed to chase them haphazardly back into their shed against the mountain. We heard the sheep bleating like crazy in their barns and we found several baby lambs that had frozen to death inside. God! How long since they'd last been fed? The poor animals could not weather the bitter northeastern wind and the biting cold from Siberia. Nor could they survive on damp grass. She stared at us in confusion as we cleared out the carcasses, not entirely comprehending what I was trying to convey to her. What kind of woman was she? When was the last time she had washed herself? We had heard that Old Man Yang took her bathing in the mountain streams. None of us knew what to do with her. We all blamed Old Man Yang for leaving her and for not asking the neighbors to keep an eye on her—but the truth was, few ever passed within five miles of their home.

I went to the nearest military post and asked the guards to send her some leftover food. The soldiers told me they had tried before, but she only downed mouthful after mouthful of uncooked rice. We discovered her stove had rusted and the one bread basket was covered with mold. How did she stay alive? Did Old Man Yang expect her to survive by herself?

We found a trap for catching civets and some snake skins in the shrubs behind the shed. There was also a pile of thin bones lying about, some fur, and the tail of a squirrel; the blood had not yet dried. And we saw that the sweet potato patch in front of the cabin was full of holes. So that was how she scraped by. Still, we couldn't help shaking our heads in disbelief.

Not long after that, I was sent north to attend a short training session. I asked my fellow workers to take care of Old Man Yang's woman and his livestock. When I returned a month later, I was eager to find out how she was doing. Over the phone, my friend asked me half jokingly whether my intentions were noble; he also told me she'd been raped again, this time by a mountain patrolman. . . .

As night fell, I drove my car along the cold, foggy mountain path. My headlights shone on a trail of cow dung and hoof tracks; beside the road, a few small animals lurking in the bushes were watching me. I was certain things had changed, either Old Man Yang had returned or she had come to her senses; otherwise the tracks on the road and the heaps of dung would not show this regular pattern. Or had someone else made a claim on her and the livestock?

I parked my car at the entrance below Old Man Yang's cabin and proceeded on foot. It was pitch dark. The droplets on the leaves glimmered faintly. Resin oozing from pine tree bark looked like the bright eyes of a rat; an owl suddenly flew overhead. I switched on my flashlight. I did not want anyone to get the wrong impression.

As I came closer, I heard sheep bleating and cows lowing. There was also the distinct rustling sound of hay. The glimmer of yellow light from inside the cabin reassured me, too. The master must be home. I clapped my hands and the dogs began to bark. As Old Man Yang's door was always open, I could hear some babbling and Old Man Yang's squeal. What had happened?

Old Man Yang had indeed returned; his face was covered with bruises.

"So you're back!" I said, grasping his still-calloused hand.

"Right!" He lowered his head and added, "That crazy woman hit me!"

I almost burst out laughing. "I think she missed you too much! So, old man, how are you?"

Old Man Yang poured some wine into a bowl and told me it was from his hometown.

He told me he almost did not make it back. His wife, his daughters-in-law, his grandchildren wept and pleaded with him not to leave. They did not want the money he'd made selling cattle and sheep, they only wanted him to stay. His wife had waited for him for forty years. She had faithfully endured the tears, the pain, the hard times, the sorrow, firmly believing he would come back. . . .

Come back he did. On his return, everyone in the village, young and old alike, crowded into the street. They beat drums and gongs and set off firecrackers in his honor. He managed to see his mother before she died, and he arranged for her funeral and built his family a two-story house. The television and refrigerator he brought back for them could only be displayed outside their home because the voltage was wrong. He was kept very busy, as were the whole village, the local county commissioners, the officials of the provincial government. But then one evening, he quietly got on a train. Tears flowed, dried, and flowed again. He could not forget the woman and the animals in the mountain. When he arrived at Taoyuan Airport, he suddenly remembered he had given away every gold ring and spent every last dime. He headed straight for home. When he reached Fengkang, he could not even afford to buy a train ticket. He scaled mountains, waded rivers, crossed plains—but he came home. When she saw him, she flung herself at him, hitting, tearing, biting him. He understood.

Old Man Yang sipped his wine and cried as he spoke. His woman, her hair hanging down, was crying, too. But I also saw the beginning of a smile.

1,230 Spots

. . .

by SHOW Foong

translated by Ching-hsi PERNG

They've agreed that he should wait for Wang Chengfu by this pond.

The pond has some geese in it and is located by the entrance to the hospital. In the last ten years, Tang Ta-sheng has come in and out of this hospital at least fifty, if not a hundred, times. Oddly, it has never occurred to him to sit by this pond. Now as he sits here, he thinks what a nice pond it is. New Year is approaching, the weather is surprisingly warm. A boy is standing by the pond feeding the golden carp, while his father snaps pictures nearby. A pregnant woman is taking a stroll. A thin, frail patient being pushed in a wheelchair gawks at the noisy sparrows in a banyan tree. The patient is rather friendly, for he smiles at everyone he sees and, with his cheeks so sunken, his grin seems to stretch from ear to ear. Somehow, he is the image of pathos.

Tang looks again at the woman, the pregnant woman, and wonders if she will give birth before or after New Year's Day. If before, the baby will be born in the year of the pig; if after, in the year of the rat. Fate is preordained. It's unfortunate that his own mother died early, for not only is he unsure of the exact hour of his birth, but there are two stories regarding his birthday, his father claiming it was the day before Midautumn, Third Aunt, the day after. He used to hate it when some serious matter came up: had he known the hour and date of his birth, he could have at least consulted a fortune-teller. In recent years, however, his life and his emotional life have been uneventful. Rather like a familiar opera whose ending one already knows, the scenario of his fate can be ignored.

It is said that an exceptionally skilled fortune-teller can trace back an event and, on the basis of your life to date, determine the exact time of your birth. But now there's really no need for this. Half a year ago, it was different, but today, the moment he stepped out of the doctor's office, his mind was almost made up. And once this matter is settled, nothing very serious can happen for the rest of his life.

Wang Chengfu still hasn't come. He is quite annoying. Actually, he is a little hard of hearing, nothing serious in a 68-year-old man. But he is also so dumb that he has to be watched all the time, or he will even forget to eat. There are more Chinese characters on Wang's body; so, on this first day of treatment, he will have to receive at least 500 pricks. Tang himself got 548 the first time. The nurse had a sweet way of cajoling him, calling him "Uncle" all the time.

"Uncle," she said, "you're in luck! All these 548 pricks were paid for by the Vocational Assistance Commission for Retired Servicemen. At NT$112 a spot, if you had to pay for them, it would cost you 60 grand or more for today's treatment alone!"

He forced a smile. Who needed such luck? But what did she know? The nurse was so young there was no use explaining to her. This all happened back in 1953 when her mother probably hadn't even been born yet, let alone she herself.

Five hundred and forty-eight laser spots, and every one of them hurt. The doctor compared it to the sting from a snapped rubber band. All right, so it's like being snapped by a rubber band; to be snapped 548 times is sure to hurt. The doctor was also a youngster, all smiles:

"It hurt when you got your tattoos. To have them removed should be no big deal."

Strangely—maybe because he was young then—the tattooing didn't seem to hurt much. Three pins, bunched together, were dipped into dye and pricked the skin.

"Kill Zhu and Weed out Mao" on his left arm.

"Anti-Communist; Anti-Russia" on his right arm.

On his chest was a map and a large flag; on his back, "Succeed or Die."

The afternoon sun is warm. The white geese glide leisurely. He counts nine of them, but there are several more under the azalea trees by the pond, so he isn't sure about their number. Inexplicably, a lone mallard dashes about among them—a bizarre picture.

A breeze blows, and some leaves fall from the banyan tree.

He remembers his advice to Wang Chengfu yesterday:

"It doesn't hurt, and it's not ugly. Laser, Ruby Laser. American scientific invention! Remarkable! One machine costs over four million NT dollars! What a great treatment, you rub on some medication, and in three days you can take a shower. Wang Chengfu, don't be stubborn. If this weren't a good thing, would I try to convince you? I myself have to have twelve; one more and then it's all over. I even made the appointment for you. Just go for the treatments, and then you can go back home next year and nobody'll give you any trouble. It doesn't hurt—I'll be damned if I'm lying. Afterward, it just looks like a few plum-shaped white dots on you. It really doesn't hurt."

In fact, it does hurt, of course, and much more on the chest and back than on the arms. But Wang Chengfu is the stubborn type. While everyone else has revisited the mainland, he doesn't dare go. Sometimes, when he gets homesick enough, he cries:

"But no, I can't. Communists are so treacherous. I have seven national flags on me, plus 'Persist in the Anti-Communist Conviction'; 'Determined to Revenge and Recover Lost Country,' plus 'Ba-ge-tu-tai-wan.' How can they forgive me?"

Though Wang appears confused now, Tang can hardly imagine that at the time, he would have gotten some English tattoos. Wang cannot even read the English alphabet! Ai! This Wang Chengfu—he is the butt of many jokes. One time, some white cotton stuff was pulled from his trouser leg, which turned out to be long underwear. He said he was quite sure he had put the underwear on that morning before he put on his trousers, but obviously that wasn't the case. By the time he discovered his mistake, it was already noon. Early that morning, Tang had gone to send US$200 to his grandson, who was getting married. When he got back, he found Wang in a very embarrassing situation. Irritated as he was, he didn't know what to do with this man.

That years ago, someone like Wang would have been fashionable enough to get tattooed with English words! "Ba-ge-tu-tai-wan," they say, means "Return to Taiwan." Tang cannot help laughing when he thinks of this. Wang Chengfu has a knack for turning every language—including English and crude Taiwanese—into Szechwanese.

Wang is still not here. Tang is curious to know how many spots he is getting today. As Wang dreads pain, Tang took it upon himself to tell the doctor to do only his two arms today, leaving the chest and back for next time. It's close to the new year; let him have a nice holiday.

Tang's own first treatment was on the arms, too. Five hundred and forty-eight spots. A month later, during the second treatment on the chest and back, he received 682 laser spots. Since then, he has come once a month, treating in turn the chest and back. He keeps it firmly in mind: Altogether he has had 1,230 little holes. Translated into money, it comes to NT$137,760. With each hole treated six times, the cost amounts to NT$826,560.

"Thus, I am a wealthy man. The 'nothingness' of my body is worth close to a million dollars—at Veterans General Hospital's rates. In a beauty parlor, they charge five hundred per spot, which means four million in total!"

Occasionally there's a story about kidnapping in the paper. Kidnappers often demand three to five million dollars, sometimes even tens of millions. He has never understood how a person could be worth that much.

At the age of sixty-nine—wow! Never in all his life has he been so valuable! The tattooing itself did not add to his worth, but its removal costs a million dollars. Ha! Everything in life is preordained.

He's heard of a chap who had the "Song of Righteousness" tattooed all over his body and who also went for treatments. He wonders how many pricks that man had to endure. The fair skin he got in return must be worth at least $3 million. What he cannot understand is why the "Song of Righteousness" should be removed. How could its author, Wen Tienxiang, who lived in the thirteenth century, have offended the Communists?

Forty-odd years ago, when they bravely endured the pain of the piercing pins, who would have expected such bad luck in old age? Ai, there's no logic to this life. Providence figures in everything.

The Korean War broke out on June 25, 1950. In October, Tang went, with a rifle made by the Han-yang Arsenal—junk from the Nationalist Army days. He hadn't yet fired a shot when the Americans dropped shells and he was captured.

The two sides exchanged POWs. What puzzled him was that five Chinese POWs would be exchanged for one U.S. POW. For the first time it occurred to him that Americans were worth more, five times as much as the Chinese.

Chinese lives were worthless! On the battlefields of the Korean War, soldiers in their twenties and thirties died one on top of the other. The youngest were only fifteen or sixteen. After three months' training, barely able to manage a bayonet, they were driven to the battlegrounds. The hand-to-hand combat drills were pointless, of course, since the Americans only fought from a distance. They never sent troops into hand-to-hand combat. Thrust!—Hey!—Thrust!—Hey!—Hey—Hey—Hey!—Thrust!—Hey! But who's going to use a bayonet?

Shrapnel flew his way and pierced his back. It was taken out, leaving a scar the size of a rice bowl. For him, that was the Korean War—memories the size of a rice bowl.

How much is a person worth after all?

How can some people be worth $100 million? But that's the price some kidnappers ask.

They say some people's clothes are worth $10 million. He has something on him that's worth $800,000. Unfortunately, that $800,000 was spent so that people *can't* see what's on him, not so that they can. Eight hundred thousand dollars so that you can't see something—he cannot even begin to explain it.

They say that it was after the Korean War that Lin Biao fell out of favor with Mao Zedong. Many people died in the war—perhaps two million. Very few survived. In his company, all 180 of them died but him. After the war, Mao incredibly got mad at Lin:

"Why bring troops back? I entered the Korean War to annihilate the Chinese population. Why not fight until everyone's dead?"

It was his idea to have his left arm tattooed "Kill Zhu and Weed out Mao."

"Why, no longer 'Anti-Communist'?"

The young doctor joked with him lightly, perhaps to make his patient relax a bit, Tang thought.

"There's no need for me to fight them," he said confidently. "They're killing each other now!"

"And no more 'Kill Zhu and Weed out Mao,' either? Well, Mao means Mao Zedong, but who's this Zhu?"

"Zhu means Zhu De, their commander-in-chief then," he said. "There's no need for me to kill them now. They've both reported to Yama. Saved me the trouble."

The doctor wore gold-rimmed glasses. He had a baby face, looked just over twenty. What did this little brat know?

Tang would always stand by his tattoos. Unlike Zheng Jiaxiao.

One day, Zheng was watching some people fly kites at the Sun Yat-sen Memorial Hall when a member of the Democratic Progressive Party came up to him and asked, "Hey you, 'Anti-Communist and Anti-Russia,' what are you doing in Taiwan? Go, go and recover your mainland! Why stay here and eat Taiwan's rice?"

Moving away, Zheng called back: "I didn't want these, they forced me! They forced me to be tattooed."

Tang is somewhat angry at Zheng. That good-for-nothing. What could the damned DPP do to you anyway? Besides, he had no tattoo on his face; how could you tell he was a DPP member? And even if he was, so what? What was it to the DPP if you wanted to pierce your own skin? Moreover, if we hadn't fought the Communists back then, we would have all ended up under Chairman Mao. And then would you sons of bitches with your full stomachs be talking such nonsense?

In the good old days, there were 14,000 of us and we were called the "Anti-Communist Freedom Seekers." A movie was made about us, *Fourteen Thousand Witnesses*. On the day we arrived in Taiwan, we marched in a parade and were decorated with bright silk stripes. There was a large turnout everywhere we went. Now, since Gu Zhenggang's death, January 23rd goes unobserved. There's no one to preside over the 1–23 Freedom Day celebrations. Speeches aren't given. Moreover, right there in front of the memorial hall of our nation's founding father, in broad daylight, that motherfucking son of a bitch! Damned disgusting! And what's even more disgusting, that good-for-nothing Zheng Jiaxiao goes and says he was forced! Nothing beats that! Zheng Jiaxiao, fuck your shameless ancestors!

"Were you willing then, or were you coerced?"

Tang was surprised the doctor should ask such a question. That was during his second laser treatment. His chest was being torn up and heated by the national flag. He could smell a slight burning, and all of a sudden, it seemed familiar. Recovering himself, he recognized it as the smell of the battlefield: flesh scorched by fire—that was it.

So the Korean War had continued up to this day, awaiting its finale; the epilogue was taking place forty-four years later.

"I wouldn't say I was forced," he replied, his chest hurting more and more. "Fourteen thousand were tattooed. Wouldn't it have been a shame not to go along?"

"Ah," said the doctor, adjusting the blue eyeshield he wore while operating to protect himself from the laser beams—rather like Batman or someone on TV. "So it's 'peer pressure.'"

"What beer?" He didn't understand. "We had no beer then."

"Peer. People of the same group. They form a coercive force among themselves."

The doctor seemed to have some education. Tang could only partly comprehend what he said and he had no intention of delving into the subject. It hurt a lot on the chest, but you're not supposed to scream—not if you're a man. But some tears seeped from the corners of his eyes after all.

The last time he'd shed tears was five years ago, on his first return visit to his native land. When his wife learned that he hadn't remarried in Taiwan, she walked ten miles to meet him. No sooner had she entered the door than she dropped to her knees:

"I have not remained your wife, I have let you down—"

Unable to pull her to her feet, he had to kneel down, too.

"No more of this talk. I'm only grateful to you—our son and daughter are both grown up—and there's even a grandson. I owe you so much for shouldering the responsibility alone."

He gave his wife a heart-shaped necklace. She neither accepted nor declined it, but simply said, "It's inconvenient for me. If I wear it, the other side might get suspicious. Give it to Xiaohong instead. Seeing Xiaohong wear it will be like wearing it myself. I was eighteen, too, when I married you."

Xiaohong, their granddaughter, was the exact image of his wife when she was young.

Those were the last tears he shed.

It was late spring, and cool enough to wear a long-sleeved shirt. In this way he was able to cover up the characters on his arms. In the evening, he went to the kitchen to bathe. His third younger brother poured water for him. The dim light in the kitchen was only about five watts.

"Oh my!" his brother exclaimed. "Second Elder Brother, whatever happened to your back—such a mess of colors?"

Tang didn't expect his brother to be so sharp-eyed, and he had to tell the truth. Third Brother was a low-ranking official. When he heard, he looked troubled.

"This isn't serious—but then it could be somewhat serious. It's all right for family members to see it, but if it's seen by others, there'll be trouble. I think we ought to be careful. 'Communists are like the moon'—you've heard that expression?—'they're different on the first day and the fifteenth of the month.'"

Since then, he has not returned to his home on the mainland.

Where the hell is Wang Chengfu? Isn't he finished with the treatment yet?

Tang's son wrote him a letter, asking him to come home for good. Thinking it over for a year, he decided to have the tattoos removed by laser first.

Wang Chengfu was a bit on the dumb side. But luckily, he was a bit of a coward, too, and hadn't gotten into trouble, unlike Li Zhixin, who almost killed himself. That was eight or nine years ago. On someone's advice he went to a beauty parlor and got hold of the stuff used for perms. With it he corroded his own skin. As a result, the characters still remained, but his skin was all burns and welts. It was a terrible sight. Li was severely reprimanded by the medical officer.

And then there was Lao Jiuzhong, another person with fantastic ideas. This also happened about ten years ago. He missed his native home so much he almost went crazy, but back then there was no such thing as laser treatment. So he went to a tattoo shop to turn the Chinese characters into green dragons. Having to disguise the original characters, however, the dragons did not turn out very well. Thus, he got the nickname, "Lao Jiulong," which means "Lao the Dragons," punning on "Lousy Dragons." Tang had seen Lao's dragons, but because they are all contorted and mixed up, he didn't even know how many there were. But at least Lao could go home; his son even came to visit him in Taiwan! A while later, Lao received laser treatments, but it took a lot of talking. The VACRS had been subsidizing the removal of tattoos like "Loyalty to Party and Country" and "Liberate the Mainland," but it had never seen tattooed dragons. It was only after long explanations and even personal testimony from Lao's former commanding officer that the origin of his dragons was clarified. Since the number of his punctures had multiplied, he had to endure more laser spots, which hurt him so much he clenched his teeth. After the treatment, it looked as if his dark chest were covered with a protective plate.

"Mr. Lao," joked the doctor, "with these dragons all over your body, you look like a gangster. Are you a member of the Qing Bang or the Hong Bang?"

"Doctor, the gang we joined in those days had very strict rules," replied Lao, who had a middle school education and a quick mind. "We had to be tattooed in order to join. And our gang is neither the Qing Bang not the Hong Bang, it's the KMT."

When Lao returned from the treatment, he told everyone that story.

Wang Chengfu is still not here. Tired of sitting, Tang Tasheng stands up and walks about. He doesn't dare go far, however, and soon finds himself singing to an old Szechwan tune:

The old don't have to care,
The young don't have to care,
It's the in-between alone
Who are given the scare.

At the end of his song, he laughs—imagine remembering that conscription song from more than forty years ago! "The old" refers to those between forty to fifty, and "the young" refers to those thirteen and fourteen. He was twenty-three then, exactly "in-between" and scared to death. He was, of course, conscripted.

The old don't have to care,
The young don't have to care,
It's the in-between alone
Who are given the scare.

Maybe because he feels good, he sings the song again.

At this moment, a slender, middle-aged man comes by and gives him some pamphlets:

"Sir, Lin and Hau for President and VP; New Party for the National Assembly, please. Thank you."

Tang is taken aback. What? This is the Veterans General Hospital, the stronghold of the KMT. How come this New Party member turns up here?

He is still wondering when he sees Wang Chengfu looking around timidly.

"Over here!" he shouts.

Wang Chengfu is a short guy. When he hears Tang's voice, his face lights up, and he waddles over on his two short legs.

"It didn't hurt much, but it hurt some!" How rare for Wang to utter a clear sentence. "The doctor says you're okay now, you've graduated, you don't have to come anymore. Next month you'll have delicate new skin! But I'm in for it, my ordeal is just beginning!"

The two of them head for the gate, to take the bus to Sanxia, where they will transfer to Baiji.

Tang has a hollow feeling. Something like an empty stomach or dizzy head. But it's neither.

Everything's gone, he suddenly realizes. Gone is "Kill Zhu and Weed out Mao," gone is "Anti-Communist and Anti-Russia," gone is the map, gone is the national flag, gone is "Succeed or Die." From now on everything is wiped out, as if a ring worn for forty years were suddenly removed, leaving nothing but a white circle. White of complete emptiness. White of complete nothingness.

Where are those bloody oaths? The doctor says they are absorbed. But where do they go when they are absorbed? Into the blood, or the marrow?

Subconsciously, he touches the bowl-size scar. It's still there, knotted like the bark of a tree. He feels a little more secure.

"The doctor told me to come back in two months," says Wang Chengfu. Somehow he has become a chatterbox today and cannot stop talking. Maybe you're less dumb when you're hurt. "By then you'll probably be off to the mainland for good. But I've got everything memorized—how to make the transfer next time, I've got everything memorized."

He speaks like a good boy.

They get on the bus at the stop. Before the bus starts, Tang moves closer to Wang and shouts in his ear:

"Next time—I'll come with you again!"

"What?" Wang shouts back. "Didn't you say that you were going home to stay with your son for good?"

"We'll talk about 'staying for good' later. I know what I'll do now. Next month I'll go visit them, and give them my family support allowance. I'll return in ten days. I've thought it all out. The rest of my life I'll just stay in the Three Gorges, Sanxia—over there it's called Sanxia, and here it's also Sanxia. Oh, yes, you must try to remember that Sanxia is the last stop; from there you transfer to Baiji. Get off at Baiji and walk—to Home of the Honored Citizens. Don't forget!"

"Don't worry, I won't forget—Sanxia is the last stop."

The bus moves. Both men are tired, and both feel a strange pain. The "Ba-ge-tu-tai-wan" on Wang Chengfu's right arm leans against the completely erased "Kill Zhu and Weed out Mao" on Tang Dasheng's left arm. To the rhythmical rocking of the bus, the two arms rub against each other all the way home. Finally, their heads resting together, the two old men fall asleep.

Valley of Hesitation

. . .

by LI Yu

translated by Daniel J. BAUER

I

The colonel was leading his column of troops as they trudged along toward the mountain to take part in a road-building project. The project would be extremely difficult, and probably dangerous. Some men might well be injured or even lose their lives. Good thing then that there were ex-soldiers among them. These veterans had either been conscripted or had volunteered. They had given up everything, and battle had become the only thing they could claim as their own. Now that the war was over, they really had nothing left. But then again, they had nothing to worry about either. Their new task suited them well, serving their own interests and those of the nation.

As for the colonel, in the beginning he had been active in intelligence work and espionage. He had had a hand in several major events shaping contemporary Chinese history. He had acted out of love and concern for his country, whether his work involved incarcerating or even assassinating a few people. After he came to the island, the authorities still wanted to make use of his professional knowledge and wealth of experience, and thus he was again put in charge of several key cases. In crucial moments of crisis or difficulty, he helped to stabilize national control and authority over the island.

When the island was designing its first major project, the great east-west public highway, no one was surprised that the president himself ordered the colonel to supervise it, putting him in charge of making the plans and implementing them from start to finish. You couldn't give such a high-level responsibility to an officer without an engineering background, of course, and it seemed the proper recognition of his abilities, a reward for his loyalty. There were some who said that opening the road should fall to the transportation ministry. But it was a military matter as well, and its internal machinations had all the complexities of espionage work. With the military aspect, the supervision, the investigations, and what all, try as you might, you could not find anyone more suited to the job.

But there were others who might describe the situation differently. Some tigers were best controlled by luring them away. This was a man whose very existence was a source of discomfort to many because he was privy to so many national secrets, and his memory was a vault of stories. This was a scheme to send him into exile!

The colonel and his column of troops had reached the foot of the mountain in personnel carriers. The forest was quite thick here, so the rest of the way would be hard going. Add to that the fact they'd have to lug along all their equipment, and a quantity of explosives. The men proceeded warily, every step an effort.

They came to the proposed starting point and found themselves in a small, untouched forest. There they carved out a flat base and set up a camp area. After that, according to the first phases of the project, they frequently had to advance an inch at a time, both over land and through water.

In constructing a road, the crucial task is blowing up the mountains. According to the blueprints for the project, a spot had been chosen. There they found the ideal site in the cliff, brought in the appropriate explosives, and in the appropriate fissures and crevices, carefully arranged lines and fuses. The entire company retreated to hiding places. When all were safe and secure, a final inspection tour was completed. And then the switch was thrown.

For a time there was a great stillness. Then suddenly a rumbling arose. With tremendous force, the cliff came crashing down.

The hills and valley trembled and swayed. A piercing light flashed, flames soared into the sky, and the sun changed color. Fragments of rock rained down like dying stars, and dust covered the world below. It was as if war had just broken out, and for the soldiers, it brought memories vividly back to life.

What flashed through the colonel's mind were scenes of his first years in the military. Visions exploded with the fury of the nitroglycerine itself as it burst into a fiery mass. It was as if that intensity swept through his being, taking it by storm.

The colonel became enthralled with any activity involving explosives. It was so dangerous, the chief engineer himself was required to arrange and execute all the details. The colonel always stood by, watching attentively. As the engineer noticed his every move being followed with meticulous attention, he wondered if he was suspected of collusion with the Communists. But eventually he realized that wasn't the case at all. The colonel was simply fascinated with the work of blowing up mountains.

The more the colonel watched, the more obsessed he became. He asked the engineer to let him try his hand at it. Overseeing terrorist activities required a knowledge of explosives, of course, and since the colonel had once been involved in espionage, he naturally had some training and experience. Now as he became more and more familiar with the steps in their particular sequence, the engineer reluctantly allowed him to try it once or twice. As it turned out, the engineer need not have worried; the colonel was even better at it than he was. So he relaxed and let the colonel take over.

Thus the colonel, with incomparable energy and focus, launched a whole new career. It was no different from the times when he took orders and executed secret missions. The explosions filled him with a kind of ecstasy; his spirits soared, and from deep within there arose an intense feeling of release. There was a ferocity to his enthusiasm, like that of one who drinks madly and then smashes the glass or lets loose in extreme anger and breaks a windowpane.

Afterward, his body was covered with sweat, his mind exhausted. It was like a fever that peaks, leaving both mind and body in total collapse.

The colonel was a little startled by this. At his age, he ought to have an even and harmonious temperament. Throughout his life, he could never stop reflecting upon things, which caused him to be objective, detached, cool, and unruffled. So where did this sudden passion come from, now that he had left a life of duty and come into the wilds?

This was how it had always been. The colonel was a man of complex emotions. Time and again, he would complete a project and his comrades and colleagues would admire his accomplishment, be content, and begin to relax. Only the colonel could not. For the sake of the democratic future of his country, he had had to deal cruelly with some human lives. Thus, his life had its dark shadows, and he couldn't hide them away in his heart. Decades of brooding had a cumulative effect, and though on the outside he appeared cool and debonair, quick and able at every task, deep inside he was a melancholic, pessimistic soul.

He relived the experience of each and every case, remembered the names of all involved, could still see the panic-stricken face of each individual. His memory would often harass him in the form of nightmares that refused to go away. Sometimes when he was alone or awake in the middle of the night, he'd suddenly be in a dungeon for secret investigations or a torture chamber shrouded in darkness. Then it was no longer someone else's torture chamber, but his own. He had no choice but to suffer with those persistent nightmares.

Missions were completed; the government replaced those in positions of authority; new chapters in history began. At all levels, high and low, he saw that it all boiled down to this: life was without light.

Born into an aristocratic family, the colonel was like every true Chinese man of letters: he had received an education in poetry and the fine arts. Whenever these moods overwhelmed him, he forced himself to suppress his inner turmoil, and for a brief time he managed. In the deep of night, he would pick up a pen and write a few words or paint a picture. The sense of contemplative calm that arose from his artistic endeavors could often lift him from the depths of his gloom and revive him, helping him face the next day's task.

Now balls of fire and bits of rock soared through the air before his very eyes. The colonel felt that not only was the mountain exploding, but those tortuous nightmares of his were exploding as well. Yes, with every blast it seemed one of them was blown to bits. No wonder, then, that he felt relief such as he had never before experienced.

And the nightmares just lined up, one after the other, waiting to be sent off into oblivion.

The colonel became entirely possessed by the violence of the explosions, and the more explosions he set off, the crazier he became. Pushing far beyond the limits of the project, he was no longer himself. The days and nights ran together. The work teams kept busy and resigned themselves to their fate. It seemed to them that they were back in war times. Battle conditions were intense, the situation was fraught with anxiety, and everyone was afraid. There in the middle of the forest, the fields of a war with no enemy were brilliantly lit.

Who could have guessed that the more explosions there were, the more nightmares there would be, too? One by one they visited him, uninvited, shoving and crowding each other, twisting into bunches, rolling back and forth, winding into balls. In the middle of the night when the others were asleep, he lay there awake all by himself and they gathered—a force shaped by mad, furious winds, sweeping through his bedroom with a roaring clamor. They pressed up against him, threw themselves violently at him, crawled all over him.

Those days he couldn't help being overwhelmed by fear. On the outside, cool and collected, he continued directing the work project. On the inside, his heart anxious, he was awash with doubt and dread. He could see that the long-suppressed darkness held within was about to be unleashed and break through to the surface. To resist its force, he had to summon all his determination and strength. But the effort brought him to the edge of madness.

The colonel aged and grew thinner. His face lost its natural glow and took on a pallor more shadowy and somber than trees after sundown.

Then finally the disaster happened. In the space of seconds, as rapidly as a spark leaps into flame, the colonel and the rubble went flying together through the air. An ambulance could never climb the steep road, so the troops carried him to the medical station at the foot of the mountain.

The colonel wavered between life and death; in flashes of consciousness he saw light, and then all was dark again. He heard the sound of footsteps, the metallic clang of medical instruments, clothes rustling, voices talking in low tones. When the noise faded, he sank into utter stillness. He was terribly afraid and wanted only to climb out of it, and how desperately he struggled! He heard someone speaking, but it was his voice. He was talking to himself. If only this one time he could manage to survive, he would certainly be cut free from his previous existence. He would no doubt begin an entirely different kind of life.

Three days later he regained consciousness and realized he had lost half a leg. He had become a cripple.

The colonel understood this disaster as a kind of warning from above. He came close to total madness, and could only manage to control himself by drawing on the strength of everything around him, almost doing violence to himself in the process.

One day the project moved to a location facing a valley. They arrived precisely as sundown swept the mountain peaks.

Against the hills on the horizon, a line of cliffs stood out in relief, dominating the gorge below. The sunlight that remained was magnificent. The mountain peaks glowed and the sun caught in the treetops, all dappled and sparkling as they reached into the air. Their green was as enchanting as emerald. The outermost tips of the branches were gilded, delicate as finely woven gold thread. The vista extended far into the distance. It was truly an extraordinary sight.

Halfway down the mountain, night had already settled in. The valley lay in darkness, stripped of color and form, making it appear shadowy and ambiguous. When one searched the very pit of the valley, there appeared to be a bottom, but a hardly visible one, dark beyond all measure and comprehension. Here the air swirled and mists billowed, monsterlike, creating an atmosphere impossible to fathom.

The colonel was struck by the breathtaking beauty of it all, but in an instant, the profound melancholy of the scene overwhelmed him. Suddenly his mood plunged from the towering peaks to the depths below, filling him with uncontrollable trepidation.

Others saw the spectacular, even dizzying beauty of the mountains and valleys, but the colonel saw an omen. A sign appeared to him, speaking to him of what was in his heart, what he was to encounter, his position now, his past, and his future.

He was a man with enough intelligence and sensitivity to grasp that, given the prowess he had once had and his present physical condition, this had to be a sign.

The president, in fact, did not want him to step down, but the colonel was strong-willed and forced him to agree. Special arrangements were made for a hefty pension, and before the engineer and troops left the area, they built the colonel a rather comfortable residence on the side of a precipice.

The colonel bade them farewell. He would accompany them no farther. He shuffled along back to the edge of the mountain, where he could look down into the deep valley below. His earlier life had been replete with vivid, marvelous stories, but it was never mentioned again. In contrast, the life that followed for him was as smooth as the surface of a pond, as still as an unmoving cloud. Yet the details of it all came to be known.

Having shed all ordinary obligations, the colonel returned to his most essential self. His material demands were utterly basic. "Ask for nearly nothing, and you can live on nearly nothing" applied perfectly here.

A group of aborigines also lived there in the mountain forest. They were gentle, simple people, and the colonel established a friendship with them. They helped him plant a vegetable patch in front of and behind his dwelling, and he raised a few ducks and chickens. They also taught him some handicraft skills. Fairly unusual trees and plants grew in the mountain forest, and it wasn't uncommon to see rare birds and wild animals. As the sun set, he would take slow strolls. Thus the colonel came to understand the lush abundance and great ease of the natural world.

Though the public highway was being built, motor vehicles weren't actually using it yet. Every few days the colonel would take his crutch and make his way along the road, one careful step at a time, to the edge of the hill village, where he bought household supplies.

The village had a shopping lane with a stand for meat, a grocery and hardware store, a tailor shop, and a betel nut stand with various edibles. There was also a shop that sold stationery goods. The paper mill stood on the hill right behind the shop and produced an extremely delicate, fine grade of paper. With a touch of your hand, you could feel how soft and smooth it was. The paper had a sheen as well, a gloss similar to moonlight. To think that such a remote village, so far from the cities, could produce paper of this quality, mused the colonel, how amazing!

Delighting in the feel of the scrolls of glossy paper, he returned home. The colonel sat in front of the window and let his mind conjure old memories from long ago, how his art teacher had instructed him to copy the paintings of the masters, and how he had drawn a few sketches. Now as he remembered, he'd enjoyed those art classes more than any of the other, "serious" subjects at school.

Then he recalled that after entering the world of politics, whenever he felt low, he would sketch at night by lamplight.

There was no avoiding it. Once again the colonel took up his paintbrush.

He began from the very beginning, drawing like a child, his hand very awkward. His sketches had the stiffness of a novice. He remembered his teacher's instructions: draw from life, let life be your base, use life as a beginning, life as reality. When a painting was finished, when it was fully realized, it would not lack this life force.

And so, later, you would often see the colonel, his painting satchel strapped to his back, his crutch in hand, as he rambled through the hills and along the rivers. He seemed to be searching for a certain scene, or working out in his mind a particular pattern. Sometimes you would see him simply standing still, transfixed. He appeared to be investigating a certain object, studying the fine contours of some form. Then he would deliberate about the right angle, set up his easel, adjust his paper, and reach for his pigments. He would lean back against a rock and lose himself in utter concentration.

He found his surroundings incredibly stimulating. Each spot offered him an entire world for a picture, and he was able to find life everywhere. With heightened vision, the colonel noticed tiny details, infinitesimal lines. He came to grasp stillness and motion, and before long, his brush moved with disciplined spirit. Those who saw his paintings thought they were the professional works of a master artist.

Thus, it no longer seemed appropriate to call him "the colonel." From then on, he was known as "the artist."

Gradually the artist became a celebrity, and everyone in the area came to hear of this man from the city, that he had a crippled leg, that he lived in a wooden house beside the road facing the mountain, and that he painted with extraordinary grace.

Oh, it was quite something—you'd look at the painted flower blossoms and they just seemed real, so that you couldn't help but reach out to touch and smell them. The birds perched on the tree branches seemed ready to take off into the sky. And the tree branches themselves, growing in such abundance, seemed to sway, assuming a thousand aspects. The scenes offered sunny days and rainy days, the moment the sun rose at dawn and the moment it set at dusk. There was day and night and light and shadow. Those who saw the paintings felt permeated by them, or vice versa, as though they themselves actually lingered there in the scenes.

The paintings waiting to be mounted in the paper shop began to attract the attention of those on the lookout for them.

But the more the artist painted, the more dissatisfied he felt. Although the paintings his brush produced had form, they lacked spirit, a special air that could provide the vitality needed to make them come to life.

What was it the paintings lacked? It was something, of course, that dwelled deep, deep within. It belonged to what existed outside of form; it came from the innermost regions. It related to the personal quality of the individual's soul. He remembered the words of his master, but they were of no help.

He spent less time outdoors now, remaining inside his house. He began to mull over a new project—portraits.

II

From the village hardware store he procured an old mirror. Not since his life in the mountains began had he even owned a mirror.

He expected to see reflected there the eyebrows jutting out as always, the very pronounced lines of the nose and lips, the silhouette of an uncompromising face. He had never had any doubts about his unique physical features or how they were shaped by his profession, about the essential characteristics of his life.

Instead he saw that no form looked back at him from the mirror, that everything seemed to shift and waver. Startled, he turned down the light and leaned forward.

He lifted his hands and rubbed his cheeks, pausing at the angular ridge where eyebrows and cheekbones met. In the past this spot had been exceptionally striking, a great source of pride for him, more so than any other feature.

His fingers smoothed the lax, unresponsive muscles where the skin was loose and soft. The passing of youth was no surprise; what shocked him was the change in what had been his most brilliant features. Now they were obscured by layers of gloom and anxiety, so that he felt like a prisoner, locked deep in the abyss of brooding melancholy.

He changed angles, and this shifted the light so that the rays from the lamp reflected from behind, drowning his face in shadow. It became less and less his face, but rather a strange shape that floated and sank in the murky glow behind him.

Sharp, thin, rough, and uneven, his face looked pale and ferocious. How in the world could that be a face? It had to be a spirit. He didn't want to look and moved his chair back, out of the range of the mirror.

The chair bumped the lamp, making its rays reflect off his face and waver there. The longest shadow moved into prominence, growing taller and shifting back and forth. It detached itself from his physical body and became a body itself, swimming up through the air.

In the dark room, a table and bed were visible, all other objects having been eliminated. Life was reduced to its most pure and still form. The mountain forest was utterly quiet. A hint of obscure animal sounds hung in the air, and one could imagine the sound of wind, the swaying of trees, and the mist that rises from below into the skies.

A chill swept over him, and he stood up, oddly off balance. He reached behind his chair and felt for his crutch.

The paths along the steep mountainside were shrouded in night, and he had to be unusually attentive. Very carefully he stepped forward. A dense pocket of darkness had settled in. It was nerve-wracking, intimidating, and the warmth of it clung to you. You lost all sense of wariness; you felt yourself enticed and lured on, as in a dream, yes, lured into a dream.

Far away and yet also very near, his hometown seemed to beckon, calling out its invitation. There below him lay the bottomless valley. He walked on, leaning against the side of the cliff for support. He was only a step away from tumbling into that dark, endless gorge. If he leaped, he would be safe, rescued, consumed, and lost as well. The past, present, and future, none of it would exist any longer, nothing would ever happen again, nothing would continue or carry on.

On the side of the cliff, time came to a halt, awaiting that leap.

A gust of wind blew softly from behind, like a gentle hand tugging on his shirttails. He trembled in fear and stepped back, his body a mass of tension, dripping with sweat.

A lively ceremony was taking place because the highway was now in full operation. Imported buses wound their way up the mountain. Designed to be attractive as well as comfortable, they represented the state of the art, a sign that the island had made great political and economic progress. In a tiny forest cove, the artist turned from his painting to look at the coaches as they ascended. He himself had played a part, had helped to construct and open the road, and this pleased him.

The passengers enjoyed the rush of air in the bus and the sound of soft music, and when they passed through the expansive valley, they kept peering ahead, sitting forward and upright in their seats, their faces pressed against the windows. They, too, were taken in by the strangeness. Afterward, a bizarre mood descended over them. It was as if they had encountered a whirlpool and been sucked helplessly into depths they had no desire to enter. They had never experienced anything like this before.

And when they returned from their journey and told friends what had happened, everyone considered it quite unusual. They all wanted to go see for themselves.

Now the artist sat before the mirror. He studied himself carefully. Entirely oblivious to everything around him, he would lift his brush and, with absolute seriousness, focus all his attention on the work at hand.

His sketching had sharpened his skills. Reproducing forms was not difficult for him, but what he could convey on the surface had very little significance. He was still unable to express the feeling that informed a scene. Regardless of how much he yearned for that kind of transcendence, he simply could not force it, and his brush faltered. He was filled with gloom, and his paintings brought him no joy.

The more difficulty the colonel-turned-artist encountered, the more determined he was to triumph. He was stubborn. If he could not produce a masterpiece, well, it just wouldn't do, that was all there was to it. He had made up his mind.

People talked, and the painter and the cliffs and valley all prompted curiosity. When public buses drove through, the passengers began asking the drivers to stop there. Some even made the trip for just this reason.

Tourists walked along the edge of the cliffs, and it was so, what people said was true: both heaven and hell appeared before their eyes. At the same time, a certain shudder ran through the onlookers, and no one could help but fall into a strange mood. Tourists flocked there, and this went on over a long period of time. There were even cases of people losing control and jumping into the valley.

It became known among tourists that the artist did not put on airs and act the part of a great master, but, on the contrary, emerged from his wooden home and welcomed visitors as if they were long-lost friends. He'd invite them in for tea, let them relax and rest a while. They would exchange the usual pleasantries and share the latest news from the city.

After talking a bit, the artist sometimes invited one or another of them to stay longer. He offered them a seat and asked to be allowed to sketch a quick portrait.

Just as you might imagine, the ones the artist invited to stay were precisely those with some tendency to leap into the gorge. He could see it in them the moment they met, as they first stood talking and laughing.

After people jumped into the gorge, they would simply disappear, case closed. What made the artist empathize most with those people was how they suffered in those moments on the edge of the cliff, their gaping mouths as terror overtook them, their mysterious sense of hopelessness.

Words were not necessary. They simply sat serenely before the artist. They could not say when the peace fell away, or when their mood settled and became calm again. But according to their accounts of it, their fate took a new course from that moment on.

Returning such a melancholic gaze, you were forced to admit that no matter how you had suffered, you had to be more fortunate than the man possessing that face.

One winter day at sunset, the weather was especially cold. There were no tourists and serenity had returned to the mountain forest.

With the chill, the light had been particularly brilliant. Now dusk came to the peaks, and the valley was surrounded by clouds. Inside his house, the artist looked out as he went about his business and saw a man standing far off, facing the gorge. In the rays that radiated off the mountain he stood framed by the window, a solitary figure, nearly transparent.

The artist suddenly recalled that many years before, on a night with an equally beautiful sunset, he stood in that man's very spot, and he could remember how it felt. Its power had not diminished, as he had mistakenly thought. Then his heart skipped a beat and he began to tremble. The force surged through his body; his limbs started shaking uncontrollably.

From halfway up the slope, he shouted, "Hello!"

"Hello!" the mountain valley echoed, sending its answer reverberating toward the sky.

"Hello!" And then something parted the treetops and a frenzied outburst, a harsh cacophony rose through the air. It was a flock of birds, and over the cliffs they flew.

Such unusual uproar caused the man to turn around. He was a young man. At first, the artist thought he looked familiar, but he was still far away. But yes, he was sure he had seen him once before.

As he approached, the artist couldn't help but marvel at how good-looking he was. Such striking good looks had to be considered extraordinary and certainly represented a once-in-a-lifetime opportunity.

The young man said that he would sit for the artist, would fulfill his dream of painting a masterpiece.

The face that had prompted such fascination now emerged from the distance and hovered close before him, and every line and contour became an object of scrutiny. He peered intently at the delicate pores, noted the refinement of the five apertures, the bone structure, the color of skin, the attitude. It was a gift from heaven.

This is providential, the artist thought, my secret prayer has been answered. He sat erect, took up his brush, and tried to encourage himself.

He studied the face carefully, with tremendous focus. This required his entire being. However, the brush offered no signs so far of what the results might be. The eventual form remained quite uncertain, and for a moment, the artist put the brush down.

Now what was the problem?

The face's every feature satisfied the demands of beauty. The delicate lines of the five apertures were particularly subtle and sensitive. A careless eye would miss them. They were done with fine strokes on a smooth surface, and the result was a plain, silklike sketch, a face that revealed a extraordinary delicacy and refined elegance. At the same time, it conveyed purity and innocence.

But the face lacked a story, a history, a life. Even a young man would exhibit some restlessness, a sense of anxiety, or he would adopt an air of alienation and nihilism. Again the artist leaned closer and concentrated on the face, feeling even more intensely that it was a blank canvas, and nothing more.

The young man sat straight, maintaining his perfect posture, as the artist moved his hand. The room held but one sound, and that was the brush against the paper. The two men dwelled silently in their own worlds, undisturbed, distant and independent. Yet there was clearly a force between them, an inquiry, a contact, a dialogue, a conflict, an outpouring. This resulted in the intimate relationship that developed.

An entire night passed.

The next day, the young man had to return to the city where he taught singing in a grammar school. But the outline had taken shape, and the artist wanted to continue. So he promised he would come back the following year during winter vacation.

The artist did not, of course, take the young man at his word, and put the draft aside. Glimpsing it occasionally, he would recall the young man's handsome appearance. At other times, it called up images of what he himself had looked like as a young man.

The two of them had several features in common. But didn't all young people look a bit alike? What made everyone so look so similar was called youth, wasn't it?

When the man returned the second winter as promised, the artist's skepticism about his subject's sincerity made him feel greatly ashamed.

It was a winter sunset, and that winter, the mountain forest had an especially beautiful serenity about it. When the sky lit up, there wasn't the slightest trace of mist or fog. As the sun set, the reds and purples colored everything, and the forest glowed resplendently, gilded and green. In a moment of reverie, the artist looked up and there he was, standing in the light.

His remarkable appearance and posture had not changed. He sat across from him, still uttering no words, but what did speak was his body. The sun entered the room from an angle that produced both light and shadow, and in the light he welcomed talk, but in the shadow, low murmurs and soulful outpourings. His beauty was not the kind that intimidated you or made you feel you were leering, made you ashamed to look again. His beauty, the artist could see now, was born of harmony, serenity, something that could not be traced. If you weren't careful, the thin contours etched gently into the silhouette might just vanish from one minute to the next.

If they did dissolve, his face would appear a white sheet, and there would be nothing there at all.

Winter light offers rays that are both delicate and fleeting. They move across a face more rapidly than at any other time. The daylight hours were very short; day hurried into night.

The light inside suddenly grew dim, and the artist put down his brush.

The young man's face was invisible now. Like a puff of smoke, a nightmare rose through the air and became a face, appearing where the young man's had been, before changing into it. One painted canvas replaced another; one moment you could actually see it, the next, it was so obscure it might be an illusion. The canvas carried on its voiceless debate with him about how it had come to this, about his links to so many matters, what had actually happened, what mistakes had been made, what crimes and retribution. As with former lovers long since estranged, there was endless bickering as old problems were rehashed, detail by detail. In an effort to defend himself, he stiffened and became rigid.

Shifting in his chair, he tried to get control of the brush.

Sometimes several appeared at once, swarming in a great mass, clinging to the young man's head. Then faces of all kinds flashed before him. They crowded close and pressed against him. The thick air was suffocating. He gasped for breath, broke out in a sweat, and then began to shiver as his sweat met the chilly winter air. His hands stiffened with cold all the way to the fingernails, and when he tried to raise his arms, he could hardly move them.

The young man shifted. He was cold. "We'll make a fire," he said.

The house became pleasantly warm with the dancing flames, and the young man's face became flushed. But that was because of the heat within his own body.

If only I myself could be like that, without a past, without a story! Wouldn't it be great! the artist thought to himself. Then his view of the young man began to change. In fact, he began to envy him.

If he could take all the years between his early twenties and his mid-forties, and carefully extract all his successes, and pitch the rest down into the valley, and merge his life with the young man's before him, and make a new beginning, he could experience that man's life and his own, all as one.

But as he sat there, all those nightmarish faces would conceal from him the young man's face. Without the young man's face, he could only put down his brush and close his eyes.

The younger man thought the painting had tired him. He stood up and said, "Let's rest a bit."

Then the artist understood why the face was a blank sheet. It gave him the chance to portray him with the face etched in his heart.

It would have been a great relief if they had just adopted an aggressive stance and, screaming wildly, attacked him. Then he could have met violence with violence, and perished with them in battle. But they always drifted in silently, pestering him and clinging to him like smitten lovers. They simply would not leave him and the young man alone.

He stepped forward, wanting to speak to them, offer an explanation, even to shake hands and embrace. They dodged and stepped back nimbly. He thought perhaps that sharing his life with them, letting them know he, too, had a hellish past, would make them forgive him and seek reconciliation. But the truth was that he himself was becoming one of the nightmares.

III

He knew, of course, that his face was the most haggard and sallow of them all.

Yes, he was clear about that, just unwilling to admit it too openly. All those faces were his own. He had known it all along, the blurred one, obscure and dizzying as it rolled first to one side, then the other: that was no one but himself. The others, the whole mix of disappointment, regret, shame, as well as all the successes, achievements, rewards, they all collapsed into the world of forgotten memories—they let go of him now, allowed him his freedom. The man who had been a tangled mess of bitterness: it was he himself and no other.

The valley mist lifted then, floated upward from below, and surrounded his being. He stretched out his hand and couldn't even see his fingers. Now he knew that what lay so quietly in that bottomless valley was woe, only woe.

This man's portrait would not be easy to paint; deep in his heart he understood that.

The young man agreed. All that mattered was that the work continue. It would rise from the depths and the artist's mind would simply be at peace. The wonderful time they shared during those winter days made the artist feel like prolonging the work. He even hoped he would not be able to finish the painting.

Most of the time they remained indoors. Daylight was short; at four or five o'clock it vanished, and every glowing moment was precious. When night set in, they stopped working.

Occasionally the artist took the young man for a stroll down the village's single lane of shops, and at the betel nut stand they had a bowl of fine, delicate noodles. At the stationery shop he would select some new supplies, and then, slowly, they'd make their way back.

And so you'd see the young man and the older one with the bad leg walking along the road. They moved slowly. It was evening, the time to go slowly; there was no need to hurry. The one in front walked with a crutch, and his every step revealed the pain, he had to hobble so. The one in back stayed close, his hand outstretched.

The road twisted and turned. It was broad enough for the moon to cast across it a pair of moving shadows.

They also enjoyed sitting by the window, watching the sun set and work its changes over the valley before them. They saw how the afterglow spun a web of illusion across the valley. If the young man had brought a bottle from the city, they might drink a drop or two.

The two of them would get a little tipsy, and the young man would stretch out on the floor while the artist, just slightly drunk, would sit beside him. The moonlight illuminated their faces with a particular glow and shadow that belonged only to the night, warmer and more serene than daylight.

Who was it that said a painting was like an exchange of souls? The artist's gaze and the brush itself connected with the object, no, actually entered it. An eye is better than a hand at reaching in and touching minute details. What emerged from the tip of an artist's brush surpassed all the eye's comprehension, and the interchange between painter and subject was, in fact, the most intimate of human activities, establishing the closest of physical connections.

Now the artist gazed at the sleeping young man. He used not touch but sight, for the eyes were better at caressing the flesh of the one before him. They found every pocket of warmth, every soft, moist place, all that was deeply, deeply intimate.

There was a glow about the face of the one who slept, and no sense of age or time, obstinacy or stubbornness, pride or resistance. Only the even, rhythmic flow of breath, a breath full of warmth.

The lamp was extinguished, and the mountain and valley entered their own true state, full of their own even breathing.

Moonlight washed into the valley, and the daytime clouds completely vanished. From the valley's depths, a stream of light arose. The valley sparkled, almost transparent, and its own image appeared.

Incredibly, this project of theirs took more than ten years. The days turned cold, the sun's rays grew pure, and the sky took on a certain distinctive blue. If there wasn't a breath of wind, you knew the young man was coming. You'd see the artist in his garden pulling up his best vegetables or catching his fattest chicken with the help of the neighbors, and you'd know for certain the young man was on his way.

At sunset the mist rose and the whole valley filled with the fragrance of stewed chicken. Oh yes, you should know the chicken in these parts were no ordinary variety. They weren't like the factory-raised fowl of the city. The natural grain they were fed and their living conditions combined to make them rich and succulent. The winter Chinese cabbages were also especially plump and tender. He would use some of the dried shrimp and fish offered by his aborigine neighbors, not adding water though, only the straight vegetable broth. He'd place it on the fire and bring it to a gentle boil. Soon after the house would be filled with still another aroma, the mouth-watering scent of smoked vegetables and other delights.

As the project continued, the form very gradually emerged in full from the outline. It attained the very height of achievement, expressing what no other painting had ever expressed.

Those who saw it said, "It's a superb likeness of the young man." The moonlight's soft sheen on the paper blurred the distinction between male and female beauty, producing a delicate quality even purer, more elegant, and softer than a woman's. It could never be duplicated.

But when you looked at it again, it didn't seem to capture him at all. The space between the eyebrows was dark with gloom, an aspect foreign to the face of the young man.

Then it seemed that this shapeless gloom rose in the air once more and trapped you; again you stood right in the thick of the mountain mist, as if bewitched.

The artist truly offered heart and mind in his attempt to achieve a significance beyond all form. Drawing upon everything at his command, holding nothing back, he sounded the entire register of his heartstrings, and when at last he finished, it was accomplished.

After the two were not seen for a number of years, word went round the mountains that a woman was the cause. People said that a young woman had come to the mountains, been enchanted by the surroundings, and fallen in love with the crippled artist. After a while the two of them became a couple.

This was a fanciful version of what happened woven by the mountain villagers, but those in the city did not believe it.

The truth was that after the painting's completion, the young man threw himself wholeheartedly into his duties as a singing instructor at his grammar school. Until he found some better opportunity to employ his musical training, he continued teaching children how to sing.

Where the artist went no one knew. Some said he had abandoned the mountain, changed his name and identity, and become rich painting for an noteworthy patron, that now he lived in a sumptuous palace.

Others said that he had been "discovered" by art critics, lived on grants in a foreign land, and traveled worldwide exhibiting his work. Still others claimed he had resumed his career in espionage, and that he was once again the president's invisible right-hand man. Those well acquainted with his past reasoned that if he happened to disappear as a result of some unexpected "accident," as he himself had known so many others to do, well, they would not be surprised.

The wooden house on the mountainside was transformed into a very beautiful resort hotel. Of course the weather and scenery were magnificent, and every year the place wove its spell, attracting countless numbers of guests.

Facing the cliff, a pavilion was built, with chairs to sit in, and a paved parking lot was put in. Along the cliff's edge, a crude corrugated-steel railing was erected to prevent picture takers and spectators from losing their footing and tumbling down into the gorge.

The painting was discovered in a dusty corner. Along with some other landscape paintings meant to be given away or sold, it was hung in a long corridor leading to the bathroom and telephone booth. It was only supposed to give the wall a bit of color. Guests walking by it, their minds on other things, always slow down, or even stop when they see it. There in the play of light and shadow, the depth of its sorrow moves them.

State Funeral

. . .

by PAI Hsien-yung

translated by the author and Patia YASIN

It was early one December morning. The sky was somber and overcast, the air raw and biting, as gust after gust of cold wind swept past. In front of the Taipei Metropolitan Funeral Hall a row of white wreaths stretched all the way from the gate to the sidewalk. An honor guard, metal helmets gleaming, stood at attention in two columns on either side of the main entrance. The street had been closed to traffic, but every now and then one or two official black limousines drove slowly in. An old man, leaning on his staff, walked up to the gate of the funeral hall. The hair on his head was white as snow; even his beard and eyebrows were all white. He had on a pair of soft-soled black cloth shoes and a Sun Yat-sen tunic of blue serge, somewhat the worse for wear. Stopping before the memorial arch at the entrance, he raised his head, squinted, and peered at the sign: MEMORIAL CEREMONY FOR THE LATE FOUR-STAR GENERAL LI HAORAN. The old man stood for a moment and then, leaning on his stick, his back bent like a bow, made his way into the hall.

A table stood by the door; on it lay an inkstone, writing brushes, and an opened guest book. As the old man drew near, a young officer in a brand-new uniform motioned to him from behind the desk, inviting him to sign his name.

"I am Qin Yifang—Qin *Fuguan*," said the old man.

Very politely, the young aide handed him an ink-soaked brush.

"I was General Li's old *Fuguan*," Qin Yifang insisted, his face solemn, his voice trembling. Without waiting for the young officer's reply, he made his way step by step into the hall, his stick tapping the floor. There were only a few scattered early mourners inside, all government officials. The walls were covered with memorial scrolls bearing elegiac couplets, many of them so long they trailed down to the floor and fluttered in the wind. In the center of the altar hung a portrait of General Li in full-dress uniform, arrayed with medals and decorations; on the wall to the left was spread the green military standard emblematic of a four-star general. The altar was covered with offerings of fruit and fresh flowers, and smoke was already spiraling up from the sandalwood incense in the cylindrical burner. Above the altar hung a horizontal sign; on it, the huge characters IN ETERNAL COMMEMORATION OF AN EMINENT HERO. As Qin Yifang walked up to the altar and, with great effort, straightened to attention, the master of ceremonies stationed to the right of the altar intoned:

"First bow!"

Ignoring the appropriate ritual, Qin Yifang threw his stick to the floor, struggled to his knees, prostrated himself, and struck his forehead against the ground several times. Shaking with the effort, he rose to his feet and rested himself on his staff, breathing heavily. There he stood and gazed at the late general's portrait; he pulled out his handkerchief, blowing his nose and wiping away his tears. A line of government officials had already formed behind him, waiting their turn to pay tribute to the deceased. A young aide hurried over and gently took Qin Yifang by the arm to lead him away. Brusquely Qin Yifang wrenched himself free and gave the young fellow a dirty look before withdrawing to one side, his staff thumping. As he stared at those young aides hurrying about the hall, sleek and clean-cut every one of them, anger flared up inside him like fire in a pan. If you ask me, the general was as good as murdered by these bastards, he muttered furiously to himself. Stinking little tortoises, how would *they* know how to care for him? Only he, Qin Yifang, who had followed the general all those years, only he understood his headstrong ways. When he got sick you weren't supposed to ask him how he felt; all you could do was keep a quiet watch over him. The moment you asked, "General, are you sure you're all right?" his face would darken. These sons of tortoises, how could they understand such things? The year before last, when the general had gone wild boar hunting in Hualien and slipped and broken his leg climbing a mountain, he himself had rushed back from Tainan to see his old chief. There he was, leg in a cast, sitting propped on a couch in the living room, all by himself. "General, Sir, at your age, you should take better care of yourself," he had scolded. You should have seen the way he scowled! You wouldn't believe how sour he looked. These last years when there were no more battles to fight, he'd go mountain climbing and hunting. He was well past seventy, but you'd never hear him admit it.

Qin Yifang looked up at the general's portrait again. Still that same stubborn look on his face! He sighed, shaking his head. The old man had carried himself like the hero that he was all his life; how could he have given up and lain down so easily? But say what you like, he should never have sent away his faithful old aide. "Qin Yifang, it's warmer down in Tainan. It'll be better for your health," he had said. So he thought he was too old, did he? Grown useless, had he? Or was it because he'd come down with asthma? But since the Master had spoken, how could he continue to hang around the Li residence without losing face? Ever since the year of the Northern Expedition, when he had followed the general with a thermos bottle on his back as they fought their way from Guangzhou in the south to Shanhaiguan in the north, all those many years, who but Qin Yifang had stood by him through thick and thin? To think that after decades of loyal personal service he should have dismissed him with the words, "Qin Yifang, it's for your own good!" Just to hear people refer to him as "General Li Haoran's aide-de-camp" was enough to make him glow with pride. A fine thing for a general to throw out his old white-haired retainer, just like that! Just think about it, is that something you could feel proud of? If anybody asked about him and General Li when he was in the Veterans Hospital, he'd simply ignore them and pretend to be asleep. But that night he clearly saw the old general with his own eyes, galloping up to him on his black charger, Covered Snow, shouting, "Qin *Fuguan*! I've lost my commander's sword!" In his fright, he fell out of bed, a cold sweat breaking out all over him. It could mean only one thing: the general was done for! Don't think that just because he had led a million troops in battle he should know how to take care of himself, to keep himself warm. In those years after Madame passed away, on winter nights Qin Yifang was often the one who got up and put the covers back on him. If he, Qin Yifang, had still been by the general's side, this never would have happened. He would have seen he wasn't feeling well, he would have seen he was ill, he would have watched over him day and night. These newcomers! Young whippersnappers! Do they feel the same devotion to their work? They say the night the general suffered his heart attack and fell on the floor, not a soul was around to help him. He didn't get to utter one last word.

"Third bow!" the master of ceremonies intoned. A bespectacled middle-aged man in traditional white hemp mourning had appeared and was on his knees by the altar, bowing again and again to acknowledge the condolences of the guests.

"Young Master—" Unsteadily, Qin Yifang hurried over to the middle-aged man and called to him gently. "Young Master, it's me, Qin *Fuguan*."

Suddenly Qin Yifang's wizened old face broke into a smile. He remembered the time Young Master was little, when he had helped him into a child-size army uniform, complete with jodhpurs and small riding boots, and even fastened his small military cape for him. He had taken him by the hand, and they had dashed to the parade ground. There was the general, waiting, mounted on his great black charger. Behind the horse stood a little white colt. In a flash father and son had galloped off around the grounds. He could see the two of them, father and son, rise and fall on the horses' backs, Young Master's cape flying in the air. When Young Master had pretended to be ill and dropped out of the military academy to go off to America, the general was so enraged that his face turned an iron black. Pointing at Young Master, he roared, "After this, don't ever bother to come back and see me!"

"The general—he—" Qin Yifang stretched out his hand. He wanted to pat the middle-aged man on the shoulder. He wanted to tell him: Father and son are still father and son, after all. He wanted to tell him: In his last years, the general was not really at peace with himself. He wanted so much to tell him: Once Madame was gone, the general was all by himself in Taiwan; he felt very lonely. But Qin Yifang withdrew his hand; the middle-aged man had raised his head and stared at him, his face expressionless, as if he did not quite recognize him.

A formidable-looking general in full regalia came up to preside over the memorial ceremony. In an instant people thronged the hall. Qin Yifang hastily retreated to a corner; he saw rows and rows of generals in the crowd, all standing there at attention, solemn and holding their breath. The presiding general raised the scroll high in both hands and began to pronounce the eulogy in a sonorous Jiangsu–Zhejiang accent, reading in rhythmic cadence:

Titan of warriors!
  Like a flying eagle.
He gave his life
  to the revolution.
Clouds of men followed him
  on the Northern Expedition.
His command held sway
  against the Japanese foe.
Then, pen in hand,
  he counseled our chief.

With the close of the eulogy, the ceremony began. The first delegation to approach was from the Army Headquarters Command, headed by a three-star general bearing a wreath. Behind him stood three rows of generals in full-dress uniforms, all emblazoned with splendid decorations. Narrowing his eyes, Qin Yifang took a good look, only to find that among these new generals there wasn't one he recognized. Then followed representatives from the headquarters of the three armed forces, the government ministries, and the legislature, who came forward one after another to pay their respects. Qin Yifang stood on tiptoe and craned his neck, looking all over for old acquaintances in the crowd. Finally he caught sight of two old men walking up side by side. The tall one with the white beard and mustache wearing a dark blue satin robe and mandarin jacket—wasn't that Commander Zhang? Qin Yifang moved forward a step, his eyes narrowing to a thin line. That man has been living in seclusion in Hong Kong for ages; so he's come, too. So the one next to him who keeps wiping his eyes with his handkerchief, looking so ill and feeble, supported by that old orderly, he must be Deputy Commander Ye. He's been bedridden in the Taipei Veterans Hospital for years; imagine, he's still in the land of the living! When the Guangxi Army led its Northern Expedition, these were the two stalwarts on the general's staff; everybody called them "the Commanders of the Steel Army." They fought shoulder to shoulder like the Song Dynasty inseparables from that novel everyone read, *The Saga of the Yang Family*, Jiao Zan and Meng Liang. For years they were an invincible team. He had just seen their memorial scrolls hanging side by side next to the door:

Pillar of the State! Your genius will be remembered a
 thousand autumns;
Upon your strategy victory followed ever;
Your one regret: the Yellow Turbans were yet to be
 conquered.
Champion of the Han! A Zhuge Liang reborn, you swore
never to share the same ground with the enemy;
Lofty in justice, your loyalty never failed,
And shall we let your history be burned to ashes?
Zhang Jian, in reverent tribute

In passes and on rivers you fought a hundred battles;
Forever shall it live immortal! your honorable name;
Too suddenly it rose, the mortal Wu-Zhang autumn wind;
The world entire mourns a true hero.
Our country, our nation is split in two;
How can we bear to see the unending tragedy and woe?
When I hear how you went hunting by night, like Li
 Guang at Ba Ling,
I ask, was there anyone willing to call back the old general?
Ye Hui, in reverent tribute

"I've got myself three fierce warriors," the general once said with obvious pride, three fingers raised. "Zhang Jian, Ye Hui, and Liu Xingqi." But who could this old Buddhist monk be, with such a sorrowful look on his face? Dragging his stick, Qin Yifang took a couple of steps forward. The old monk was robed in a black cassock, a pair of straw sandals on his feet; around his neck hung a string of russet-colored rosary beads. Standing before the altar, palms together, he bowed three times, swung around, and walked out.

"General!" Qin Yifang uttered an involuntary cry. He had caught sight of a palm-sized scar, reddish in color, on the back of the old monk's neck. He remembered that wound vividly; during the Northern Expedition, at the battle at Longtan against the warlord Sun Chuanfang, Liu Xingqi got himself a grapeshot wound on the back of the neck. He was taken to the Nanjing Sanatorium; the general had sent Qin Yifang there especially to take care of him.

You wouldn't believe how flamboyantly Liu Xingqi had behaved in the old days! He was young, capable, and highly regarded by the general; his troops won virtually every battle they fought. You could say that of all the general's subordinates, he was the most successful. He was known as "the Commander of the Iron Forces," as the Guangdong Army of the Northern Expedition was called. At the very mention of his *nom de guerre* soldiers would gasp with awe. But what on earth had caused this change in him? Why was he dressed this way? Hobbling with his staff, Qin Yifang pushed his way through the crowd and rushed outside after the monk.

"General, it's me, Qin Yifang." Propped on his staff, his back bowed, Qin Yifang addressed the old monk; he was panting so hard he could scarcely draw a breath.

The old monk halted, surprise written all over his face. For a moment he stared at the man intently, studying him from head to foot. He hesitated.

"Is it really you? Qin Yifang?"

"It is Qin Yifang, wishing the lieutenant-general the best of health." He joined his hands and bowed. Palms together, the old monk quickly returned Qin Yifang's greeting. That sorrowful look was gradually reappearing on his face; after a long moment he uttered a sigh.

"Qin Yifang—ah, the general—" As he spoke, the old monk choked, and tears began to fall; hastily he touched the wide sleeve of his cassock to his eyes. Qin Yifang pulled out his handkerchief and blew his nose. How many years it had been since he had seen Liu Xingqi last! Not since the lieutenant-general had escaped all alone from Guangdong to Taiwan. He had just been stripped of his military rank and had come to the Li residence to report to his superior officer. He had been held captive by the Communist Eighth Route Army for a year, and he was unrecognizable: his face looked seared, virtually all his hair had fallen out, and he was so emaciated there was almost nothing left to him but skin and bone. The moment he saw General Li he called out in a trembling voice, "Your Excellency Haoran—" and then he broke down completely and could not utter another word for sobbing.

"Xingqi, how you must have suffered. . . ." The general's eyes reddened; he kept patting Liu Xingqi on the shoulder.

"Your Excellency—I feel so ashamed." Liu Xingqi swallowed hard, shaking his head.

"The whole situation had gotten away from us; it was really no one's fault." The general let out a long, deep sigh. The two sat facing each other, at a loss for words.

"When we retreated to Guangdong, I thought we could put up a last-ditch effort." His voice low and mournful, the general spoke at last. "Zhang Jian, Ye Hui, and you—your divisions were all made up of our own Guangdong boys. They'd been following me all those years; now that we had returned to Guangdong we'd be defending our own homes and villages. If we fought to the death, maybe we could still turn the tide. We never dreamed that the end would be such a debacle—" The general's voice shook. "Tens of thousands of our own Guangdong boys, all lost to the enemy; just to talk about it—ah—it breaks my heart." And at last two streams of tears started to flow down the general's face.

"Your Excellency!" His own face covered with tears, Liu Xingqi cried out in pain. "I've followed Your Excellency a good thirty years, ever since we first started out campaigning from our home province—on the Northern Expedition and in the War of Resistance against Japan. I may say that my troops contributed to our cause in no small measure. And now, the entire force is destroyed. As the commander of a defeated army, I deserve to die ten thousand deaths! And more, I had to suffer all kinds of humiliation at the hands of the enemy. Indeed, as Xiang Yu said, Your Excellency, 'I cannot bear to face the fathers and elders at home!'" Abandoning all restraint, Liu Xingqi let loose with a storm of wails.

During the final retreat from the mainland, the general, Commander Zhang, and Deputy Commander Ye had waited three days on board the battleship *Bagui* at Longmen Harbor off Hainan Island for Liu Xingqi and his troops to withdraw from Guangdong. Every day the three of them stood side by side on the deck, watching and hoping to see him come out. Up to the very last moment when the order was given to sail, the general was still holding his binoculars, peering again and again in the direction of the Bay of Guangzhou. He hadn't slept for three nights; his face was as haggard as if he had suddenly aged ten years.

"The general, to me, he was so—" Shaking his head, the old monk sighed deeply and turned to leave.

"General, Sir, do take care of yourself!" Qin Yifang followed him a few steps, calling after him. The old monk didn't even turn his head; his black cassock floating about in the bitter wind soon became no more than a shadow vanishing in the distance.

Inside the hall the funeral march sounded; it was time to move the casket. The crowd outside the gate suddenly parted; rifles and bayonets raised, the army honor guard stood at attention; General Li Haoran's casket, draped with the Blue Sky and White Sun, was borne from the hall by eight honor guard officers. Outside, an honor guard jeep was waiting; in it stood a standard bearer holding the four-star general's banner. Behind it stood the hearse, which had General Li's portrait on the front. As soon as the casket was placed in the hearse, all the officials who were to attend the graveside ceremony entered their cars. The long line of official sedans stretched bumper to bumper like a black dragon along the avenue. Both civil and military police, their whistles blowing, were busy directing traffic. Qin Yifang hastily wrapped a mourning sash of white hemp around his waist; pushing through the crowd with one hand, clutching his staff in the other, he hobbled toward the hearse. Behind the hearse was parked an open-top military ten-wheeler. Several of the young aides had already jumped on and were standing inside the vehicle. Qin Yifang went around to the rear and started to climb up, only to be stopped by an MP.

Agitated, Qin Yifang said, "I am General Li's old *Fuguan*," and started to climb on again.

"This is a military vehicle." The MP pulled him back down.

"You—you people—" Qin Yifang staggered backward, choking with rage; he pounded his staff furiously on the ground. "I followed General Li for thirty years when he was alive!" he shouted, his voice quivering. "I'm seeing him off for the last time now; how dare you prevent me?"

The captain of the aides ran up to see what was wrong, and finally Qin Yifang was allowed to board the truck. The old man clambered up, but before he could get situated the truck started off, sending him lurching this way and that until a young aide caught hold of him and helped him to the side. He grabbed the iron railing and hung on, doubled over, panting a long time before he recovered his breath. A chill wind blew into his face, making him hunch his shoulders. Soon the funeral procession turned onto Nanjing East Road. At the intersection a giant arch of pine branches had been erected; across the top were huge characters made up of white chrysanthemums: TRIBUTE TO HIS EXCELLENCY THE LATE GENERAL LI HAORAN. As the hearse proceeded through the arch, an infantry company came marching along one side of the avenue. Seeing the hearse, their commanding officer barked out the order: "Sa-lute!"

Smartly, the soldiers in the company turned their heads toward the hearse in a military salute.

At the sound of the order Qin Yifang straightened up in spite of himself. There he stood in the truck, head held high, chin in the air, his expression solemn, his white hair standing up in the wind. Suddenly he recalled the year the anti-Japanese war was won and they had moved back to Nanjing, the former capital. The general had gone to the Sun Yat-sen Mausoleum on Purple Mountain to pay tribute to the Father of the Country. He himself had never seen so many high-ranking generals together at one time; they were all there, Commander Zhang, Deputy Commander Ye, Lieutenant-General Liu. That day he'd been the one who served as captain of the general's aides. He had on riding boots, white gloves, a wide belt buckled so tightly it held his back straight, and a shiny black revolver strapped to his side. The general was wearing a military cape; a sword glistened at his side. He was right behind the general, their riding boots clicking jauntily on the marble steps. In front of the mausoleum the military guard stood in formation, waiting. As they approached, a thunderous chorus burst out:

"Sa—lute!"

Tale of Two Strangers

. . .

by YUAN Jen

translated by Daniel J. BAUER

I

Just what season of the year was it, anyway?

Sitting there in the taxi with nothing to do, fighting off sheer boredom, I suddenly felt seized by that question. A world like this hardly offered definite answers to questions even as simple as that. What season was it? When you really wanted to be clear about something, the thing to do was to figure out precisely where you were at the moment, then follow the path back to the beginning. So there I was again, mired in my question. And as for getting back to where it had all started—that wasn't so easy.

If it weren't for the taxi driver playing a tape of Copeland's "Appalachian Spring," would I suddenly be thinking about the changing seasons? What taste in music the fellow had!

The human mind is such a strange thing. Most of the time it's a container, mysterious and deep, and the truth is you can never put a lid on it. And then sometimes it's more like embroidered cloth, the various stitches all silky and fine. It isn't that it's woven badly, but rather that all the threads follow one another, twisting and turning until finally they're lost in a sad, dark mass of confusion. The present moment was an example of that. Copland was unleashing this magnificent array of spectacles, all the colors of the universe, but if I looked outside the window, what did I see? Nothing but a sheet of chilly, dull gray. Winter had all but completed its song. And spring? There wasn't even a hint of its first faintest notes.

The kaleidoscopic world inside the car and the dreary cold outside were as real to me as they were deluding, and how could I, a lonely wanderer who had never found a place to put down roots, a home to call my own, manage to comprehend it all? The moment expressed it well. Speeding along, I knew my life was unfolding like a vast journey, the road before me calling for decisions. But what world had I come spinning out of, and where was I rushing to now? I was certain of one thing: there would always be so much I would never completely understand.

It didn't snow in Wuhe in the winter, and naturally it was much warmer than here. Wouldn't spring just be starting there now? Wuhe didn't have any real mountains, but there were hills as far as you could see. If you took all that "Appalachian Spring" glory and put it aside for a minute, well, wouldn't the melody capture the beauty of this dreamland of the East? It wasn't something I had any control over: the very name Wuhe stirred up visions of my father reminiscing, and set my imagination on fire.

There was a tree that Wuhe was famous for, the tong oil tree. Wuhe had so many tong oil trees! They were big and tall. "Were they taller than mango trees?" I'd asked. "Much taller! There are no tall trees in *this place*!" My father replied with the haughty contempt of a tough veteran army officer, even though he had only commanded an infantry company. The fruit of the tong tree contained an oil you could extract. At first, the fruit was green, but then it turned yellow, and finally red. It was the prettiest thing you could imagine! You could squeeze out that oil and use it for all sorts of things. This bit of information came from my father, but geography books agreed.

There were also "oil cha" bushes. The plains were just covered with them. They weren't as tall as a human being, and they produced fruit about the size of small tomatoes that first glowed bright green and then deepened to a rich red. When they were completely ripe, the skin burst at the seams. The seed had an oil you extracted, a very important, useful cooking oil. "Did it taste good?" "Ah! A little oily but not bad. A lot of folks on the mainland couldn't get their hands on even two ounces of oil in a whole year." Back then, I realized, our Wuhe must have been considered a wealthy place.

"Mountains everywhere. Well, are there terraced rice paddies on the slopes?" That's the way the Szechwan province was, according to geography books.

"No, the slopes aren't that steep. You can plant and harvest in the middle of the plain. Rice paddies are all over the place there, and good for two crops a year."

My father used the lid of his teacup to clear the foam from his tea. He pursed his lips, and then his eyes and voice fluttered off into the distance.

"You use water buffalo to till the fields. There aren't many oxen, and they're for pulling carts. The weather in the old country's real good; the different seasons—four of 'em!—are just about perfect for farming. In the spring, the spring rains come. You have to wear those straw hats the farmers wear, and big raincoats. Seems like they'd be too warm, but in fact they're cool and comfortable."

I thought about this for a while. "Well, wasn't it more or less like 'this place'?"

"It's not the same! Oh no, not at all the same!" An assertive note entered my father's voice again. "In the old country there was so much bamboo, and the buildings were all taller, and no matter what you laid your eyes on, hell—it was twice as good as here!"

I was well acquainted with springtime in Taiwan's countryside, and I thought of it often.

I had tested into a well-known middle school run by the county, and my father constantly displayed his pride by blurting out, "Did I tell you what school my boy got into?" without an ounce of sensitivity for my unspoken feelings. "Daaad, don't *embarrass* me again, please, Dad!" Once school began, my father kept saying he meant to call on my teachers, to pay them the equivalent of an official parental visit. I fought the idea resolutely, hoping to deter him with my stubborn resistance and brooding silence.

But not long after the second semester began, I opened my eyes one morning to find my father all dressed and ready to go. There he sat on the edge of the bed, smoking a cigarette. It was obvious he had taken excruciating pains in choosing his outfit. His dress was immaculate to the point of absurdity, and it almost magically transformed his entire countenance. His clothes clashed with the tone of his skin, which was dark and leathery tough. His shoes were polished to a frightening shine, his hair brushed straight back and worried into a hatlike form, and his posture was absolutely rigid. Everything about my father announced loudly that he was a wild taro escaped from the boonies for an excursion into the big city.

I heaved a sigh of resignation. "Okay, let's go!"

At that time, the city limits were not very well defined, and the school was on the edge of town. After you got off the bus there was still quite a walk, and then, finally, you got out to the springtime fields.

I led the way, the two of us taking a shortcut along a path so narrow we could not walk side by side. That fact, at least, made things a little easier. My father clomped along behind me, complaining with every step about the bad road. Of course I knew the real reason for the grumbling was his fear of scuffing up his shoes.

My father's irritation gave me a distinct sense of pleasure. Even the harsh, unrelenting rays of the morning sun seemed auspicious.

Here were newly planted rice paddies, and the fields were squared off into individual terraces, with the tips of rice shoots poking up through the water's glistening surface. Men were working in some of the paddies. They were bent over at the waist and seemed to grow right up out of the water. Off in the distance a team of water buffalo trudged along in yoke and harness; then they turned around and started back in the other direction.

I didn't know a thing about working rice paddies. It seemed to me that the workers' backs never straightened, even after they left the field at the end of the day; that the water buffalo plodded endlessly up and back, back and up, as if to say, "What else can we do? The gods won't give us our rice for nothing, you know!" I couldn't tell if the men and their animals were happy or sad. I felt that they were simply there, and that their lives were hard.

Because of those unfamiliar shoes, my father's discomfort was probably very great already. As he kept stopping to stare off in every direction, I had to stop, too. I felt the length of the shadow my body cast behind me, the top of it reaching my father's feet as he stood in the road, knocking the mud from his soles and then hobbling ahead another step or two. Eventually my father pointed off into the distance. "Look at that mist floating over there! It's like that classic verse, 'Mist as soft as the dust left by wild horses galloping over the horizon'." The mist looked like floating dust all right, but wild horses? What bullshit! He was always quoting that sort of thing. As usual, my response was silence.

At school my father hurried off to find my advisor, and went right home afterward. He didn't interrupt class, which was a great relief. My advisor was the Chinese literature teacher, also from the mainland. Talking was probably easy for the two of them. Later, my advisor pulled me aside and said with a chuckle,

"I had no idea your father was so familiar with classical sources. You can do some extra reading at home and get him to help you." Of course my advisor did not know that we hardly exchanged a word at home. And as for my father's background in the classics, I couldn't care less.

When you stepped into our house, it leaped from the wall at you—a huge white poster with four lines of blocky Chinese characters in the style of the celebrated Tang dynasty calligrapher Yan Zhenqing:

> Asleep in the midst of spring, dead to the rising of the sun
> Hill and valley filled with the chirping of birds
> Nights with sounds of wind and raindrops, breezes gently humming
> Who can count the petals that tumble free and fall to the ground?

It wasn't enough to write it down; you had to plaster it up, too. And not only plaster it up, you even had to read it out loud! And that word "*qu*," you had to pronounce it with a twist of the vowel to make it almost a "*qi*." And the "*ye*" wasn't "*ye*" at all! It had to be "*ya*"! After supper my father had his cup of tea, and then he'd drag me through the whole rigamarole once again. I'd listen as hard as I could, but by God, there was no ignoring the rumble of "*qu-ah*," "*qu-ah*," until it rose up inside from the marrow of my bones, and all I wanted was to shout, "All right, all right! If *this place here* is no good, why don't you just go back to the old country, huh? '*Qu-ah*!' Go ahead, go back!"

The taxi had just turned off the highway, and was approaching the airport now. As it took the curve, I swayed to the left, cradling the package on my knees and steadying it with my hand. An exit ramp loomed ahead; trees had been planted along the road. The tops of the trees bunched together, tip to tip, and over them rose the lofty tail of a plane. Yes, that was it. People who went back home took something to show they had made their mark in the world. But I hadn't. Maybe I could get a seat in the back of the plane, right over the taillights. Then I would literally be "clinging to the tail of an illustrious party," as the classical proverb put it. Of course I couldn't brag about coming from a long line of erudite scholars, but hadn't I inherited something from my father after all? Otherwise, how to explain this quick wit?

Springtime in the Appalachians quickly turned to clouds on the horizon. Which season was approaching so rapidly? Copland didn't really say, and now I did not want to ask.

II

When you're trying to find something, what you need is light. When you're looking for yourself, what you need is darkness. I was quite familiar with lying awake at night, and I had come to enjoy darkness and the kind of clarity it offered me. That flash at the instant of birth, and the final seconds before death—perhaps those moments offer the most luminous light? I imagine so.

The darkness of the sky was so utterly desolate and deep, so overwhelmingly vast, that it could obliterate anything. Suddenly an impulse seized me. If I could break the window next to me, if I could empty the urn, those ashes that were as white as snow, what would they look like? If every secret could be completely revealed, if everything could be poured back into the universe—well, there was no harm in that.

That day, for the first time in my life, I had seen human ashes. It was too bad a person's ashes could never be just ashes, that they could never have the color of other burned-up things. How different it was from what I had imagined! To get them out of the contraption at the crematorium, they had to pound the bones into the finest, purest powder, and then this stuff took on a texture that was eerily airy and light. And I still couldn't fathom how to connect my father's face with the white stuff in the urn I was carrying.

After my mother died, the government gave my father permission to retire from the service and raise his son. He found a piece of land in the middle of the countryside on the edge of a military compound in central Taiwan, and, with his own hands, built us a place to live. There the two of us, father and son, settled down. In time, the house, though small, acquired a certain notoriety because it was truly an unusual place. Except for the support beams, it was made entirely of bamboo, and, what's more, it was a remarkably tall structure, though it had no upstairs. The upper level was not for living in at all! And so the height of the place seemed to have some poignant meaning all by itself.

"There's not a thing wrong with it; all the houses in the old country were built just like this."

It was well built, my father told me. As he stirred his tea, his voice seemed to float off into the distant horizon.

But the local people just couldn't get used to it, and they called it the "*le*" house after the Taiwanese word for "tall." The house became better known than the military compound itself. Later, students from all around that area called me "le," despite the fact I was rather short. Of course this made the nickname sting even more.

"Making a bamboo house isn't anything special. You just hand the men in Wuhe a clump of bamboo and a knife, and they'll make anything out of it." That's what my father said when people came to see our house. The result was that we accumulated stacks of bamboo.

Later I would come to know the meaning of "possessing bamboo nature." But there's a great gulf between deep and shallow knowledge. With almost magical artistry, my father wove together bamboo slats just the right color and shade; meticulously he worked the corners. Even the outer edges were finished with three-tone strips, the end result looking like fancy lace embroidery. Talk about a thing of beauty! It seemed as if it should have been moved from the country and put on exhibit somewhere. But it was for his own enjoyment, and nothing more. At first, no one gave any thought to a couple extra pieces of bamboo siding. Except for the pleasure you could get from them, what use were beautiful things like that?

Around the house, enclosing the open space, my father built a bamboo fence, and then along the back border he set up a lattice structure, also made of bamboo. One morning my father went out before I even left for school and was already home when I came back that afternoon. It was pleasantly cool inside the house, but my father lay on his bed as if not an ounce of energy remained in his whole body. When he heard me enter, he blinked once or twice, and spoke listlessly. I poured him a drink of water, and through the back window saw a pair of sturdy bamboo poles with an elaborate lattice arrangement underneath. The thing struck me as magnificent and beautiful. And yet somehow I had the sensation of gazing at a strikingly attractive woman who, you knew with a single glance, could not be trusted. It was disturbing.

Beyond a large storage crate lay a tract of land. I saw a strip of newly sectioned off ground and some linked bamboo rings. Before we moved here, I'd once heard my father mention this to one of his buddies, something about this area having a possible opening, and how he might start his own refuse-gathering business. That was the phrase my father used, "refuse gathering." The children in the military compound called it "picking up garbage." Local kids called it "collecting trash."

Army veterans were always dark in color. But after he became a professional—again, that was my father's word, "professional"—his skin turned even darker every year. The truth was, he looked as if he'd been repainted. My father said that back in the old country, once people got to be middle-aged and had made their mark, they bought themselves a good coffin. And then with each passing year they'd throw on another coat of lacquer. If a man was blessed with a long life, his coffin shone so brightly that all you had to do was flick a tiny drop of paint onto the surface, and you heard a *ping* like gold clinking against hard flint. I knew it was wrong, but sometimes I couldn't help thinking of that eerie custom from the old country when I looked at my father's skin; I felt nothing but contempt for those people.

Although in his final years he had given up collecting trash, my father was still darker than most people. Who would have thought that in the end he'd be reduced to a pile of lily-white ashes? As I thought about it, I smiled wryly. I chuckled, and though the sound wasn't enough to overcome the bottomless dark outside the plane, it bounced like a pebble against the window, sending back an echo that was dry, crisp, and chill. It unnerved me.

Wang Zhaonan, better known by his nickname "Old Ah-nan," came in to visit me from his school on the outskirts of the city. I had just taken him out for a meal at a popular noodle shop, not expensive at all, only six dollars a bowl, and the servings were so large you dozed off at the table the minute you finished eating. I couldn't offer Old Ah-nan a place for a nap, probably because my dormitory had been so full that day. So we ended up wandering around Roosevelt Road. It was one of those brilliant winter days. Ah-nan hadn't seen anything but rain on his campus for a long time, and he couldn't help but gaze in wonder at the sky, which was as blue as the ocean.

"Hey, Old Le! Since when have you become an authority on midwifery?" Ah-nan suddenly snickered. It occurred to me that the old nickname was a sign of how close we'd been all through the years. Ah-nan turned and looked right at a sign that was blinking at us. It read, THE GANSHENG GYNECOLOGY CLINIC. "Hey Gan! Will you just look at that name! Same as yours, isn't it, Gan? Gansheng, Gansheng. Fuck-a-baby, fuck-a-baby! That's it, all right!" The rhyme my name made with a certain memorable word delighted him. "You fucker, Gan, go ahead, Fuck-around-Gan, fuck around all right, Gan, and you'll get a baby, pal! Hey, the joint's named after you!"

I had laughed at the joke, but later I thought of Wang Zhaonan's name, and more than that, I thought of Ah-nan himself. He and his name both seemed low. With his education, he ought to be above that sort of humor. Kids around here!

It was only much later that I came to recognize how good my father's calligraphy really was; at the time I thought he was just showing off. Later when I read my father's words, "Asleep in the midst of spring, dead to the rising of the sun," for the first time they really made an impression on me.

I was thinking of those bamboo crates my father made, the ones that were five different colors. The rain eventually faded the lettering into a single warm yellow. Actually it wasn't a bad color, not too dark, not too light. It pretty much went unnoticed. But all good things come to an end. One day I came home from school to find two of the crates freshly painted with red lettering. *Ganji, ganji*—four characters, each more obvious than the last. He had painted them on all sides, so they couldn't be missed, so you saw them from every angle.

Even a trash collector has to have a logo!

"Hey, Le! Your old man's a clever old fucker, eh? He'll scribble that name of yours all over his garbage bins. *Gan-ru-qu, gan-ru-qu*. Gan Refuse Collecting! What a name! Might as well write: Fuck-er Gan, fuck-er on in, fuck-er on out, huh?"

My fists shot up and I went for Ah-nan.

The word "*gan*" wasn't in my dictionary. How did Ah-nan know it? Of course, after the fight, all the boys in my class knew it. Well, I was short and thin, and from then on, I took a lot of poundings; but I also dealt out my share of bloody noses and black eyes.

"Wasn't I born in Taiwan? Why did you name me Gansheng?" People had always called me this, and only now did I find out my name was all wrong. I resolved that regardless of the consequences, I had to ask my father.

"Your mother got pregnant when we were still in the old country. We were only here two months when you were born. Of course your name had to be Gansheng. For important filial reasons!" But I would not back down. For once I would go all the way to the bitter end. My father had no clue what he had done by combining the double meanings of this Mandarin word "*gan*" with its counterpart pronunciation in the Taiwanese dialect. I would sure as hell tell that stupid old son of a bitch what suffering and shame I had gone through. I would do it carefully, even indirectly, but I would do it. I wanted him to know.

"Don't pay any attention to them! These kids around here! They can't do a damn thing!"

Yeah, you're the only one who can do anything right. You're the garbage collector.

But I only dared say that to myself.

Why couldn't I have gotten inside her eight months later?

Why couldn't I have the name Ji Taisheng—meaning "born in Taiwan"? Impossible. My father would never have given me a name with a meaning that connected my birth to Taiwan. Unless I was named *ji*, meaning "stay for a while," and not meaning "remember."

Ji Taisheng . . . Ji Taisheng, stay for a while in Taiwan, stay just for a while. Yes, that's it!

My father's calligraphy didn't only win him a name in the neighborhood, "bringing glory to a humble home," as the proverb went; later it literally "glorified" the doorways of our house. I don't know when it began, but for several New Years in a row, rhymed couplets were hung by the doors. On flashy red paper was written the famous old saying:

> Every year comes as trial and challenge, but every year we get by;
> Not a home anywhere in sight, yet every place is a home for me.

Across the top of the door were the words:

> Floating life is a stopover.

That's the way it was. My father had stopped over as an honored guest, and I, as his son, had shared the hospitality. One more year in exile amounts to one more year. And what began as a visit turns into a lifetime.

You probably learn this while you're still in the womb. Those eight months of darkness had been exerting a decisive influence on me ever since. Or rather, they made it impossible for me to ever be decisive about anything.

I thought I spoke Taiwanese like a native, but Xuehua pooh-poohed it the very first time she heard me.

"Since I got out of college, I've used it less. I think I must have forgotten some of it." I fumbled for an excuse, and it was sad, for it felt as if I'd lost something I really thought was a part of me. I was considered a good Mandarin Chinese speaker when I lived in Taiwan, being a "mainlander." Yet the first time I met Yuanlin—talk about loss of face! I wanted desperately to think I had handled it well, but I knew I had made a complete ass of myself.

"You're Taiwanese, right? I can tell by your accent. Beijing pronunciation is the basis for Mandarin, but it's not the same as Taiwan Mandarin."

I tried to find an excuse. I had said *shi* very smoothly, but had forgotten to curl my tongue back on *qu*, and I was sure Yuanlin heard it. Not only could I not help feeling foolish, but this time I wasn't even sure what I had done wrong.

Why had I married Yuanlin instead of Xuehua? At least in the beginning, I think it had something to do with pleasing my father, a kind of compensation for the past. Yuanlin was from Beijing. As a child, she had moved around with her refugee parents, and she happened to live in the neighboring region for six or seven years. For all practical purposes she was half native to the area. Well, from the moment they met, my father felt an immediate sense of kinship with her. Nothing had to be explained. They talked warmly of the Jiangxi province he had heard about since he was a child, and it was almost like meeting someone from your hometown in a far-off and very foreign land. Even the grass and trees seem like old friends!

But it wasn't the same for me. I just couldn't measure up to Yuanlin and her way with the language, for example. Thinking back to the very beginning of my life, why, I'd never spent a single day over there.

And Xuehua said that when you came right down to it, I really knew very little about Taiwanese customs and ideas. From her perspective, "Your mainland origins probably influenced you some." This came as a shock to me, because after all, she had never even met my father. And that was another good thing. Xuehua really was a local girl. I couldn't imagine her and my father finding anything to talk about.

After the darkness, calm; and after calm, tranquility. With tranquility comes awareness. The jetliner was still moving, but my sense was that it had reached a standstill. The body of the craft melted into the night and the night faded into darkness. I was like an unripe seed planted in the depths of the darkest night. I felt clear-headed, but I did not know what night it was, or where I was.

"Knocking back a drink or two, singing a song
Who knows the length of our days?"

Let the booze give you courage! Come on, show us that voice of yours!

This was the traditional farewell ritual at the university, and not an easy thing for a sensitive person like myself. There I was with my classmates, men and women, partying the night away. Four long years, gazing out the same windows of the same classrooms, but not together all that often, mostly just fooling around. And now it was time to say good-bye.

Everyone was shouting that it was my turn. No getting around it now; I had to sing. "Only the booze can take away the sadness. . . ." Caocao leading soldiers by the millions all the way to Annan, oh, so full of confidence back then, that line, one more time, let's go! That rush of emotion! The old university gang: a fleet of sailboats heading out on a glittering sea. Thinking of those long-distant carefree days, how could you not feel a little sad? Covering my face with my left arm, hiding behind my sleeve, I lifted the glass. I leaned my head back dramatically and downed every last drop.

High on the fringe of yonder treetop
See the birds circling round and round
Never can they land or rest
No place do they find.

The same windows, the same rooms . . . together we forged our way, together we took our rest, nothing special about any of it. . . . It's only when you must face a farewell that you see the beauty of true friends. Ah, the sparkle of those marvelous days, but . . . you just can't go back to them, can't go back.

"The Duke of Zhou worked so industriously that he earned the devotion of all the people in the world."

Your body's stuck in a tight little corner, but your mind can contain the whole world. My father said it well: only a virtuoso like Yuan Shihai could capture the noble ambition of that ancient hero.

Everyone was so young then. It's all gone now; it's so damn sad. But still we should look out at the world with heads held high, our gaze set on the far horizon.

By the time I got out the final refrain, I felt as if I'd never been so happy in my entire life. My eyes were burning, and I slumped forward and bowed my head.

"Excuse me everyone, please, for my lousy singing—no, ah, I can't sing at all." I had to get hold of myself.

Expressing deep emotion like that was out of character for me. I was probably a little tipsy. The performance was almost overdone. And Li Youlan was there, too. Once I had felt a pang of desire for her, oh, imagine! Never again, never again. That was the last time.

Slowly I raised my head and sat up, as if to refill my glass. All of a sudden the room seemed strange. There was no going back now. I glanced around at everyone; their expressions no longer looked natural. There was Old Fish Head already finishing his coffee, toying with his cup. And people's voices—what was wrong? They seemed to clatter in the air. Li Youlan's profile revealed the last of a little smirk she couldn't control. And Wang Zhengxiong, a guy I had never gotten along with, was trying to put on a kind expression to make everything seem all right.

My stomach was in an uproar, my throat prickled, and my face was becoming flushed from the alcohol. Not only was I angry with myself, I was ashamed. I felt like a girl who had revealed her love for the first time and been rejected by a cruel lover. The early afternoon sun cast shadows over the hard, slippery floor. Shadows spread from my feet, my upper body was concealed. I thought of the path beside the rice paddies that spring, and of the wild horses kicking up dust. Again I faced the rising sun and saw the long shadow of my back, my father's leather shoes. One thing blends into another, and then it all happens over and over again. You can't get away from it. You can't break free.

"One—all right, turn—bright light—moon—the three—principles of the people. Can you hear it now? Concentrate! It's actually a four beat times two, one heavy, three light, like the national anthem." Studying it with minute care, my father guiding me even more carefully, we tapped out the tune with our fingers. It was as if we not only kept time with our hands on the arms of the chairs we were sitting in but also were actually creating that delicate magic in the air, that incredible rhythm so difficult to achieve between father and son, which the instruction manual termed, "Tenderness easily broken."

A tree takes ten years to grow, and the pair of mu-ma-huang trees my father had planted now dwarfed the front entrance of the Le House. Still visible, however, were his banners proclaiming poetic ideals. We sat beneath the shade of the trees, father and son, each in a rattan chair. We were listening to Yu Shuyan's "The Inn."

I couldn't find any tutoring work that summer, and so I lived at home. But life back home wasn't all that easy. Time dragged. After all, I couldn't study every minute and my father couldn't spend all his time collecting trash. There was no avoiding each other. So what could we do? Study Beijing Opera! I found a way out for myself, and for my father as well. "One—two—three—four. . . ." Without even thinking about it, there I was, wagging and bobbing my head with the tune,

"Knocking back a drink or two, singing a song
Who knows the length of our days?"

Yu Shuyan was gone, and Yuan Shihai had his turn on stage. He was such a pro at those complicated and subtle gestures, all the vocal intonations, oh, he was a great one, that frail and delicate old fogey. But his voice had gotten to sound like a bully's.

They mastered about half of "The Inn," my father said, but its deepest meaning was not something you could rush into. He understood it himself, but finding the words for it was another matter, of course. The trees hummed with the soft music of cicadas, but they couldn't mask the tenuous nature of those moments. In all our life together, didn't it come down to just this single fleeting summer?

Singing "Composing a Poem in the Heat of Battle" was so very much more than simply getting the words out and swaggering around all puffed up with the role. Caocao was a crafty schemer, cunning and aggressive, always just two steps ahead of the enemy in his strategies. The essence of his poem "Duange xing" was that even when the words spoke of sorrow and nostalgia, down deep he was proud and confident! You had to be faithful to your inner self! When you chanted the verses, the thing to do was to maintain the balance, knowing when to let go and when to hold your emotions in check. My father took up his teacup and used the top to clear the tea leaves. He pushed it back and forth, and when he realized I did not look impatient with him, he put the cup down and continued with his explanation. First he took me through those memorable old peaks and valleys of the Battle at the Red Cliff fought in the era of the Three Kingdoms, and then he talked of the brilliant Su Dongpo and his famous essay, "Reflections Beneath the Red Cliff." It dawned on him gradually that I was not feigning interest, and so he went on and on and spoke not in mere generalities but quoting the text, line by line.

How my father had impressed me that day; he was nothing short of magnificent. I looked up in total admiration, and saw that the old man had risen so high I almost lost sight of him.

My father finished his lecture and rearranged his tea paraphernalia. In conclusion he said, "That's the way Beijing Opera is. The background is all long ago and far away. The essential meanings go all the way down to the bottom. And not only that, but there's not a single sound that isn't also a musical note, not a gesture that isn't part of a dance. You can see an act or a scene a hundred times and never be bored! Now this local Taiwanese opera is just a bunch of noise. You don't know what the hell they're singing!" It was as if the local shows were invasive weeds, and you might as well just lift your feet and stomp them flat.

The gentle singing of the cicadas, the lush front courtyard. I had an impulse to sing or play a flute. In my whole life I only learned to sing one section of the Beijing opera of Caocao's "Composing a Poem in the Heat of Battle." But from that moment on I could never bear to look at a Taiwanese opera again, or to hear anyone say a negative word about Beijing Opera.

Outside the window there had been undiluted darkness, but now it seemed to have softened, and you could catch a glimmer of faint color in the sheet of darkness. Perhaps behind that light, endless darkness set in again.

I again became aware of the plane's motion. But perhaps because I had been gazing at the dark for so long, I couldn't say for some time where it was headed.

The dark sky was so limpid it seemed it might never turn solid again. A chemist would rate its solubility high, its permeability low. It was like young love—strong and violent up to a certain point, and then quite ready to spend itself to exhaustion, to diminish and slowly die off. It advanced from all sides and wrapped itself around the essence of every existing thing, and then it grew dim and faded away. It was fated to embrace height and depth, all shape and substance, as if it were a great round ball. Then it would transform itself into yet another new force and burst forth into the spectacular light of a new day.

As the first rays of the early morning sun poured through the window, I suddenly became aware that although my father and I had been flying for a good long time, we had not quite left the world behind yet. Many people surrounded us, and not a few practicalities still needed to be straightened out. I didn't want to sleep any longer, just close my eyes. Realities stood fixed, but the light pouring in offered no guidance. It only helped me see more vividly the turmoil approaching from all sides.

I pushed my father along to the French windows. The snow that lay on the ground beneath the pale trees was patchy and thin. The sun's reflection shimmered across the frozen green pond. A wild duck flew through the air from the opposite shore and found a slippery landing on its surface. Its little rear end flipped over backward, and the two of us laughed. It was nearly sundown, and we were alone, father and son, and suddenly we each recognized the singularity of the moment. A chill passed over me.

My father did not have many days left now, and I would come to the hospital to be with him whenever I had the time. My body was there, but my voice seemed to be someplace else. I just could not find the words.

"Ah, ahem . . . should take this chance, just the two of us here, Ji Gansheng. There's something here to, ah, take care of." So finally it was the sick man taking the initiative to break the silence. There was a solemn note in my father's voice, and the curious look on the face I saw reflected back in the window made me uneasy.

"When I made the arrangements for that piece of land and wrote to you about it in that letter, you didn't offer any opinion. Later I found some people who were willing to invest; together we had an apartment building put up there, and I got two floors of it. Well, later I sold my share off for cash. All that happened and you kept quiet. It was like you didn't want to get involved. Now—the situation—well, now you don't have any choice. Your name's on the papers; the legal briefs and my seal are in my briefcase. Later on, you just go ahead and take it all out. Whatever you want to do with it, you just go ahead and do. Well, another way to look at it—that saying, 'With a little thrift comes a little fortune,' that's it. Your old man had a dirty job, but his money's clean."

I looked away from the lake outside the window, and dropped my gaze slightly. On the chilly windowpane I saw a reflection of my father's face with that indignant look.

In those years at sunset I used to do my homework at my desk by the window, and I'd lift my head and watch my father pick through trash, separating it with meticulous care. I saw him weigh it into five-pound stacks, and then saw how he threw himself into a ritual of shining and polishing, polishing and shining. If somebody had only given him a scale, he would have looked like a merchant fussing over precious jewels. He had two storage containers for his trash, and in these he carefully stashed everything away. Every few days he would drag his treasures out and sell them to this or that specialist.

A few years passed, our life improved, and I began to hear people in the military compound connect my father's name to the Jiujiang River area back in mainland China. "That Old Jiujiang," they said, "he's one sharp old geezer." Wuhe was such a tiny little place, and here my father was associated with the better-known city of Jiujiang. My classmates from the nearby towns would taunt me in Taiwanese dialect, "Hey Le, your old man picking up hunks of gold or something?" Indeed, when I looked carefully at the way the whites of his eyes flashed against the dark of his face, something told me that our small fortune wasn't coming from thrift alone.

My father never let me do anything to help; he just provided all the pocket money I needed. At school I was acutely sensitive to other people's reactions, especially the sympathy of teachers aware of my background. But I had considerably more spending money than anyone around me. Both my comfort and my shame sprang from the same well, and it was impossible to separate the two. It was only after I went abroad to study, only after I established a home and career, that I could get my mind off that well.

Over the last ten years, I'd gone back only twice. I felt my status as a guest even more deeply on the second trip. "The Tall House" had become a ten-story apartment building. There were four families to a floor, and my father owned two floors. He lived in the middle unit. The front entrance belonged to everyone, so he had lost the privilege of posting Chinese New Year blessings over the doorways. The profits from garbage collecting had dried up long ago, but my father's financial situation had never been better.

Originally, the whole piece of land had been public property, but by squatter's right, my father claimed it as his own. And after long years of quarreling with the authorities, he won. "This place" may never have been like the old country, but it wasn't too hard for him to make a kind of career for himself here. Like they say about the people from Jiujiang, the old man was one sharp old geezer, all right.

Actually everything was perfect. Neighbors and friends treated me well; they were all model hosts. But still I felt like an intruder. I couldn't touch a thing or say a word without feeling that I'd somehow broken a taboo. My father was like a pampered guest relishing the excessive hospitality continually lavished upon him by his kind and patient host. And I, in turn, was my father's guest. Although neither of us could complain, in the end, we both sensed a certain emptiness we couldn't really name. Uprooted, my father had become a guest of honor for life, and I had fallen heir to that hospitality. It was all preordained.

And so the moment arrived. Before he passed on, my father wanted to offer me this farewell gift. It made no sense for me to accept it, yet I could not summon the courage to say no. And so I had made this long, difficult journey to receive something my father wanted me to accept. "Just take it with a smile," as the Chinese often said when urging a gift upon someone. But how could I smile? It was such an absurd joke I wanted to laugh. But now all I could do was close my eyes and chuckle softly to myself, because the darkness that had offered me comfort and protection was already gone.

III

Slowly I made my way toward the plane exit. Losing sleep was nothing new to me, but lying all cramped up and then straightening my legs and forcing them to walk again made me realize how exhausted I was. Between the cumbersome overnight bag weighing down my right shoulder, shifting with every step, and the urn of ashes in my hands, requiring such careful and respectful vigilance, I felt like a clumsy country bumpkin on a pilgrimage to the Holy Mountain. My father was my father; dead, he was still a burden. Dimly I considered that; a sudden wave of nausea rose inside me, and with it a hunger pang. Then it didn't seem to be either, only a pit of anxiety I didn't want to think about.

"I can make that decision after I reach Tokyo." That is what I'd said to Yuanlin as I stepped out the door. Then we'd both started laughing, because we both knew how I dreaded making decisions. And here I was. In Tokyo. Should I head west? Or go south? I had no idea.

"So you talked Dad into it. Now he really wants to go to Wuhe and take a look around."

"You'd better think about what's best, though. I think he got used to living in Taiwan," she blurted out. "And going back, he'll be disappointed for sure. And there's no way he can stay there."

"You were the one who couldn't stop talking about how fabulous the old country was, how great and terrific it was, blah, blah, blah. And now that you've got him all worked up about it, you sing a different song."

"Oh, he's an old man now. I was just trying to cheer him up! He kept criticizing Taiwan—the economy, social standards, the crooks in the government, that kind of talk. All right, so I did build it up a little for him. I told him the old country was the Taj Mahal, the Golden Paradise, okay, okay. Let him keep his dream." I was used to my wife's sharp tongue; still, every time she asserted herself like that, it caught me off guard.

"I must say you've been very successful. Not only has he been cheered up, now he wants to consign his ashes. He says that when he left he was young, and going back now he'd be old, and who would know him in Wuhe anyway? If he went back, what he'd do is find a grave site, and then when the time came he could lay himself down to rest, kind of, well, return to his roots."

I was using the lid of my cup to stir the floating tea leaves. I stopped abruptly and lifted the cup to my lips. Recently I'd found myself taking on more and more of my father's mannerisms. Influence, influence. The Chinese word meant literally "shadow and sound." "And it was like a shadow following his shadow, an echo to his voice." Pursing his lips at the taste of the tea, my father led me ploddingly through another explanation of poetry, punctuating his sentences with the lid of his tea mug. The two of us fused together in a single silhouette beneath the lamplight. How marvelous, those early makers of words!

"It's something you'd better mull over." Yuanlin was speaking in that Beijing accent of hers. She paused to sit down beside me. I could tell from her tone that she was trying to be patient. "People over there don't care much about spiritual notions. They think differently about the dead. When I was in Jiangxi, if someone died, they were just carted outside and tossed any old place. We used to see the bones and whatever, and nobody thought much about it. If he went back now and spent money on a grave, well, who knows? First of all, who could he count on to manage the arrangements? You couldn't be going back there all the time yourself. Who knows what would happen in the future? That's the simple truth, you know. It would be best for you to find some way to sit down and talk it out with him."

Well, "finding some way to sit down and talk" was no easy matter. I might get started, but the right words would escape me. Finally Yuanlin herself managed to do it for me. I appreciated that, though afterward I felt guilty because my father stopped talking glowingly of the old country. Also he became more aloof toward Yuanlin. And never again did he mention the idea of going back home. It was as if he realized he couldn't fight what he'd been told, and what he hadn't been told would be decided without him.

Exiting the plane, I made my way along the ramp toward the stewardesses who were exchanging polite good-byes with passengers. One hand cradled the wrapped urn, the other was poised to ward off the swarm of travelers around me. All of a sudden I felt the strap of my carry-on catch a passing coat sleeve. My hand wasn't quick enough to steady my package, and for a split second all was panic. A stewardess saw my alarm and stepped forward, thinking she could help. As she lunged for the urn, I was thrown even more off balance, and now a growing sense of crisis filled the air. Too late—the precious package had already fallen into someone else's hands; for someone else to touch it seemed unspeakably wrong. I wanted it back, and in that moment, I felt more lost than ever. Only disaster could follow. The urn crashed to the ground.

I sat alone in the reception room, the gold-wrapped package with the urn before me on an end table. When I thought of how respectable it had looked when I set out, how battered it was now, I felt so ashamed I wondered how I could ever raise my head again. All the rules of propriety, decency, filial respect—they had all been broken; they were gone forever.

Leaning closer to the table, I placed my hand on the package. I couldn't fathom why it gave me such an uneasy feeling. Still wondering, I rose to my feet. I smoothed the wrinkles of my coat and bowed solemnly, as was the custom when paying final respects. Then it occurred to me that, as a matter of fact, I hadn't done anything wrong. Hadn't I considered every last detail, carefully wrapping the urn for the long journey, tying each ribbon as securely as possible? Now I loosened the knots. It caught me by surprise, the way the wrapping fell away, like petals of a wondrous yellow flower.

There lay the broken fragments. Though it was in five or six pieces, the urn had more or less retained its original shape. The powdery white ashes were still a shock, and those tiny flakes of black, they must be his hair. When you're alive, it doesn't really matter how much hair you've got. But after you die, it becomes something marvelous, doesn't it? It adds a rather pleasant contrast to the pure white of the ashes. The soft ribbons and wrapping paper enfolding the urn fell back gracefully in undulating waves. And in the bottom right corner nestled several shards of emerald green porcelain. It was like gazing at a magnificent artistic creation, a painting in which each brushstroke achieves perfect delicacy and harmony. That was how the light reflecting off the shattered porcelain impressed me. At the center, the pure white ashes formed a heart, making the deep green glisten.

I leaned closer and gazed even more intently. Closer and closer, I pored over it with my whole heart and mind. Finally I reached out and stirred the powder with my fingertip, gently, as if I might find a clue to the mystery buried there.

I had no memories of my father taking my hand when I was young, and the truth was that once I'd grown up, we never touched. Even eye contact was hard for us. After the funeral, it had dawned on me that I had no clear impression of my father's physical being, only that unusually dark skin of his and the equally extraordinary whites of his eyes. Now when I finally dared to face my father without flinching, to take his full measure, all that was left of him were those two colors, black and white. Suddenly tears fell; they rolled down my cheeks into that white and black amid remnants of yellow paper. Teardrops formed a circle that spread rapidly, instantly engulfing the black and white powder.

Gazing at the urn through my tears convinced me more than ever to consign the ashes to the universe, and in so doing release both the dead and the living.

There was a knock at the door. In stepped a woman, accompanied by a middle-aged man in a handsome suit. It was the stewardess named Rui, who blamed the accident entirely on herself. The two of them saw the porcelain urn, completely unwrapped now, and they steeled themselves for my anger. I knew from a glance that they were terribly anxious, terribly embarrassed. Miss Rui immediately broke into tears; she was so distraught she couldn't speak.

Why should she take it so hard? Almost beside myself over their discomfort, I was about to blurt out, "Oh, you know, accidents will happen, please don't give it another thought," when I realized it was beyond the pale for a son to even contemplate such words. Why did it always have to be this way? Regardless of time or place, I was doomed never to do right by the old man. And just thinking of it in those terms and under the present circumstances made it all the more ludicrous. Was the son's failure the father's fault even after he was dead and gone? Then my thoughts swerved in another direction. Added to my distress was a cavernous sense of shame, making it all the harder to find a way out. I pictured myself a prisoner, unable to tolerate more torture. I wished I could fall dead at that very moment, or simply pass out and then regain consciousness, minus an arm or leg if necessary. At least that would be an escape.

The gentleman was an executive from the airline. He fumbled for words, tripping over his tongue in his effort to be polite. I hardly heard a word of it. Looking quite frantic, the fellow said there wasn't time to locate the right sort of urn to offer as compensation, but perhaps I could find it in my heart to forgive them? His words still hanging in the air, he reached into a bag and drew out an urn quite similar in color to the original one, but a good bit smaller. It was only after he pulled out a second jar of the same type that everything became clear.

The gentleman felt the weight of my silence and dropped his head, helplessly embarrassed. Not until he summoned the courage to look up did he note my friendly eyes looking back at him. Yes, I would be happy to accept this form of compensation. I spoke quietly, politely adding a request. I had just decided to spend a week in Taiwan and then go on to the mainland . Might they be able to help me with travel arrangements?

After they left the room, I sat down alone again before the table.

The human mind is a very complicated thing. You give free rein to a single thread of an idea, and it may take off in a thousand directions. You'll never wind it back in again. And if you manage to trace it back to the very first impulse, this is what you find: it makes no sense at all.

Carefully I scooped up a small amount of ash and held it over the open mouth of one of the urns. Lifting my palms upward, I let the powder sift gently between my fingers, as if it were sand flowing into an hourglass. The tiny flakes fell to the bottom without a whisper, like seconds slipping away in time, merging into the long river of eternity. The lamp shone down on the oval mound in my hands, caressing a shadow there. I pictured the scene below as a delicate waterfall. A fleck or two of ash brushed across my chest. A human life cannot be called brief, but in the end, what's left of it, a few handfuls, can be divided into two even parts.

Staring dumbly at the pair of urns, I marveled at nature's truths. The bones and flesh of a body will not be pushed around, but after death, they disintegrate and blend, and one becomes the other. That was how it was. As my father had often said,

> Spirit that is touched with breath becomes soul; spirit that is touched with form becomes essence.

Now the breath was extinguished, and the bones, reduced to powder, would find a final resting place on both sides of the Taiwan Strait. Free at last, half his ashes would journey back to the land of his dreams, the other half stay on the beautiful island, Formosa. Forty years of thoughts about the old country now belonged to the universe. No more cares, no more worries.

But for myself? Before me, I saw nowhere to go, and behind me, I saw no path leading to where I stood. Here I was, blessed with body and breath, but what good did it do me? What good did it do me at all?

The Last of the Whampoa Breed

. . .

by TAI Wen-tsai

translated by Michelle WU

Walking down to the street corner in Chengdu, one can poignantly sense a lethargy that comes from an overdose of sagacity, a calculated and weary dallying with life. As Uncle says, time is worthless here. Two long lines of street vendors stretch out under the shade of the bodhi trees. There are people peddling dried money skulls, bear paws, dried snake corpses, bean jellies, cold noodles, mung bean gruel, and hollow baked cakes. Dry, white flour powders the walls, which are smoked black and smeared with yellow grease. "*Koo-loo-arg-huh*," a spurt of thick phlegm makes its way from the bamboo sling chairs in front of the teahouse and through the crowds, landing in the bicycle lineup. Someone once said, "China is a giant spittoon."

Uncle has aged. In this place where neither time nor life is worth anything, only the aging of political strongmen has any significance or meaning. People like Uncle, as Uncle says, are but mud under the feet of the political strongmen, useless, like the clay figures of horses and warriors buried with the dead.

Taking a seat in the teahouse, Uncle takes out his own *fuling* cakes[1] and orders two bowls of *maojian*[2] tea and watermelon seeds from Mt. Ali. The worn-out bamboo chairs, the chipped tea bowls, and the sunflower-seed shells scattered all over the floor, along with the wet marks of phlegm, are tragically and hopelessly saturated with shame. Uncle pulls out a wad of paper and carefully wipes the edge of the bowl. He folds the moistened paper, dries it out in the palm of his hand, and puts it back into his pocket. The tender tea leaves gradually expand in the water, a light yellowish-green color. What a strange combination, the complicated atmosphere of the place and the clear, good tea.

Even in the teahouse, Uncle retains his sitting posture from the Whampoa Academy[3]—straight waist, occupying only the front half of the chair, two hands placed on the knees, and straight back, without touching the back of the chair. It is the same when he walks—stomach and buttocks tucked in and fingers held tightly together, swaying parallel to the seams of his trousers. To him, is the soldier's decorum like riding a bicycle—you learn it once, and it stays with you for a lifetime?

I ask Uncle, "Do you have anything that dates back to the Whampoa days? It could be worth a fortune now!"

Uncle says he threw everything away in 1949, on the eve of He Long's[4] entry into the city. The new year was just around the

[1] *Fuling* is a kind of mushroom that grows at the roots of pine trees. According to the Chinese pharmacopoeia, it is a diuretic, and it can strengthen the spleen and cure heart palpitations and insomnia. It can be mixed with rice and made into cakes.

[2] *Maojian* are tea leaves consisting of the tender top portion of the leaves.

[3] A military academy near Guangzhou, established in 1924 by Sun Yat-sen to train officers for the Guomindang. Many of its graduates were personally loyal to the academy's first leader, Chiang Kai-shek, and immeasurably strengthened his political power base.

[4] A Communist general.

corner; it was snowing in Jianmen Guan and Zhao Tian Yi.[5] Cut off at the tail and intercepted up front, Hu Zongnan's[6] troops were cornered and caught dead in the Chengdu Basin. He Long's troops were singing along the way.

"Run fast, move fast, we're not afraid of sore feet, we're not afraid of the cold, we're going to make our way to Chengdu, and capture Hu Zongnan alive."

Uncle was Cheng Jian's[7] personal bodyguard and did not belong to Hu Zongnan's battalion. Uncle said that Cheng Jian had houses in Nanjing, Changsha, and Shanghai, and that he had thought about rebellion a long time ago. Generalissimo Chiang Kai-shek sent Chen Mingren,[8] a Whampoa alumni stationed in Changsha, to get rid of Cheng Jian in the name of patriotism. Who could have known, however, that Chen Mingren and Cheng Jian would end up both defecting to the Communist camp? Uncle received one ounce of gold as "disbandment fee." With Hu Zongnan gone and Liu Wenhui and Pan Minghua[9] both turning their coats, the city of Chengdu was filled with defeated generals and dislocated soldiers. Uncle wanted to go to Kunming[10] to join the troops of Lu Han, who was another Whampoa graduate. But he didn't make it because the liberation army of Deng Xiaoping and Liu Bocheng was everywhere. Seeing that He Long was about to make his way into the city, Uncle hurriedly destroyed his military uniform, his school directory, and the awards given to him by the Generalissimo, burning and tearing everything in a frenzy. In the middle of the night, he

[5] Important fortresses guarding Chengdu, the capital of Szechwan province.
[6] A Nationalist general who died in this war.
[7] An important general in the Nationalist camp.
[8] An important general in the Nationalist camp.
[9] Both Nationalist generals.
[10] Kunming is the capital of Yunnan, a province south of Szechwan.

nervously took out the Whampoa sign of honor—two brass swords with the "Zhongzhen" insignia—and sank them in the well, trembling with fear all the while. Uncle says the well was just a few blocks away, and has been filled in already. He still recalls that the lane was called Da Fujian Lane. With the fifty grams of gold, he rented a run-down civilian shack. The landlord refused to give him change, and this took care of his "disbandment fee." All through the night, he scrambled to sew himself civilian clothes, and shaved his head to change his appearance. The next day, early in the morning, he joined the crowds outside the city to applaud and welcome General He Long's entry into the city, chanting along with everyone:

"The peach trees blossom, the plum trees blossom, hundreds of flowers blossom to welcome the People's Liberation Army into the mountain fort."

Uncle says that was the last of his Whampoa days.

The Dragon Boat Festival[11] is just around the corner. A vendor selling Chinese mugwort tied with straw into sheaths like swords moves in next to the vendor of bear paws. The sounds of bargaining clamor to the skies. Uncle asks the owner of the tea shop for a water bottle to add water.

"We're running out of water and you want to add water?"

Uncle doesn't say anything. In his languid expression, there is a magnanimous and natural dignity that hasn't a trace of "socialist" air, but is more like a noble pride that has transcended the mundane.

[11] The Dragon Boat Festival falls on the fifth day of the fifth month. This is one of the most important Chinese festivals. On this day, which represents the pinnacle of the heat of summer, people fend off poisonous insects and animals by anointing themselves with yellow wine. Sheaths of Chinese mugwort (*ai cao*) are placed over the doorways to keep away evil spirits.

After the "liberation" of Chengdu and He Long's entry into the city, Uncle fell on hard times with no job and no food. "People started to peddle their goods on the streets, pretty much like what they're doing now!" There were a lot of generals, colonels, and sergeants, all vending their "leftover goods." When Uncle got married, his family gave him an oxhide suitcase in which there were still some quilt covers, pillowcases, shoes, and cloth. He sold something out of the suitcase each day in exchange for rice or money. Uncle was bashful and couldn't make himself sell the stuff, so he asked a colonel who used to borrow rice from him to go sell the goods in exchange for a portion of the money or food. At the worst of times, four leaves of a Chinese cabbage had to last a day for the family of four. The "leftover goods" lasted for two years, and finally, the suitcase was sold too.

Uncle was of the sixteenth class to graduate from the Whampoa Academy—the last class. Uncle says Cheng Jian was like a weed on a fence that could bend in any direction with the wind. I ask him, "Why did you decide to follow him?"

Uncle smiles. The myriad expressions that climb over his face are but the flickering of light and the shadow of bodhi leaves over the face of an old pimp. Is meditating on history like meditating on Zen? Could it be that all that is left in his smile is the simple contemplation of a flower, of life?

As a child, Uncle says, he lived in the suburbs of Ding County. Two stone lions with balls in their mouths guarded their red-colored front door. He often played by the lions, grabbing their ears and swinging to and fro. It was a big house; one had to cross over three thresholds to reach the main hall. When he was fifteen years old, he was sent to the Shi family's old House of Silks and Satins to learn the skill of trading. The next year, the September

18th Mukden Incident[12] happened, and he made up his mind to fight the Japanese. Without letting his family know, he enrolled at the Military Police Academy.

"I graduated from the Military Police Academy with top grades," Uncle says suddenly, grinning like a child. "The top thirty graduates from the Military Police Academy were qualified to go directly to the Whampoa Academy. Seldom did a county produce more than two Whampoa Academy students. It really was an honor! My parents and siblings were so proud of me."

Uncle's eyebrows resemble two daggers shaped like mantis legs, slanting at steep angles. As a young man, he must have looked heroic, handsome, and forceful, but now he is old, and his drooping eyelids accentuate his slanting brows and feeble eyesight. His tongue has grown heavy and slow, making it necessary for him to reiterate a sentence several times in order to make himself clear. Sometimes, when he is in a rush, his cheeks bulge into balloons and his lips become puckered. He says that he is going to remain muddle-headed and not be sober, because the day that he sobers up will be the day that he dies. Only when talking about the Whampoa Academy does he come to life with dancing eyes, bursting with vivid descriptions of his life back then.

Cheng Jian was the chief of staff and commander of the First War Zone. He recruited them to the Whampoa Academy. Mao Zedong and Zhou Enlai also called on them to go to Yan'an. Uncle wanted to go to the front, so he signed up with Cheng Jian. He had followed Cheng Jian ever since he graduated from

[12] The Mukden Incident refers to an outbreak of fighting between the Chinese and Japanese troops on September 18, 1931, instigated by Japanese officers alleging that Chinese attacked them along a railway line outside of Mukden. Following this incident, the Japanese quickly mobilized troops to take control of all of Manchuria. The incident of Japanese aggression aroused patriotic fervor among the Chinese.

the Whampoa Academy. It wasn't until after the Taier zhuang[13] victory that he got a chance to go home for one hour. He met his family on Niutou Mountain in Fulu County. Uncle says that he had lost track of when he last went home. His family later followed his younger brother from Nanjing to Guangzhou, and eventually to Taiwan. That one hour was Uncle's only reunion with his family after he entered the Military Police Academy.

Cheng Jian was for a settlement between the Nationalists and the Communists. There were two telephones on his desk—one was connected directly to Nanjing[14] and the other to Yan'an.[15] Uncle said that Cheng Jian "vacillated here and there." Cheng Jian later negotiated with Yan'an: 1) he would agree with Communist policies but never become a Communist; he was against Generalissimo Chiang Kai-shek, but he would never betray the Guomindang; 2) he wanted a house in Shanghai. Uncle also said that Chen Mingren, who swore to be anti-Communist to the end, later actually gave every Whampoa alumnus a picture of himself and Mao Zedong standing before a chapel at the Temple of Heaven. Chen Mingren and Chen Chien defected to the other side together. Zhu De personally cooked a spicy, hot Szechwan dish for them. Uncle said that the two sold Whampoa for a hot, spicy dish with a dash of Chinese prickly ash. He said that the war was lost because Whampoa graduates sold Whampoa graduates.

Cheng Jian later rose to the position of Vice Chairman of the Chinese People's Political Consultative Conference. Many people urged Uncle to seek him out again as a member of the "insurrection army." But Uncle refused. Fu Zuoyi, Zhang Zhichun . . . many people sought out Cheng Jian's patronage, but not Uncle.

[13] A town in Shantung province where the Guomindang troops scored a victory over the Communist troops.

[14] The location of the headquarters of the Nationalist government.

[15] The location of the headquarters of the Communist forces.

Across the street, someone is selling shacha noodles. I ask Uncle what shacha noodles are. Uncle tells me that beef is chopped into paste, then fried with hot chili and Chinese prickly ash . . . he says that probably is the way that it is prepared, but he has never tasted it before. Having lived in Chengdu for more than forty years, Uncle still refuses to speak the Szechwan dialect, and he has refused to taste Szechwan pepper. His memory lingers only in the last of the Whampoa days.

Having sold the last of the remaining goods, he had to find a way to make a living. Uncle, however, said that nothing could stop him from reflecting upon the past. Thinking, thinking, thinking of the circumstances. What was going on? He couldn't understand it, yet he couldn't stop thinking. One day, an old friend came calling. That friend's family sold herbal medicine, so he taught Uncle the basics of pharmacology. Who would have known that Uncle would nosedive into it? It was as if his gushing ambition when entering the Military Police Academy to fight the Japanese and his hot-blooded patriotism when enlisting in the Whampoa Academy had returned. In a frenzy, he studied day and night, leaving no time for rest. At his rather advanced age, he actually passed the entrance exam to the School of Chinese Medicine. He studied like crazy, because he couldn't and was reluctant to vacate his brain for wild ruminations. He studied until he coughed up blood. He was forced to take a leave of absence from school for two or three years to nurse himself back to life. Then he returned to his studies. The different but similar gushes of emotions, Uncle says, were his only herbal medicine.

Because of his outstanding school performance, the school made an exception and sent Uncle to pursue further studies in western medicine. Upon graduation, Uncle got the best grades in surgery, but he refused to operate and chose to stay in internal medicine. The Whampoa graduate was transformed into a doctor, and forty years flew by.

Once Uncle started to practice as a doctor, it was as if he had gone mad again. Without eating, drinking, or resting, he could treat more than a hundred patients a day. All doctors got the same wages for seeing one patient or seeing a hundred patients. Uncle says it was a kind of "honor." He still remembered the five creeds, "The Three Principles of the People, the president, the nation, honor, and responsibility." Uncle could still memorize by heart: "The rise and fall of the nation are my responsibility; for my country I am willing to sacrifice my life."[16] I always considered that line to be a tongue-tying and restraining ideological slogan. During those times people suffered from malnutrition and were overworked. Tens and thousands of patients were waiting for treatment. There was no end to it, and doctors were wanted everywhere.

The Cultural Revolution broke out, and quite a number of Whampoa graduates became targets of attack; even Lin Biao[17] met with a pitiful end. I ask Uncle if he was a victim of the Cultural Revolution.

"I was beaten up! I was denounced! If I hadn't been a doctor, I would have been beaten to death!" Uncle is still bothered by the fact that he was dubbed one of the monsters and demons—class enemies. He considers it to be "dishonorable."

"I never did anything bad. I have only done good, saving people."

[16] This is a famous quote of Chiang Kai-shek that became a popular patriotic slogan.

[17] Military leader for the Communist forces who was the minister of defense for the Chinese Communists in 1958. He was an ardent supporter of Mao Zedong, and was named to be Mao's successor in 1969. He supposedly died two years later in an airplane crash after having escaped a failed coup against Mao.

Uncle had a sign hung around his neck; he wore tall hats and swept the streets; he was made to hold a straw in his mouth and imitate an airplane.[18] After two whole months of torture and punishment, his former patients petitioned that he be released to give them medical treatment. So his punishment was changed to sweeping the streets during the day and seeing patients at night. A month later, it was changed to prescribing medicine in the daytime and seeing patients in the evenings. His highest record was seeing more than 200 patients on a single night. From then on, no one picked on him anymore, as long as he confessed to Chairman Mao every morning before seeing his patients. Uncle says that in making up his mind to save lives, he actually saved his own life. One night, when the whole city of Chengdu was under curfew, 108 "Guomindang counter-revolutionaries" were executed. While the chilling gunshots sounded outside, Uncle trembled with trepidation as he treated his patients inside his clinic.

Uncle showed me his "certificates of award." He had burned all his awards from Whampoa; the ones that he has now are "A Progressive Health Worker," "A Progressive Individual in Fighting the Flood and Catastrophe, Preventing Disease, and Treating Sickness," and "A Progressive Individual in Promoting the Four Modernizations." He received awards every year. Uncle folded each certificate neatly, placing them in his simple and humble little house, wrapped in plastic bags to avoid the dampness and the insects. He very much liked to take them out for proud inspection—this was "honor." He worked overtime, seeing more than 100 patients per day, without earning an extra penny. And all he got in exchange were several pieces of paper. To Uncle's five children, they were "not worth a cent."

[18] This was a popular form of corporal punishment during the Cultural Revolution. People were asked to hold straws in their mouths with their arms spread out, standing on one foot only.

Uncle's children all grew up chanting "The sun is shiny, Chairman Mao is more shiny" and "We are intimate with Mother and Father, but even more intimate with Chairman Mao." No one could understand Uncle's Whampoa sense of honor. There is no similarity in behavior, appearance, speech, or disposition between Uncle and his children. Sitting among them, Uncle resembles a deserted Buddha in a temple. Their world is closed to Uncle, and Uncle doesn't want to leave his world either. Uncle has only one thing to say to his children, "Eat more vegetables and fruit." He does have something else to say to his grandchildren, however; that is "Study harder, study harder," with eyes full of anxiety, a simple and single-minded anxiety that borders on childishness.

One day we visited the Du Fu[19] Cottage. As we passed by the Flower Bathing Stream, we saw the couplet pasted over the front door: "West of the Wanli Bridge, North of the Baihua Pond."

Uncle and I stood under the couplet amid the garbage that literally covered the ground. Of course, there was phlegm all over the place too. There was no escape from phlegm. People were eating and drinking inside and outside of the cottage. The watermelon-seed shells scattered on the floor were so thick that even ants would have difficulty passing through them. Uncle stood there in a daze, like an ancient pile of ruins called Honor, standing in the midst of loneliness. I thought of Uncle's words: "The mud trampled under the feet of the strongmen are nothing: they are only good for making clay horses and warriors to be buried with the dead."

Uncle retired last year at seventy-five. He could have retired ten years ago, but his old patients wouldn't let him go. Other people got their pension money and started to take it easy in old age. Uncle received his pension money and continued to treat patients for free. Ten years passed by. He could still see dozens of

[19] A great Chinese poet from the Tang dynasty.

patients per day. Now he rests at home, only to continue his wild ruminations from forty years ago.

One day we went to the South Hot Springs Park in Chongqing. As we walked along the Flowery Stream, Uncle said that Generalissimo Chiang Kai-shek and Song Meiling used to take their walks here. It suddenly occurred to me to ask him, "Can you still sing the school anthem of the Whampoa Academy? I can." And I started to sing at the top of my lungs:

> The wind and the clouds roll, the mountains and rivers tremble,
> The Whampoa builds strong and mighty forces.
> With revolutionary ambition we have sworn to be loyal,
> With shiny swords and iron horses, we have trampled over hundreds of battlefields;
> We are vanguards in quelling inner conflict and fighting foreign enemies;
> Sweeping over the land in victory, resurrecting China,
> We are unrivaled as we score major victories.

Uncle joined in softly, and his eyes welled up into two pools of water.

I was totally caught by surprise. The song was outdated. We sometimes sang it like a childhood song, or we would sing it during picnics to clear up groggy minds, and we would even joke about it.

We sang the song twice as Uncle stood by the stream. Chongqing becomes beautiful only after sunset, because as darkness sets in, covering the sky and the earth, all the battered and withered sights seem rejuvenated in the night, the past temporarily retrieved.

Uncle says that in his lifetime he still misses most his days at Whampoa.

My Relatives in Hong Kong

. . .

by HSIAO Sa

translated by LOH I-cheng

I

Father asked me to lend him money. This had never happened before, and it wasn't a small sum, either. He asked for NT$300,000, which in U.S. dollars would be about $8,000.

That day at noon, he rode the bus from Taoyuan forty miles north to Taipei to see me at my office.

"This is a good-sized operation." Taking a chair in front of my desk, he looked around the busy office. "There must be a few hundred people here."

I felt a bit proud. "This is Japan's third largest trading company. In addition to Taiwan, we have offices in Hong Kong, Singapore . . ."

"Well," he said, nodding, probably noticing the samples of yard goods, food items, and chemicals piled on desks in the various departments, "seems it's got a hand in everything."

"Yes, everything," I replied. "Textiles, food, chemicals, steel and iron, shipping . . . you name it."

He was still shaking his head when we walked out of the office together. "Yeah, it's a large company. But I never imagined that you would be working for the Japanese!"

Father had retired from the county government only the year before, after he had had a stroke. He had recovered somewhat, but his right side was still weak. He had to use a walking stick whenever he went outside, and so he looked much older than two years ago. His comment about my working for a Japanese company somehow made this encounter even more poignant, and I could only manage a wry smile.

All the restaurants near my office are Japanese, so I suggested that we have sashimi for lunch, knowing he had learned how to eat raw fish from Mother.

"Too expensive," he said, shaking his head, "better not splurge."

"It's okay, I can sign for it." I meant that I could charge it to the office expense account. The truth was that in the last two years, the accounting department had started watching expenses, and I wasn't at all sure I could get away with it. But I wanted to make him feel more at ease.

I ordered the best sashimi, tempura, seaweed rolls, roasted fish, and many other dishes. Father kept saying, "That's enough. That's enough."

We finished eating. I thought he would tell me what he needed the money for, but he never said a word. Instead, he repeated, "As soon as the certificate of deposit matures, I'll pay you back."

II

Huimei, my wife, taught at the junior high school. Since home economics was not exactly a hot subject, she kept very regular hours. She went to work every morning. When her classes were over in the afternoon, she picked up our son from day care and went to her parents' home, which was nearby. When I got off work, I'd pick them up in the new Renault I'd bought on the installment plan and we'd go home together. If I was tied up, they would have dinner there and return home by bus.

Tonight, I left the office immediately after work. Normally, I would have stayed on a little longer. This had become the unwritten rule; from the branch manager and division heads to office workers like me, everyone tried to act as if they would give their last ounce of energy for the company. Nobody ever locked up and headed for home right at six o'clock.

"Aren't you a little early today?" My mother-in-law greeted me in her broken Mandarin. She was built like my mother, sturdy, with big hands and big feet. Except that my mother had married my father, and as a result spoke perfect Mandarin, even with a northern Chinese accent.

"Yeah, I'm a little early today." Long ago I'd stopped trying to be polite at my in-laws'. I was always in a hurry to collect my wife and son, and just said hello and good-bye. Fortunately, they were both very nice, and hardly ever complained about having a son-in-law like me.

In the car, even Huimei asked me the same thing. "Aren't you kind of early today?"

"What's wrong with being early?"

She laughed. Chaoming pulled on her hand, wanting to eat the candy Grandma had just given him. Huimei said no, adding, "You'll be having dinner soon."

I told her that Father had come to see me at the office. She, too, was surprised, and asked, "Anything on his mind?"

"He wants to borrow NT$300,000."

Her reaction was immediate. "Where would you get that kind of money?"

Three months ago, we had contracted for a house to be built in Tianmu, a suburb of Taipei. It would cost us NT$2,700,000, or about $71,000, and even with a bank mortgage, we had to put up almost half the amount ourselves. Although in these last two years, we had joined mutual saving groups and saved a little money, it wasn't easy to come up with so much so quickly. As each payment came due, we were notified of the amount we had to somehow produce.

"This is the first time he's ever asked me," I said. "What do you think I should have said?"

"But so much money . . . what is it for?"

"He didn't say."

"Does your mother know?"

"I didn't ask."

We bought take-out food on the way home and hurried through dinner.

Huimei washed the dishes and gave Chaoming his bath to get him ready for bed by nine o'clock. Neither of us mentioned the NT$300,000 again, but it was clear that she was not exactly pleased.

While Huimei was putting our son to bed, I took my bath. Halfway through, the phone rang. I knew that Huimei could not leave Chaoming to answer it, so, dripping with soapy water, I picked up the extension in the bathroom.

It was my sister, Bizhen. In an annoyed voice, she blurted out, "Mom wants you to come home right away."

"What for?" I was not exactly in a good mood either, with water dripping from me. "I'm taking a bath. How can I come that fast?"

"Mom says she wants to die! She wants you to come home right now! Immediately!"

"Who wants to die?" It was not that I hadn't heard her. I was mad at her for repeating such nonsense, like adding fuel to the fire.

"Your mother! Who else?" Bizhen retorted and hung up. She was always short with me. I didn't have the strength to be angry at her, and went back to my bath.

After Huimei put Chaoming to bed, she stuck her head in to ask who had called.

"Bizhen. She wants us to come home right now."

Huimei raised her eyebrows. "To Taoyuan? At this time of night?"

"What time is it?"

"Nine-thirty."

I put on my underwear and went into the study to call home. It was Mother who answered, and she was crying, "I can't go on anymore. Anything else, I'll do anything else he says, but this . . . I'll never agree to it."

"But what's the matter, Mom?"

"Come home! Come right now!"

She hung up on me, too. Angry as I was, there was nothing I could do. I told Huimei to get the boy up again, because we were going to Taoyuan.

"So late at night?"

Huimei grumbled while she tried to change his clothes. I watched impatiently. "Don't bother to dress him, let him go in his pajamas. And you too, just wear whatever you have on."

So the whole family piled into the car and sped to Taoyuan.

III

For more than a decade, Father had lived in Taoyuan in that two-story house. Although it was rather old, it was well maintained, and the neighbors also kept their houses neat and clean. That was why he and Mother did not want to move. It was nothing like our apartment building, where half of the tenants just rented. Maintenance standards were low. Motorcycles filled all the available space in the lobby every night. Paint was peeling in the stairwells and if a light bulb burned out, nobody bothered to change it. No wonder Huimei and I were so eager to move into our own house.

"Why are we going to Grandma's after I've gone to bed?" Chaoming, who had slept during the long ride, was regaining his usual energy, and kept on asking "Why?" as we arrived.

"I don't know." Huimei did not feel like answering him and stared grimly out the window. So I said, "Grandma and Grandpa had a fight."

"But why did she want us to come?"

I shrugged. "I don't know either."

He sighed and reached the inevitable conclusion: "Grown-ups just like to fight."

Bizhen opened the door for us. She did not utter a word of greeting.

In the living room, the air was so thick you could cut it with a knife. Father sat on the sofa, not saying a word, his eyes fixed on the ground in front of him. Mother's eyes and even her nose looked red; she must have just cried her heart out.

"What's the matter?" I sat down and as always, reminded my son of his manners. "Did you greet Grandpa and Grandma yet?"

The boy greeted them dutifully and then said, "I want to sleep."

Mother told him to go to Bizhen's bedroom, and Huimei took him upstairs.

Now only the four of us were left in the living room: father, mother, son, and daughter. Yet no one spoke for a long time. Finally I asked again, "So what's the matter? This hour of the night! What's this all about?"

Only then did my mother blow up. "You ask him!" She pointed at my father. "Ask him!"

Father kept his eyes on the ground, not saying a word.

I glanced at Bizhen, but she just gave me a dirty look. She was only a year younger than me, thirty-two, and still without prospects for a husband. The fact was, I knew lots of unmarried women more or less her age in Taipei, but none so sour as Bizhen had become in the last two years. I really didn't know why she was cross all the time.

"Bizhen, you tell me."

That left her no option, and she replied, though reluctantly, "Dad wants to go to Hong Kong to visit his relatives."

My father's younger sister, whom I called Auntie, lived in Hong Kong. For my father to visit her didn't seem like such a big deal. "To see Auntie . . . ?" I asked.

"To meet some people from the mainland . . . our relatives."

No sooner had she uttered these words than Mother leaped up. "What do you mean 'relatives'? What kind of relatives are they? I do not recognize them. I'll never recognize them as that!"

"Won't you please be quiet?" Bizhen glanced at Mother impatiently, but her words were meant to be soothing. "Dad's wife on the mainland, and their daughter, have arrived in Hong Kong."

"They're out?" Now it was my turn to be surprised. It dawned on me that this must have something to do with his wanting to borrow money.

Father finally spoke, but only in a whisper. "Only let them out for a visit. They have to go back."

The fact that Father had a wife and daughter on the mainland was not exactly a secret even when we were young. Mother did not seem to mind terribly, and sometimes she even joked with him in front of us children. But now she was denying any knowledge of it.

"I will not recognize it! When you proposed, you lied to me about being married before, or why would I have accepted you? I will not agree to this. So you want to go to Hong Kong to visit her? Where does that leave me? I'll never be anyone's concubine! I'll never agree to it!"

"Don't get too worked up," I tried to console Mother. "He can't leave for Hong Kong right away, so why get so excited?"

"Yes, he can," Mother started raving again. "You ask him! Behind my back, he's made all the arrangements to go. He was just telling me when he's leaving. . . . Him! Him! Married to him for thirty-odd years. Who does he think I am? You ask him! Even if I were a servant, he couldn't just get up and go like this!"

I looked at Father. He sat without saying a word, his unseeing eyes gazing through all of us there in the room, as if he were in a different world.

Bizhen tried to persuade Mother. "Didn't he tell you he'd only be gone for a few days, and come right back?"

"A few days? I won't agree to even a few days!" Mother's mind was made up. "I won't accept it! If he wants to go, let him get a divorce. After the divorce he can do as he pleases!"

"Why must you talk like that?" I said.

"Well, what do you want me to say? He sent her money every month. He sent a television, a bicycle. I didn't say anything then. Now he wants to visit her . . . and now you . . . what do you want me to say!?"

"All right, all right." Bizhen tried to calm Mother down. "At least they were husband and wife, and father and daughter. Take it easy. . . ."

"What husband and wife? Do you mean that I am not his wife? I won't accept this! I'll never accept it!"

"You! You! What is it you won't accept?" Driven to the edge, Father mumbled to himself.

"I won't accept that you have another wife. Because what does that make me? A concubine? I won't accept that."

"Fighting won't solve anything," I interjected.

"You mean you have a solution?" Bizhen gave me another dirty look.

"Dad wants to go. So let him go. He'll be back in a few days anyway!"

"Now you, my own flesh and blood, you're trying to help him!" Mother was really livid. "You want to let him go! Look at him, limping around, and you want him to go!"

"You, you . . . you're talking nonsense!" Father was shaking now, banging his right hand, still without full control, on the arm of the sofa for emphasis. Mother wasn't showing any signs of backing down either. Her accusing finger almost touching his nose, she said:

"What more do you want of me? I slaved for you all my life . . . all these years. Now you want to visit another woman! What do you take me for? I won't allow it, I just won't allow it!"

"Whether you allow it or not . . . I'm going!" Father asserted, shaking with rage.

"All right, all right! Please don't fight anymore! It just doesn't do any good to fight like this. . . ."

Before I could finish and for reasons beyond me, Bizhen now turned on me and exploded:

"Won't do any good, huh? Well, you're the elder son, you come up with an idea!"

"What kind of idea can I come up with? If I say let Dad go, Mom gets mad at me. If I tell him not to, Dad gets unhappy. . . . What do you expect me to say?"

"You can't say anything! You are the elder brother, but what have you ever done to fulfill your responsibility to this home?"

Now it dawned on me that Bizhen had been waiting a long time to pick this fight with me.

"So you want to quarrel, do you?"

"So what if I do!" She lifted her chin, her face full of pent-up anger. "I've wanted to get this off my chest for a long time. As elder brother, you, and your wife, have you fulfilled your responsibility? You live in Taipei. This is your home, too, but you only come when there's a holiday, when you can find time. Mom says she wants to die! And you still won't come back!"

"What do you want me to do? You want me to quit my job in Taipei? Is that what you want?"

"Well, what do you think I've done? This house, Dad and Mom. If I don't stay here, who'll look after them? What if something happens to them?"

"All right, all right! You're saying I'm not fulfilling my filial duty? Is that it? You're the good daughter. Or are you implying that it'll be my fault if you become an old maid? If you want to get married, do it! Anytime you want! But don't saddle me with ridiculous charges!"

"How can I go and get married? You don't take care of anything! You think I can just leave, the way things are?"

"Bizhen, can't you just drop this! Let's get things clear, today, once and for all. Are you getting married tomorrow? Okay, if you're getting married tomorrow, I'll quit my job in Taipei! Does that satisfy you?"

"I'm not getting married tomorrow, so you can keep hiding."

"Who's hiding?"

"You are!"

"You know very well that I have to work!"

"All right!" Father shouted suddenly. "All right!" Shakily, he got up from his sofa, waving his arms. "No more of this! No more!"

IV

I was really pissed off by Bizhen's tirade. And my wife was almost as bad, with her icy glare. Even the next morning, when I drove her and Chaoming to school, she wouldn't say a word to me.

Later that morning I was on the phone with a important client when Bizhen called. Miss Wang took the call.

"Ask her to wait a moment, I'm busy!"

Miss Wang repeated the message, but still pointed to the phone: "Your sister says it's urgent. She insists on talking to you now."

I had to excuse myself and pick up the other line, only to be subjected to her sharp tongue.

"Oh, so you're busy! Such important business! Asking me to wait, eh?"

I decided the best thing was to ignore her. "What is it?" I asked.

"Nothing involving me. I wouldn't dare bother you with any of my trivial problems! It's Mom. She's left home. Dad wants you to find her . . . well, if you don't want to, it's up to you. . . ."

And she hung up, just like that. I thought she must have enjoyed this chance to cut me off. And me? All I could do was pick up the client's line again and go on with business as usual. Then, with business out of the way, I began making one call after another to find out where Mother could be.

Mother was native Taiwanese, with all kinds of relatives in all kinds of places. Exactly the opposite of Father, who had come to Taiwan all alone. He didn't even have many friends.

They were introduced to each other with marriage as the stated purpose. They had gotten along fine, thanks to Mother and her outgoing, forthright personality. She let him have his way most of the time and never really put up a fight. This time, this business of his going to Hong Kong, was an exception. To have become so incensed, Mother must have felt this as a violation of a woman's strongest taboo.

Of course, in more than thirty years of marriage, minor tensions could not be avoided. For example, Mother liked to worship in those temples all over the island, which Father did not approve of at all. There was also the difference in their personalities. Father was more conservative, to the point of being old-fashioned.

Mother, on the other hand, was more adaptable and lively, and she liked company. There were always friends and relatives at our home, or she would go to theirs, which did not please Father either. Huimei often told me that she liked my mother better than my father. And there was good reason for this. An active, fun-loving older woman is easier to deal with than an old man with no interests who is always long-faced and complaining.

After eight phone calls, I finally located her. Mother was at the home of her sixth sister on Xinyi Road.

"Ah Ye, come quickly!" My sixth aunt had never learned Mandarin and only spoke Taiwanese. "Your mother is crying!"

I asked her to put Mother on the phone. Sure enough, she'd been sobbing her heart out. Now she was blowing her nose and complaining at the same time:

"What do you want me for? You have someone else you can call Mommy now, so what do you want me for?"

"Just stay at Sixth Aunt's house, and don't leave there," I said. "I'll come after lunch to take you home."

"I don't want to go home. That's not my home anymore," she said.

By the time I got to Sixth Aunt's, the living room was full of people. My first aunt was there, my first uncle's wife, my third aunt on her mother's side, and scores of others. I hardly had enough time to greet them all properly. And then no one gave me a chance to open my mouth, they were so busy interrupting each other, offering Mother advice. The final consensus was that she should go home. After all, why should she give up the home she'd put decades of work into? Even if she wanted a divorce, let the man move out; why should the woman leave her own house?

Listening to them, Mother couldn't help coming to Father's defense. "He never said he wanted a divorce. He just wants to visit and then he'll come right back."

"I'd say no to that. Why should it be so easy for him?" My first uncle's wife seemed more outraged than Mother. "He wants to go and he goes, he wants to come back and he comes back! Now you're really acting like you were his concubine!"

"Well, what should I do? He insists on going! He would go even if I said no! He's made all the plans and has all the papers ready. What worries me now is . . . what if he doesn't come back?" And then Mother burst into tears.

Sixth Aunt believed that peace was still the best policy between husband and wife. Finally she suggested:

"You stay here with me for a few days. We'll think it over, and see what he decides. Let Ah Ye go back home and try to talk him out of it again."

V

That night, I called Huimei at my in-laws' to tell her I had to go back to Taoyuan to have a heart-to-heart talk with Father.

"Fine." She was still sulking.

"What's the matter with you?"

"Nothing."

"Really nothing?"

"Uh-huh."

"Look, I can tell from your voice. If there's something bugging you, out with it."

"No, it's fine."

Of course I knew that something was bugging her. But right now I had enough problems to deal with, so I let her sulk.

By the time I got to Taoyuan, it was almost eight o'clock. Bizhen and Father were eating dinner. On the table were two tiny vegetable dishes obviously fresh out of the can: tofu and pickled cucumber. They were eating instant noodles.

"Why didn't you make rice?"

It was just a passing remark on my part, but Bizhen became indignant.

"Mother's not home. Who's going to cook? I have to go to work every day. When am I supposed to make dinner?"

"You sure know how to talk! You don't do anything else, but you sure can talk."

"At least that's better than not knowing, and wanting to know, what's happening in this house."

She had the last word. Then she collected the plates and chopsticks and went into the kitchen. She didn't come out again.

Father sighed and tried to placate me. "She acts as if she were still a child."

"She's not a child anymore."

Bizhen had not always been like this. Her hostility was a product of the last two years. She really blamed me for not living with our parents, but the truth was I had no choice.

"Mom is staying with Sixth Aunt," I told Father.

He nodded. "Bizhen called there, too."

"This matter of going to Hong Kong . . . I mean, you really want to go? Do you really have to go?"

He gazed at me for what seemed a long time, and said, "Yes, I have to go. I'm only human, and humans have to behave like humans. I need to have one look, to see her just once."

Actually, I wasn't opposed to the idea myself. Father had reached the age where, if he really wanted to do something, he ought to do it.

"Well," I said, nodding in agreement, "then go! As for Mom, I'll try to convince her. Anyway, you'll be back in a few days, right? Mom was worried that . . . that you might not come back."

"You think I'm nuts? Where would I go if I didn't come back? To a place like that?"

"They, uh, they're in Hong Kong now?"

"Staying with your aunt. I just talked to them on the telephone yesterday."

"Oh."

"So . . . I think . . . the earlier the better."

"I see . . . the money . . . in a day or two! Mom was right when she worried about you walking. I think I'd better go with you."

"Well!" Father looked up at me, more pleased than surprised. "The entry visa for Hong Kong, have you got one?"

"Last month I was going to go to Hong Kong for business, so I'm all set. I always have a visa, to avoid the month's wait if I have to go in a hurry."

"Well, that's the best way." He nodded again. "One family, at least we are one family. It would be best to see them."

VI

The next morning, I told Huimei to borrow NT$300,000 from her colleagues, at the usual interest rate, of course. Because of our new house, I'd exhausted all my credit with my own company. I had to ask Huimei to arrange for the loan this time.

When I got to the office, I phoned the travel agent to make our plane reservations. Then I made a round of calls to several clients. At noon, I ran over to Sixth Aunt's house to see Mother.

Sixth Aunt was out at the moment. It was only the two of us. I tried to persuade her:

"Let him go just to see them this once. Why are you so set against it?"

"I just don't like it," she said.

"What don't you like?" I teased her. "Are you worried they'll sleep together? That's ridiculous!"

Even she smiled this time, and scolded me. "You're talking pure nonsense!"

"All right, but just take it easy. If you like it in Taipei, then stay here in the city for a while. Go out and have some fun with Sixth Aunt. Be happy, that's the best medicine. Dad wants to go, just let him go. He'll be back in a few days!"

I seemed to be persuading her. She was softening, but she still tried to talk tough:

"You go tell him! I won't recognize it. If he goes, he had better not come back to me."

That night, I really wanted to go home and rest, but some Japanese had arrived that day. The last time I was in Osaka, they'd given me the royal treatment, so I had to take them to dinner at the Restaurant of Ten Thousand Happinesses, and then to a bar in Sixth Alley just off Zhongshan North Road, where we drank until 1:30 in the morning. After that I left the night's itinerary to my colleague.

When I got home, Huimei was still up, curled on the sofa, waiting for me. Even from a distance, she must have smelled my breath, because she said, with a long face:

"You drank too much again!"

"There are guests here from Japan."

"Why do you have to get drunk every time someone comes from Japan?"

You can't reason with women about things like that. I went into the bathroom to wash. She came in, too, and sat down on the john. She sat there for a long time without uttering a word.

"Why don't you go to bed?"

She thought a moment, then replied: "I want to talk to you."

I looked at her, waiting for her to speak.

"The check is on the dining table. I borrowed it from my mother. You know how I hate to borrow anything from my family. There are so many brothers and sisters-in-law . . ."

What could I say when she talked like this? I had to keep my mouth shut.

Huimei was not looking at me either. She just looked at the floor, uncurling her bent fingers one by one. She always did that when something bothered her. Then she spoke slowly, as if weighing every word:

"I've told my mother. Tomorrow, I'll move back home for a while."

"But why?"

"I don't like it." Suddenly she raised her voice. "I really don't like it."

Huimei rarely ever talked to me like this. We had been in love for two years before we got married, which was four years ago. I knew her inside and out. She had the sweetest disposition, and was patient and tolerant with everyone.

"What is it you don't like?"

"You should have told your father the truth. We don't have any money, but you'll pay interest to borrow money for your father. . . . It's like the old saying about slapping your face till it's swollen to look prosperous and well-fed."

"I don't know what you're talking about."

I dried off and slammed the door after me. Huimei stayed in the bathroom for a long time. After I went to bed, she quietly went to the living room, turned off the lights, locked the porch door, and returned to the bedroom.

"I'm not finished yet." She turned on the bedside lamp. "There's something else I've wanted to say for a long time. I can't stand the kind of life we lead. There are just endless social engagements for your work, every night of the week. I can't stand it. The other teachers at my school . . . nobody lives this way."

She started crying softly. I was not in the best mood either, so I shot back:

"So why didn't you marry another schoolteacher, so you could leave work together every day?"

I reached up and switched off the light. Lying in the dark, I could still hear her sobbing. Of course I knew that right then, she needed me to comfort her and say sweet things. But who would say sweet things and comfort me, when I, too, had to face the same routine, the same pressures, every day? As I lay there thinking, I got more and more annoyed.

VII

Three days later, I flew with Father to Hong Kong. No one came to the airport to see us off. Sixth Aunt took my mother to Tainan, to my second aunt's home, to take her mind off things. True to her word, Huimei took our son back to her parents' house.

I looked at Father, who had just had a haircut the day before. He still had his walking stick, but he was all decked out in a bright tie and new suit he'd bought for the New Year. In fact, I hadn't seen him looking so well since before his stroke. In contrast, I was the one who looked totally beat and bleary-eyed. In addition to entertaining the Japanese visitors the day before, I'd had to get through all my unfinished business, go to the bank to change money, get some cash, and so on and so forth. Even after we checked in, I had to call the office to tie up some loose ends.

On business trips, I always liked to travel light: a big tote bag, plus one suit. I usually did not even bother checking my luggage. But Father was carrying a huge suitcase. When customs opened it for inspection, it was filled with fruits and vegetables.

"What are you bringing papaya, guava, cucumber, and things like that for?"

He sounded perfectly justified. "I do this every time. Your aunt asked for them because she can't find them in Hong Kong."

For the life of me I could not recall Hong Kong ever lacking fruits or vegetables, but I left it at that.

The flight took only an hour and ten minutes, faster than going from Taipei to Xinzhu. It was only a little after three when we walked out of Kai Tak Airport.

I asked Father, "Who's coming to meet us?"

"All of them, I think."

Outside in the arrivals area, hundreds of people milled about. Father began to look a little nervous, mumbling to himself, "Are they here? Are they here?"

"Yeah, they're here," I replied, pointing to my aunt and her husband. Uncle had become even thinner, creating the illusion that he'd actually shrunk. On the other hand, my aunt was a size larger than when I'd seen her last, two years ago. Her face glistening with sweat, she was waving her handkerchief to catch Father's eye.

"Elder Brother! Elder Brother! Over here!"

Although the middle-aged woman standing next to my aunt had just had her hair done, she betrayed her origin to any discerning eye. Dressed in a very old-fashioned jacket and nondescript bluish-gray pants, anybody could tell at a glance that she wasn't from Hong Kong. She held the arm of an old woman, her hair pulled back in a bun, who even had the traces of bound feet. She was wearing a short jacket and pants of dark gray. Judging from her age, the old lady must be Great Mother, and the middle-aged woman my elder sister, Xiuzhen. But at the moment, it was hard to comprehend that fact. My own mother, who was approaching sixty, looked about the same age as Elder Sister Xiuzhen, who would be in her early forties. And Great Mother, whom I understood had just turned sixty, looked at least twenty years older than my own mother. She was really, really old.

At the first sight of mother and daughter, Father appeared somewhat excited and also embarrassed. I felt sure that he was as shocked and saddened by their elderly appearance as I was. I had been pushing his large suitcase on a cart for him. But now, to cover up his embarrassment, he started looking all over for his baggage.

"Here, let me take it." Uncle took the cart from me.

Until they got into Uncle's Peugeot, Father did not exchange a word with Great Mother. They even tried to avoid each other's eyes. On the other hand, my elder sister Xiuzhen turned out to be quite open and outgoing. She kept on calling him Dad, and addressing me as Younger Brother.

Uncle, Aunt, Father, Great Mother, and Elder Sister rode in one car. I rode in the other car, borrowed for the occasion by Second Cousin Dawu, who was Uncle's nephew. I asked about my aunt's daughter, who was in high school, and her younger son, who was only in grade school:

"How are Juanjuan and Dongdong?"

"They're at school."

"Juanjuan should be preparing for her college entrance exams now."

"Yeah, she's all right. But Dongdong is spoiled rotten. The children in Hong Kong. I've never seen the likes of them. He buys anything he wants. All he can think of is play, play, play. No child on the mainland is like that. At his age, they would have been working in the fields already."

Dawu was the son of Uncle's elder brother. He was two years older than I and he'd left Beijing with his wife and two daughters only a few years ago. Now he helped Uncle in his office, which was dealing in the gold futures market. He'd caught on real fast, they said, in just two or three years. The family had also moved out of Uncle's home, having bought an apartment of their own, with Uncle's help. Hong Kong was full of cases like his, relatives helping relatives fresh out of Red China.

We talked about Uncle's business, and also about 1997. I asked him how he'd come to the decision to buy an apartment last month.

With an air of resignation, he shrugged and said:

"Real estate prices were falling like crazy then. And I thought, what the hell, I'll cross that bridge when I come to it. 1997 is eleven years away. We can't just stop living because of that!"

"That's very philosophical."

"No, it's not at all. Everybody thinks the same way in Hong Kong. All the rich are ready to pack up and leave . . . for Canada, the United States, or Australia. And the poor, they just live one day at a time."

"What are Uncle's plans?"

"If Juanjuan can't get into college here, they'll all move to Canada."

I knew that Uncle had a relative in Canada who owned a restaurant.

"What about you?"

"We'll see." He smiled bitterly. "We'll have to think of something! It took a hell of a lot to get out of there, and I'll be damned if I'm going to sit here and wait for the Communists to come again."

My aunt's home was at North Point. They'd lived there, in the penthouse apartment of a 24-story high-rise, for more than ten years now. On the ground floor was a restaurant. It was not one of the best locations in Hong Kong. And the apartment was small; I estimated it at less than 2,000 square feet. Since Uncle had his own business, he was far more prosperous than Father. But from the place they lived in, you could tell they were not spendthrifts.

We arrived first. Cousin Dawu helped me unload the baggage, and then we stood there waiting for the other car. It soon arrived. I opened the car door for Father, and noticed that he was dabbing the corners of his eyes. Great Mother, who sat beside him, was trying to muffle her mouth with her handkerchief so as not to cry too loud. Elder Sister Xiuzhen, and even my aunt who sat in front, had been crying, too.

VIII

That night, Uncle and Aunt invited us all to dinner at Tongqing Lou Restaurant in Causeway Bay. There are only two kinds of Chinese restaurants in the world: those that are well-managed and those that aren't. The first kind is definitely the minority, consisting mostly of those catering to tourists and foreigners. All the others seem to prefer looking old and dirty, the chipped chinaware and grease indicating they've been around a long time.

Tongqing Lou was hardly different. We walked up a narrow staircase to the second floor. The red and gold velvet wallpaper looked as dirty as it was old, peeling away at the corners and seams. The red carpet under our feet had lost most of its nap and was covered with stains and holes. I felt the same way about Hong Kong as I did about this restaurant; I didn't like either of them very much.

But Uncle couldn't stop praising this place. "The food is really superb here. Not much to look at, but ahh, the food. We come here for the cuisine, not the atmosphere."

Father nodded consent. "Who can eat atmosphere? All we care about is the food."

Father, of course, sat at the head of the table with Great Mother and Elder Sister. My seat happened to face both women. While they were talking and exchanging toasts with Uncle and Aunt, I had the opportunity to really look them over. What surprised me was that they did not look too much alike. Actually, Elder Sister was the spitting image of my father. The same kind of big, round northern Chinese face, with somewhat triangular eyes and very thin lips. She was not pretty but looked quite neat and efficient.

She told of her experiences during the Great Proletarian Cultural Revolution, when she was sent to work in the country and really suffered many hardships. To me, she looked like the type who could survive under such conditions. Although her features were typical of a northern Chinese woman, Great Mother had a longer face and a better-looking nose. What intrigued me was that she even looked a bit like my own mother, maybe because they both had long, narrow eyes, and long eyebrows, too.

I understood that Father and Great Mother's marriage was arranged through a matchmaker and at their parents' bidding. Not long afterward, Father left for the south, and because of the war, was never heard from again. My mother said they hardly knew each other. But no matter what the circumstances were forty years ago, the bonds between husband and wife and father and daughter appeared hard to break, from what I could see. It didn't matter whether they had ever been in love with each other. You couldn't just dismiss such bonds on the basis of likes or dislikes.

Great Mother hardly ever spoke voluntarily. She just nodded to whatever was said. If anyone toasted her, she would take one sip from her wine cup. Once Father picked up a piece of fish and put it on her plate, and she blushed. It broke your heart to see an old lady like that blush.

Aunt noticed, too, and laughing, said:

"Elder Sister-in-law, when you first came to our house, at every meal you kept piling food on my plate, because you were too shy to eat much yourself. Elder Brother was living in the city then, and hardly ever came home."

Feeling even more embarrassed, Great Mother shook her head and said something totally irrelevant: "I'm old now, I'm old."

For the life of me, I couldn't imagine that she had ever been young. The years were certainly cruel; time spares no one.

"Younger Brother, are you also in business like our uncle?"

Xiuzhen was always calling me Younger Brother to show she felt close to me. For my part, however, I could not yet bring myself to call her Elder Sister. I just smiled and nodded. "Yes."

"We know nothing whatever about business," she said. "Your brother-in-law is a doctor. And I work in a factory. Why don't you all come visit us sometime?"

She spoke with such a typical Beijing accent, so earthy, that it sounded odd, but I knew she was sincerely expressing warmth and friendship.

"It's not very convenient," I said.

"Yes," she sighed. "The truth is, there's not much to see, anyway. Our daily life just can't compare with the life here in Hong Kong. In Taiwan, I hear it's about the same as Hong Kong."

"Not really the same," I replied.

Uncle took up where I left off, nodding for emphasis. "Better than Hong Kong! Hong Kong is getting worse every day."

"Oh." Xiuzhen nodded as if she understood. "Ah, the food, the clothes in Hong Kong. . . . There is so much that is new. . . . The only trouble is that there are so many people!"

Great Mother, who had not said anything all that time, showed signs of agitation when Elder Sister invited us to visit them. I could see that she was trying to restrain herself, but finally she pulled at the arm of her talkative daughter and began whispering in her ear.

Xiuzhen listened for a moment and then broke out laughing. Pushing her mother away, she said:

"No chance of it. Don't worry. Just eat some more."

"What's the matter, Xiuzhen?" Aunt asked her.

She laughed again. "Mom said that when we left, the unit where we work kept telling us that when we met relatives, we should say that everything is fine, and urge them to come back to live in China. They tell everyone the same thing, but who would take them seriously?"

Great Mother kept shaking her hand to indicate her feelings. Looking at Father, she said, "Don't go back! Don't go back!"

Xiuzhen laughed at her again, and said, "Mom, who would be that stupid! You don't need to warn them. I just said they could come visit. I never said anything about staying for good!"

IX

That night and all the nights that followed, we stayed with my aunt. They had a small guest room, which Great Mother and Elder Sister had been using. Now Elder Sister said she would sleep with Juanjuan, my aunt's daughter, and let Father and her mother stay together. But over and over Great Mother refused, saying, "How could we? How could we?"

My aunt replied, "Look how old even your daughter is now, so why not?"

On the other side of the room, Father was sitting and chatting with Uncle, pretending not to hear them.

Finally, despite their protests, Father and Great Mother were persuaded to stay in the guest room. Elder Sister slept with Juanjuan. Dongdong, my aunt's son, had a single bed. My aunt wanted him to offer it to me, but I refused and insisted on sleeping on the floor in the living room.

The guest room was directly off the living room; and the guest room light stayed on almost all night. They had not really spoken to each other since Father got off the plane. Now they were by themselves, and I could hear them talking on and on in low voices.

After midnight, I called Taipei. There was still no answer at home. Then I dialed my in-laws' number and found Huimei still up.

"What are you doing up so late?" I asked.

"Nothing."

"Is Chaoming asleep?"

"Yeah, he's asleep."

I knew we were just making conversation, but I felt better after calling her, and soon fell asleep.

X

Aunt was the first one up in the morning. Seeing that I was awake, she winked at me, and said, "They talked the whole night, didn't they?"

I laughed, yawning, and sat up in my makeshift bed.

"Go back to sleep! It's still early."

"No, I'll get up."

How could anyone go back to sleep on the floor in someone else's living room?

Aunt started to fix breakfast, saying she would use last night's leftovers from the restaurant to make some noodles. Great Mother must have heard us and, dressing in a hurry, came out to help. When I glanced her way, she looked especially embarrassed, and kept on smoothing down her hair.

Juanjuan and Dongdong had to leave for school, and were given money to buy something along the way. Nothing was more important to Uncle than the newspaper, so Father had to sit across from him to scan the Hong Kong headlines. Someone had turned on the television, and all the early morning programs, of course, were in yackety-yack Cantonese. Since there was no escaping it, I just sat there watching TV.

The noodles were ready. Bringing me my bowl, Xiuzhen asked, "Younger Brother, where are you going today?"

"Oh," I said, "maybe to see some friends. What about you?"

"I don't know. We've been here two days. Aunt said to wait till Dad arrived and then we'd all go out together."

"Uncle has a car, and you can . . . "

Uncle overheard me, and said, "I have to go to the office, but your aunt will keep you company. Dawu will come back with my car."

Eating the noodles, I noticed that Elder Sister was wearing a long-sleeved calico blouse today, and did not look as old as yesterday. She was aware that I was looking at her, and laughed, a little self-consciously.

"Aunt gave it to me. Too flowery. I was afraid to wear it."

"It looks nice," I said.

Father chimed in, too. "It's nice. We'll buy a couple more for you to take back."

After everyone had had breakfast, Dawu returned with the car, and they got ready to go out. But before they left, Father had some instructions for me. He drew me aside.

"Call your mother, and tell her not to worry. Ohh, I didn't sleep well at all, just not used to it! Someone I haven't seen for so many years, ohh, I'm just not used to it. . . . "

His last remark seemed to be meant as a kind of explanation.

After they left the apartment, I tried to call Taoyuan, and Sixth Aunt's home in Taipei. Nobody answered at either place. So I called and asked my friend to cross over to Kowloon and meet me at the famous Regent Café.

I did not return to Aunt's apartment until late in the evening. In the morning, I talked to my business friend about Hong Kong's future as a market. He had a lunch engagement, so I ate alone, and in the afternoon I went shopping. I bought a suit for Huimei, some Japanese-made warrior toys for our son, and a pair of pants for myself. Then I went into a Jewish restaurant for a steak, which was not bad at all.

After spending the whole day on the Kowloon side, I did not feel like riding the subway back to Hong Kong when night came, so I took the ferry instead. The subway was more convenient, but I'd always preferred the ferry, and it seemed somewhat sacrilegious to come to Hong Kong and not take it even once. I especially liked sitting on the upper deck while the ferry took its time crossing the sea at night, those millions of lights shining on both shores making Hong Kong look more romantic and more beautiful than it really is.

Returning to Aunt's apartment, I was startled by the sight that greeted me when I opened the door. The place was full of packages, big and small, the loot of a whole day's shopping.

Father, Great Mother, Elder Sister, and Aunt and Uncle were opening them one by one and putting everything in place.

Great Mother kept saying, "Don't throw the bags away! Don't throw them away!"

She even insisted that Elder Sister smooth out all the thin plastic produce bags, saying that they could take them back to Beijing, and that their neighbors would be pleased to have them.

They'd bought everything—everything to eat, to wear, and to use. Elder Sister carefully folded every piece of clothing. The candies and the cookies were repacked to save every inch of available space. There was a camera, a cassette recorder, a hair dryer, a lighter, an electric fan. . . .

"Are you sure you can bring all of these back?"

Father cut in: "Sure! Sure!"

Aunt got up and fetched her handbag. Checking all the receipts, she gave them to Elder Sister. "Keep these and don't lose them."

I edged over to get a closer look. Aunt explained: "That's for the washing machine and refrigerator. They can be delivered to Beijing."

This reminded me of how the Communists were always harping about the four modernizations of China. It seemed that Great Mother's home, at least, would be modernized all at once.

"Aren't you going to buy a television set, too?" I reminded Father.

Uncle answered for him.

"They've got one. Your father bought it last year. I helped find someone to take it to them."

I looked at Father. He was smiling as he checked the cassette recorder. He turned to Elder Sister:

"We forgot the batteries. We'll buy them tomorrow and put them in."

This was why he had borrowed NT$300,000 from me! He wanted to make up for the hardships that Great Mother and their daughter had suffered over these thirty-odd years. Although everyone realized that nothing in the world could compensate for what they'd been through, he still wanted to do all he could for them.

XI

The second, third, and fourth days followed more or less the same routine as the first. They went shopping; they ate at western restaurants, seafood restaurants, and Chinese restaurants. They visited the Seaquarium, rode the ferry, went to the racecourse, and spent time at Repulse Bay. I heard that they lost money at the races. Great Mother kept saying what a shame it was, that the money they'd lost could last her two months back home.

"Your great mother is too stingy!" Aunt kept whispering to me behind her back. "They're all like that when they come out for the first time, all country bumpkins. And you can't do a thing to change it!"

I spent most of my time wandering about. The truth was, Hong Kong offered even fewer places to go than Taipei. In two or three days you could see them all. After that, I had to try to fill the hours one by one. Life was so busy in Taipei that I sometimes wondered why I'd turned myself into a machine, working day and night just to make a living. But now that I had time on my hands, I had no idea what to do with it, and feeling lost like that was just as bad as feeling harried, if not worse.

Early on the morning of the fifth day, Father asked me if I would go with them to have a picture taken for a keepsake. I had nothing else to do, so I said yes. It was a Sunday, so neither Juanjuan or Dongdong had school. Aunt asked them to come, too, but Juanjuan resisted. She replied sullenly:

"But my friend and I were going to the movies!"

"Can't you see it next week? Your uncle and aunt are going home soon."

"This is the last day for the movie, too."

Dongdong didn't like the idea any better, protesting that he wanted to go skating.

In the end, we all went to the photo studio, even Second Cousin Dawu's family. There were twelve of us, including the children. The photographer arranged us in two rows and took one picture.

"Make an enlargement," said Father. "I'll take one back to put up." I thought he must have been carried away by the occasion.

Not only would Mother not let him hang the photo, she might tear it to pieces and smash the frame.

Then, of course, we had to eat lunch. Great Mother said she could not eat any more, since she already had a mild case of diarrhea. Father's stomach was also slightly upset. But Uncle insisted we go, because the host, Mr. Wang, had been his old business partner for years, and had invited us to the Jewel Seafood Restaurant to show his respect. I'd eaten there several times on previous visits. We drove for over half an hour, crossed several ridges, and finally came to a small seaside bay. The restaurant itself was a huge boat, constructed in three stories and garishly decorated, one of those Hong Kong seafood restaurants for tourists.

"It's really beautiful. I've never seen anything like it in my life."

Elder Sister Xiuzhen kept praising the place, making our hosts, Mr. and Mrs. Wang, glow with pride. But still Great Mother insisted:

"Eating this way every day is such a waste! We shouldn't be doing it."

My aunt scolded her:

"Eat a bit if you can manage it. You won't find food like this after you go back!"

Both Juanjuan and Dongdong looked thoroughly bored. At least three times Dongdong said, "I got tired of this place ages ago."

Juanjuan sat next to me. Since I could not keep up with the elder generation's conversation, I chatted with her.

"Is school keeping you busy?"

"Very busy, all the time." Juanjuan spoke fluent Cantonese, so her Mandarin sounded somewhat awkward.

"You have to take the college exams soon?"

"Yes, but I don't know if I'll pass or not."

"Ever thought of going to one of the universities in Taiwan?"

She shook her head. "If I fail, I'll go to Canada."

"Are there a lot of people from Hong Kong going to Canada?"

"Uh-huh, a lot of my schoolmates. There are more and more Chinese there now."

"Come visit us in Taiwan sometime."

"Okay! My schoolmates who've been there say it's nice. More culture. And a better place to study than Hong Kong. It's just that . . ."

"Just what?"

"Just that it's still different, even though it's Chinese."

I knew what she meant. Yes, we were all Chinese, but still we were different.

"It's a pity to be a Hong Kong Chinese," she said. "My schoolmates always say: What are we? We're not English, and we don't want to be Communists. But Taiwan . . . that's not our home either. There's no place we can call our own."

"What about Canada?"

"I don't know. We'll have to see when we get there. After 1997, there's no staying here. All those who can are leaving."

Around this large, round table sat fourteen people. Mr. and Mrs. Wang were born in Hong Kong. Uncle and Aunt came here only after 1949 to earn a living. Juanjuan and Dongdong belonged to the second generation. And, of course, there was Second Cousin Dawu's family, who risked their lives to escape from the Chinese mainland. Yes, they all lived in Hong Kong now, and in a few years, they would face the Hong Kong dilemma. Aside from them, there were Great Mother and Elder Sister Xiuzhen, who had stayed in China all these years, had grown old before their time, and really had nothing much to look forward to. And there was my father, who'd gone to Taiwan after 1949, and me, born and raised on the island. Yes, we were all Chinese, but each of us faced a vastly different future.

XII

In the afternoon, Aunt took Elder Sister Xiuzhen to the beauty parlor to get a permanent. I followed Father and Great Mother as they shopped for more goodies for her to take back to relatives, friends, and neighbors as gifts.

"Everybody knew we were going to Hong Kong to meet relatives from Taiwan. They were so envious! So we need to buy candies and other treats for everyone to share."

In Taiwan, Father usually hated to go shopping with Mother. Being naturally thrifty, he thought everything was too expensive and he disliked spending money. But on this visit to Hong Kong, he bought things day in and day out, shelling out rolls and rolls of banknotes; I never even saw him get impatient.

That night, Uncle invited everybody to a farewell dinner at the Shanghai Club in Hong Kong's central district. At least this restaurant was cleaner and had a better atmosphere. But after so many days of stuffing ourselves, nobody had much appetite left. We just sampled from the heaping platters.

On the way back to the apartment, I rode with Elder Sister Xiuzhen.

"What do you think of my new permanent?" she asked.

"It's fine," I said. The truth was that I hadn't noticed a difference, except that her hair looked a little shorter and maybe curlier.

"I feel kind of strange; maybe it's too curly." She touched the hair close to her neck.

"No, it's fine."

"You're sure? Okay, then."

She seemed really relieved by my remark, and turned from fussing with her hair to playing with the electric button that controlled the window, lowering it halfway.

"It's autumn now. It'll begin to snow soon in the north."

"Have you bought some warm clothes yet?"

"Oh, sure. Dad bought us three down jackets. They're really warm. In Beijing, you need clothes like that to fend off the cold. . . . One of them is for my husband."

"And nothing for my niece and nephew?" I was referring to her two children, who attended high school.

She laughed happily, slapping my arm lightly as she spoke. "Thank you for thinking of them. Yes, we bought clothes for them, too. But young people don't need anything that warm. Just heavy jackets will do."

Cousin Dawu, who was driving, turned his head and said, "Your father spent a lot of money this visit."

"It's all right." I had to be polite.

"Yes." Elder Sister Xiuzhen nodded earnestly. "Dad insisted on buying all these things for us to take back. And I couldn't say no, no, no all the time. Every day I said, 'That's enough,' 'That's enough.' But he wouldn't listen! Younger Brother, you're all doing all right in Taiwan, aren't you?"

"Not too bad," I said.

"It seems like you must be doing pretty well."

To put her mind at ease, I said, "Sure, we can afford the things that we want."

"Then it's all right. Mother told him over and over not to spend money like that, but she was afraid of offending him. He feels that he owes us a lot. But the truth is, how could anybody blame him? Please, please tell him that."

"Yes, I'll tell him."

She nodded. Then suddenly, she took two rings off her fingers and handed them to me.

"They're not worth anything! One is silver, the other is only brass. But they are the best that I own. Take them back with you, one for your wife, and the other for Younger Sister—just to remember me with."

I didn't want to disappoint her, so I accepted them and put them in my pocket.

"Aiyee. . . ." She sighed again. I hadn't noticed her doing this the first few days, so it must have been because they'd be leaving the next day. She went on, "Mother told me to tell you this. When you get back, tell your mother not to be mad at Dad anymore. She won't be coming out another time, and she's getting old. So please tell your mother not to be mad anymore."

I felt a little bit choked up, too.

"Also, Dad promised to try to get me and my husband out. I don't think it will be that easy. For me and my husband, well, we shouldn't entertain such dreams anymore. But for our children . . . if it's at all possible, please do try. Of course, we would like to give them the chance for a better life. But if it really is impossible, then . . ."

She couldn't go on anymore; she just kept blowing her nose.

XIII

Early the next morning, Uncle and Cousin Dawu were the chauffeurs once more. There were two bulging suitcases and three boxes, tied with rope, and it took us all quite some time to lug them down from the apartment and into the cars.

We took the underwater tunnel to the train station in Kowloon. Father did not say a word the whole way, but his eyes were red. Even when we reached the Kowloon–Canton

Railway Station, he refused to wait with us. Leaning on his walking stick, he found a place to sit alone. He would not even look our way.

The three women—Great Mother, Elder Sister, and my aunt—had been crying nonstop since early that morning.

As Great Mother and Elder Sister boarded the train, I addressed them for the first time in my life.

"Elder Sister! Great Mother! . . . I'll get Father to come over."

"Don't." Elder Sister grabbed my sleeve. "Younger Brother, don't. This is probably better. He'll only feel worse if he comes over. It'll be all right once the train starts to move. We will be off in a second."

Xiuzhen kept patting her mother, saying, "All right, all right! Don't cry now. After all, you've seen each other, and should be thankful!"

The train started to move. In spite of what she said, I ran over to Father.

"The train's leaving."

But he wouldn't even look in that direction.

My aunt sighed. "All this time together, everything seemed fine. So why are you acting so strange today?"

The train hissed, blew its whistle, and finally pulled away. Uncle, Aunt, Cousin Dawu, and I watched it until we could not see it any longer. But Father did not lift his eyes once.

XIV

There wasn't time for lunch. Uncle drove Father and me to the airport. We told Cousin Dawu not to bother to see us off since he had other things to attend to.

"Let's go," said Father, and headed straight for the departing passengers' area, without looking back.

My aunt said good-bye to me, repeating again and again:

"Tell your mother not to make any more trouble for him! Understand? I'll call her, too, to make her feel better. . . . And your father, talk to him. Now that they've seen each other, there's no sense them crying their hearts out."

"I will."

Father did not say a word throughout the flight; he did not eat the lunch the stewardess served him, either.

"Eat something," I said. "You need to eat something."

"No, I am not hungry," he replied.

I thought he was still feeling bad for Great Mother and Elder Sister, so I said:

"If you want to see them again, it's easy, just tell them to come out."

He shook his head. "She won't come out again—they said that. She's too old."

"Well, you can see Elder Sister again."

"Uh-huh." He nodded. After a long while, he suddenly said, "Your mother . . . she should see Xiuzhen, too."

"Dad . . . " My curiosity finally got the better of me and I blurted out the question. "You . . . before, you didn't like Great Mother very much, so how come . . ."

"Mmmm. . . ." he closed his eyes and a tranquil look came over his face. "I felt that I hadn't treated her right . . . that's why I had to see her."

Eyes closed, he remained quiet for a long time. I thought he was trying to catch up on his sleep. But all of a sudden he said:

"Do you think your mother will come to meet us?"

That was exactly what I'd been worrying about. Would Mother come to the airport? And my wife, Huimei, would she bring Chaoming to meet the plane? Every time I returned after a trip abroad, the two of them were waiting happily at the airport.

Huimei used to say that she didn't like seeing people off, she only liked greeting them when they returned.

This time, I wasn't at all sure. Shaking my head, I replied, "I really don't know!"

XV

The plane landed at CKS International Airport at 2:30 P.M. We both felt anxious to rush through the arrival procedures. Half an hour later, when the automatic sliding door of the arrivals area opened, the first thing I saw was my son, charging unsteadily toward me, crashing into my legs, and shouting for all the world to hear, "Daddy's home! Daddy's home!"

I pulled him up and kissed him, asking, "Where's Mommy?"

"Over there!"

Then I saw Huimei, and Mother and Bizhen. The three women stood in a row. They still weren't quite over their anger, but they couldn't hide their pleasure at seeing us home.

I looked at Father. He had left his melancholy manner behind on the plane. Somewhat apologetically, as though trying very hard to please, he walked toward Mother.

Mother pretended that she was still cross:

"Why did you come back at all?"

Saying nothing, Father simply followed her out.

I pressed Huimei's hand gently and she blushed. Somehow, it reminded me of Great Mother blushing.

"I missed you," I whispered to her.

"You liar!"

But women still like to hear such things. She grabbed our son's hand and followed Father out.

Bizhen was walking behind me. She asked icily:

"So you met them?"

I took out the rings and handed her the silver one.

"Elder Sister gave you this. She asked for you to remember her."

She took it and looked at it, holding it in her hand for a long time. She seemed touched, and only after a long pause, said, "Next time, I should go to meet her."

"Yes."

Now it was only the two of us, and it felt like we were back together in the good old days. She was still the sister I often hated but always loved. I asked her earnestly:

"Bizhen, are you really going to get married?"

She didn't answer. She looked at me sideways, and asked in a small voice:

"What do you mean by that?"

"You know what I mean! What Dad and Mom would like most is for the four of us to live in the old house, the same as we did before, without changing anything. But in fact, that's not possible anymore. I'm married and I have a job in Taipei. We all have to adapt to a new way of life. . . . But Dad and Mom don't want to leave the old house. They don't like Taipei. If you want to get married, we'll figure something out. So don't worry. . . ."

She looked at me silently, and opened her palm to look at the silver ring again. She put it on; it fit nicely on the middle finger of her right hand. Softly, as if talking to herself, she said:

"I was just . . . not feeling well. It was really nothing."

I didn't know what more I should say. By then we were out of the terminal building. I could see my son running around his grandpa and grandma and mommy, jumping and shouting and having the time of his life. The afternoon autumn sun shone brightly, ever so brightly, on them all.

Spring Hope

. . .

by LI Li

translated by CHEN I-djen

He was in a state between sleep and wakefulness, seemingly almost awake but actually still half asleep. He thought the rumbling noise was a pneumatic drill digging up the road outside his home. When he woke fully, he realized that the aches and pains he felt all over were the result of his falling asleep curled up in an airplane seat. Darkness enclosed him, except for the light of the reading lamps over a few scattered seats. The snores of nearby passengers could be heard above the engine noise. He raised his arm to look at his watch but could not make out the time. Turning on his light, he could still only see a blur. He had to fish for his reading glasses to discover that it had been about six or seven hours since their takeoff from Los Angeles. At the beginning of the trip he'd been so exhausted he could not find a comfortable position no matter how he twisted and turned. Later, after some food and two tranquilizers, he started to doze off and finally fell into a fitful sleep. He was dreaming. His dreams were episodic and very involved, leaving him with no memory of any of them. It was more like seeing dark, shadowy figures or looking at old, faded photographs. He had a feeling that they involved his hometown in Fujian. This he sensed rather than actually remembered. He had the impression of a little girl crying and tugging at his pants. And there was the vague form of a woman's face disappearing behind a dark shadow.

He got up slowly, feeling faint. He held onto the back of a seat and stood a moment, stretching his back and his limbs. The coolness in the cabin made him shiver. Normally at times like this, his wife Yinru would be handing him a sweater. She had spoiled him over the past thirty-odd years. He almost never had to manage by himself. The year before last, Yinru had had to go to America to help their eldest daughter Jinlin, who had just had a baby. About a month later his life had turned on its head, and he longed for her to return. He wished she could come home soon, but he didn't want to compete with their daughter. After all, he realized what Jinlin was going through after a cesarean birth. Yinru, however, was very much aware of his state. Quietly she arranged for Jinlin's mother-in-law to take over so she could return to Taiwan. After all, having been married for so many years, they were perfectly attuned to each other. Now that the children were grown up, she was even more attentive, looking after him and protecting him as if he were her child.

He staggered to the lavatory. The strong fluorescent light made him look even paler. He stuck his tongue out and saw a thick layer of white. He sighed. If only Yinru were here.

But this was one trip he had to make alone. He knew it was something he had to face by himself. No one, not even Yinru, could accompany him. More than thirty years had gone by. He was pushing seventy. If he did not face up to it now, he might not have another chance.

"Papa? Hello Papa, can you hear me? Hello, hello . . ." Jinyuan's voice came over the phone from across the Pacific. Above the background static, his voice was like a candle, sometimes bright, sometimes flickering faintly, weak yet piercing.

"Yes, Ah Yuan, I can hear you. Can you hear me clearly?" He, too, was shouting into the receiver.

"Papa, this call must be very expensive. I'll talk about the important business first . . . hello? Papa, I've bought a train ticket; I'll be leaving Beijing tomorrow for Shenzhen, the border town. Have you got your plane ticket yet? When will you be arriving in Hong Kong? Hello, Papa?"

He rummaged hurriedly through his pocket. Xiaolei handed him a piece of paper. He squinted and rubbed his eyes. Xiaolei handed him his glasses. "Hello, yes, yes, I'm leaving Los Angeles on the twentieth and I'll be arriving on the twenty-first, Monday, at eight o'clock in the evening."

Xiaolei reminded him to mention the flight number.

"Very good, Papa. Jinfang will be meeting me in Shenzhen. She'll be there on the eighteenth. We'll probably be in Hong Kong on the nineteenth or the twentieth, at the latest. We've already been in touch with Uncle Chen. Papa, we'll be there at the airport to meet you."

All of a sudden, he snapped to attention, realizing only then that he was actually talking to Jinyuan. He felt a lump rise in his throat. "G—good, Ah Yuan."

"Papa, we will definitely be at the airport. You wait for us; we will definitely be there."

"Ah Yuan." His mouth felt stiff though his lip quivered as he fought for control. "Good, you . . . be there, and I'll definitely, definitely . . ." He took a deep breath, recovering somewhat, and asked, "Ah Fang, how is she?"

"Papa, listen, Ah Fang, if she should mention the letters you wrote her, you just don't say anything."

"What? What letters?"

"Papa." The static reached a new high, abruptly overpowering Jinyuan's voice. Only a few words came through faintly, like the voice of someone drowning. "I . . . Ah Fang . . . you wrote . . . don't say . . . just say . . ."

"Hello, hello, Ah Yuan, Ah Yuan." He was shouting.

Now Jinyuan's voice suddenly came through a little clearer. "We don't have a very good connection. Papa, we'll talk about it when we meet. In any case, if Ah Fang mentions your letters, don't say you never wrote any."

"Hello, Ah Yuan, what is this—"

"We mustn't talk too long. It's costing Xiaolei a lot of money. Papa, take care of yourself. We'll meet on the twenty-first, and that's definite. Good-bye, Papa."

"That's definite. Definite."

He hung up and felt as if he were drifting in space. All he could hear was Jinyuan's voice saying, "Papa, Papa," and "that's definite."

Suddenly the plane was bouncing up and down. They had probably hit some turbulence. Overhead, the FASTEN SEAT BELT sign came on. The middle-aged man sitting next to him opened his eyes and yawned. As he turned his head, their eyes met. The man smiled and said, "We probably have another three hours yet, or more." The man spoke with a very heavy Cantonese accent, but he understood and smiled, nodding in agreement.

"Do you live in Hong Kong, sir?"

"No, Taiwan. Taipei."

"Is that so? I go there quite often, on business," the man said as he handed him a business card. To be polite, he accepted it, but he didn't bother to put on his glasses to read it.

Just to make conversation he said, "Business must be very good for your company."

"Not bad, not bad." The middle-aged man smiled in a friendly way, so his smug attitude wasn't annoying. "We're doing all right. Our company is just an intermediary serving Taiwan and mainland China. Business is all right, all right. Am I correct in assuming that you, sir, are now returning to Taiwan by way of Hong Kong after a trip to America?"

"Yes, I have two children in America." Suddenly he remembered Xiaolei and Xiaoyun and added, "Um, I mean two boys and two girls."

"Sir, you are truly blessed." The man asked him the reason for his stop in Hong Kong. He was never very good at making small talk with strangers, and the business at hand was not something he wanted to discuss. Feeling somewhat apologetic, he muttered a vague reply. But he was really wasn't up to carrying on a conversation, either physically or emotionally. He closed his eyes and pretended to rest. It crossed his mind that claiming fatigue to avoid making unnecessary conversation was probably an old man's privilege.

Dear Father,

How are you?

It has been more than thirty years since I last wrote you. For a moment, after I picked up the pen, I did not know where to begin. To be exact, it has been thirty-eight years. There is so much I want to tell you. I remember when we parted in Fuzhou; I was only ten. You fondled my head, then turned around and left. I stood there watching your retreating figure. Later I ran upstairs and watched from the porch as you walked out of the alley. The events of that day are the only things I remember. All that happened earlier is very blurry. . . .

This letter had been forwarded to Taipei through Xiaolei. Xiaolei went to Beijing at least once a year, since the company he worked for had set up an office in China. On his first trip he approached a few organizations to help him locate Jinyuan. When Xiaolei went back the second time, he and Jinyuan met in Beijing.

He really did not know what to write to Jinyuan. After he left Fuzhou, he had stayed in Canton and Hong Kong for some time before going to Taiwan. The first couple of years in Taipei he had sent letters home through friends in Hong Kong. These he discontinued after a while. He had no idea what went through the minds of his mother and his two children back home; he did not even dare to venture a guess. Gradually he learned to lock away his fear and his longing. He hardly even mentioned it to Yinru. He did not want to analyze himself, did not want to measure his guilt.

The only thing he remembered clearly from his dreams was his old mother's wide-open eyes. They seemed to have something to tell him. But he had dreamed of another face, too, that appeared in the dark for a fleeting moment and then turned away as if to avoid his eyes. He had seen who it was. It was the face of the mother of Jinyuan and Jinfang, his deceased wife.

But he seldom dreamed of his two children. Was it because subconsciously he knew the children were continually growing, and they would not be the same as when he saw them last? He could only see their silhouettes indistinctly and from far away. Whenever he woke up after dreams like that, he found it hard to go back to sleep. He would go quietly to the kitchen, make himself a cup of warm milk, and sit there in a daze until daybreak.

Yinru, of course, knew what was tormenting him. Since he did not want to talk about it, she was very understanding and did not ask any questions. However, she was forever watching the ebb and flow of his emotional state. Word of his mother's death finally reached him by way of a distant cousin in Singapore. It had gone through many hands; by the time the news got to Yinru, it was a year old. At that time they had just lost a large sum of money in a joint business deal and were on the brink of bankruptcy. Yinru hesitated to tell him, although eventually she had to.

How had he survived those days? He dreaded thinking back on them, as if afraid to touch an old wound. If it hadn't been for Yinru, he might not have been able to control himself, might have done something foolish. Yinru knew that he must be worried about the children, and she tried to find out the whereabouts of Jinfang, who had stayed in their hometown to keep Grandma company, and Jinyuan, who was attending school in Fuzhou. She was told it would be difficult to locate them during that turbulent time. And even if they succeeded, they might only be getting the children into more trouble.

He and Yinru thought it over and agreed. As their father, he had walked away from them many years ago. If they harbored any resentment or hatred, so be it. They were grown up now. If he and Yinru succeeded in locating them, then what? They didn't want to add to their problems.

He was never good at expressing himself in words, and he lacked the courage to open that painful wound deep inside. What could he write to Jinyuan now? True, it was still with him, that sensation of fondling his head for the last time, but what could he say to a son now approaching middle age? Surely not "Papa is sorry," as they did so casually on those television soap operas. His own son, flesh of his flesh, whom he had failed to care for and to raise, what had become of him? Xiaolei said Jinyuan looked like him. He wasn't sure whether he was pleased or disappointed.

And then there was Jinfang. When he left his home, she had just learned to walk. A frail, motherless child, she started to walk late. He vaguely remembered that she couldn't walk across a tiny ditch in front of their house and had to crawl over it, crying all the way.

Finally he'd written a very short letter, summing up over thirty years of life in a few words, saying only that all was well with him. Via Xiaolei, he'd sent a picture of himself and Yinru and their two younger children in Taiwan.

After that, his dreams became more disturbing. The vague figures were always retreating. He knew in his heart who they were; he wanted to catch up with them, but he didn't dare. His feet refused to take a step, and his throat closed.

The flight attendant announced that they would soon be landing at the Hong Kong airport. He fastened his seat belt and gazed absently out of the window. The dark sky looked clear with a few thin clouds. Slowly the airplane descended out of the slight cloud cover. There outside the window, right before his eyes, the lights from all the skyscrapers dotted the black earth like a storybook display of pearls and diamonds. In 1950, when he was last in Hong Kong, there hadn't been so many tall buildings. In those days most people traveled by boat and could not look down on any of this. Seeing that he was looking out, his neighbor in the next seat pointed out a few sights to him, but he hardly heard. He only hoped the plane would circle a little more, giving him the time he needed to adjust. And yet he could hardly wait to step out of the cabin.

He was familiar with the expression, "a feeling of timidity sets in as one approaches one's native land," but it never occurred to him that it could happen here. It must be that this feeling was caused by people, not places.

More than thirty years ago when he'd come to Hong Kong, alone and for a short stay, he never dreamed that one day this would be the meeting place for himself and his son and daughter. A few years back, when Taiwan first permitted its residents to travel abroad, visiting Hong Kong was very popular among his friends. He was never tempted. But once, an idea flashed momentarily through his mind: what if he went quietly from Hong Kong to . . . No, no, he no longer had any hope of finding them. It would be more difficult than finding a needle in a haystack. What good would it do to make such a trip? What would the consequences be? What about Yinru and the children in Taiwan? He quickly abandoned the whole idea.

Among his friends, he was known for his stubborn refusal to travel abroad, and also for his stubborn refusal to enjoy life in other ways. For years he ran a small pediatric clinic. Anybody else would have accumulated a modest fortune. But not him; he had only a small apartment. True, recovering from his business loss took him quite a few years. But the nurse at the clinic put it more aptly: "This is no way to run a hospital; this is like running a relief center." Often, when she saw the fees he charged his patients, she mumbled, "Another freebie!" Later she wouldn't even bother to comment. Yinru was just like him. She never questioned him about his fees. Teasing him, their younger daughter Jinmei once said, "Too bad Papa doesn't speak a foreign language. Otherwise he could go to Africa and be another Schweitzer."

Schweitzer? Smiling ironically, he thought, I'm nothing like Schweitzer. He rarely analyzed himself, nor did he want to. But he was sure his motives were self-serving: to relieve his sense of guilt in some small measure, to ease the self-reproach, to win some peace of mind. That's all there was to it.

He simply considered adopting Xiaolei and Xiaoyun the right thing to do, his responsibility. He didn't give it a second thought. Of course, he had Yinru's consent. Everybody else shunned these two children whose parents had been found guilty of some political offense. When it seemed safe, an old schoolmate came to him and commented, "Among all the people from our town and our medical school, only you had the courage and the moral sense to do it." Again he forced a smile and kept quiet. What courage? What moral sense? he thought. If Jinyuan and Jinfang were to become homeless orphans, he hoped someone would take them in and see that they didn't suffer from cold and hunger and got proper schooling.

Nevertheless, even in so simple and straightforward a matter as this, he felt that no one except Yinru could really understand him.

The plane landed with a bump. Although the crew told the passengers to wait for a complete halt before leaving their seats, the anxious ones were already picking up their bags and standing in the aisles. Remaining seated, he automatically smoothed his hair and straightened his tie. He could feel his heart beating as clearly as if he were listening through a stethoscope. He took a few deep breaths, slowly; his palms were sweaty and cold.

He had reached the end of his long journey. Now he had to go through immigration, baggage claim, customs, and then. . . . Then he had to face two of the people he loved the most. But they were strangers to him, and they would judge him.

"Don't cry, be a good girl, don't cry." The little girl opened her mouth wider and cried harder, tears streaming down her cheeks from her tightly closed eyes.

"Doctor?" the mother asked worriedly. It brought him back to reality, and he removed the stethoscope from his ears, pulled down the little girl's dress, and said very gently, "It's all right. In a little while your papa is going to take you home, your mama will give you some medicine, and in a couple of days you'll be well enough to play with your friends again. How's that?"

The vision of a little girl, a skinny, frail child, crying as she crawled across the shallow ditch, often came to mind. Her grandma was getting old; who was there to help her across a deeper, wider ditch? To take her to school? Who looked after her when

Grandma died? Who took her to see a doctor when she was sick? Who told her what she need to know about becoming a young woman?

After Jinyuan's letter arrived, he knew he would soon hear from Jinfang. In the meantime he walked around in a daze. When her letter arrived, he gently stroked the thin paper. It was such poor quality it looked as if it might fall apart at a touch. Water spots had blurred the ink in quite a few places. The letter was short; she simply repeated how happy she was to hear from her father after ten years or so, and that nothing made her happier than to learn he was in good health. He was startled when he read that "ten years or so." It must have been a slip of the pen, since more than thirty years had passed.

Jinfang's childish scrawl saddened him. When he looked up from her letter, there, right in front of him, were pictures of Jinlin getting her doctorate and Jinmei getting her master's degree. Both smiled the smile of the fortunate. The thin paper rustled gently; he realized his usually steady hands were trembling.

Writing back to Jinfang was even harder. Why should Jinfang consider him her father? Why should she write? Why should she feel happy? He wanted to ask her, What kind of a daughter are you? Don't you understand hatred?

Of course he asked her no such questions. He just wrote a short letter addressed to both of them, with a sum of money, all to be delivered through Xiaolei.

Jinlin and the others asked him again and again to visit them in America. He always refused, saying that he could not get away from the clinic. Then one night Xiaolei called, and that was the end of his resolution never to travel abroad.

"Uncle, I just returned from over there yesterday." Xiaolei sounded excited. "Brother Ah Yuan said he often travels to the south on business, and he found out that it's quite easy to apply for a visiting permit to Hong Kong to meet relatives. He wanted me to find out if you could visit your relatives here in the United States and then stop in Hong Kong and meet him there. There's a chance that Sister Ah Fang would be able to come, too."

"I . . ." This possibility had never crossed his mind, and for a moment he did not know how to react. "Let me think it over. You discuss it with them. If possible, of course I . . . of course . . ."

There was a map of China on the wall in their youngest son Jinhong's room. With his eyes, he tried to measure the distances between certain places. All of a sudden the absurdity of the situation struck him. The hopeless regrets and guilt he had suffered for more than half a lifetime were caused by a separation of mere inches on the map. It was all so hard to believe, and life seemed so very unreal.

Pushing the baggage cart, he walked toward the crowd. As he approached a middle-aged man, a strange sensation came over him. He stopped and turned to look the man in the eyes. It was not exactly like looking at oneself in a mirror; looking in a mirror would not be as startling as this. It was as if the image had stepped out of the mirror and were walking toward him.

It was all happening too fast. Afterward, it was impossible to trace the details of that moment. For example, did he call out to his son, or did the name stick in his throat? Did his son call out first, or after he gathered him in his arms? He could not remember any of it. He only remembered that once he was holding his son, his only fear was that some evil magic might make him vanish. He couldn't let go. How long did it last? Jinyuan let go first. Now he was able to look closely into his son's eyes, shining with tears. There seemed to be a reflection of himself there, as if it had been locked inside all these years.

He turned and saw another pair of eyes, wide open, full of sadness yet smiling. They were the eyes of his mother, of whom he had dreamed countless times. They seemed to want to tell him something, but held back in silence. Then there was that lovely nose, the slightly protruding front teeth; his dead wife stepped across time, across the barrier of life and death, and was standing in front of him—

"Ah Fang . . ." When he heard what came out of his own throat, he was overcome with surprise. Ah Fang? That frail, skinny, weeping little girl?

She was still skinny, so thin it broke his heart, and she was still weeping, but she was smiling at the same time. There were wrinkles at the corners of her eyes as she smiled. He took her gently into his arms. She was angular, all bones, and every one of them pierced him to the core. He wanted more pain. He couldn't tell how long he held her like that, though he was vaguely aware that the few occasions when he had held her as a child probably added up to less time.

Mr. Chen, the husband of a close friend of Yinru's, had arranged for them to stay in a quiet little hotel in Kowloon, and he very thoughtfully showed them around the neighborhood, pointing out the bus stops and restaurants. He informed them that the staff spoke Mandarin and the area was safe. Forcing himself to listen to Mr. Chen, he found it difficult to concentrate. He had been so nervous that he was in a daze. All he could focus on was his son in his loose-fitting western suit, whose temples were as gray as his own, though there was no sign of middle-age paunch. During the trip from the airport he discovered that his son was as tongue-tied as he was when it came to small talk. His daughter had her mother's lush black hair. It was a shame to see it in tight, stiff-looking curls. She had probably gotten a permanent especially for this occasion. Her eyes looked larger than life, maybe because she was so thin. He wanted to look into those eyes a little longer, but he was afraid.

By the time the three of them were finally alone in their hotel room, it was late at night. Although it was still daytime to him because of the time difference, he was exhausted, but not sleepy. The room was quiet for a few seconds, as if the strangeness was finally settling over them.

Jinyuan cleared his throat, got up, and took a paper bag from his suitcase. "Papa, here are some recent pictures of me, Huiwen, and our child." Jinyuan enunciated distinctly, as if every word were carefully chosen.

Jinfang came over to look too, but he had a feeling that her thoughts were elsewhere. When they were finished with the pictures, she hastily unpacked a gray wool vest. "Papa, I knitted this for you; I wonder if it fits."

Gingerly, she measured the vest against his body, then uttered a sigh of relief and said, "It'll do, it'll fit." Now she seemed more sure of herself. "I asked my sister-in-law to get the yarn for me. I couldn't get any good wool yarn even at the county seat. Beijing has a wider selection; besides, Sister-in-law has better taste. I was afraid that I wouldn't be able to make the trip. I was trying to finish it as quickly as possible so I could mail it to Brother to bring to you."

He took the vest and stared at the countless stitches, knit, purl, knit, purl. . . .

He reached for her hands and held them tightly in his own. Without thinking, he turned them over to examine them more closely. They were thin and hard; there were thick calluses on her palms. He caressed them softly with his thumb. Suddenly he bent and buried his face in her hands for a long while. He raised his head and whispered, "Tell Papa, Ah Fang, how have the years been for you?"

Ah Fang looked at him. Then slowly she lowered her head and played with her own fingers.

After some time, a tear fell on the back of her hand.

"Are you angry with Papa?"

She shook her head. Another drop fell.

"Did you think that Papa deserted you and didn't want you anymore?" The words were out before he could raise his head to look at Jinyuan. Jinyuan was watching him. In the room's soft light Jinyuan looked younger than he had at first. Suddenly he felt lost and confused; he could not quite grasp when and where he was.

Jinfang raised her head and looked him straight in the eye. Softly but firmly she said, "Long ago, yes. I was very young then. Everybody else had a papa and mama, and I only had a grandma. I felt inferior. Grandma told me my mama died and my papa was a very good doctor who went far away to practice. He would be back one day."

He lowered his head and gazed at his fingers, long and thin and pale. These hands had taken care of countless patients, countless children and old people. But what about his own two children and elderly mother? How often had he ever touched them?

"Many years passed. Papa still had not returned and had not even sent a letter. Then I recalled a story Brother told me. It was about a genie who was locked up in a bottle. At first he hoped someone would rescue him. After a long time he gave up hope and swore that he would eat whoever released him from the bottle." She smiled sadly and went on, "I thought then that if Papa should actually come back someday, I wouldn't speak to him. So, when Grandma told me one day that Brother had forwarded a letter from Papa, I made up my mind not to read it."

He was taken aback and was about to say something when he caught Jinyuan's eye and remembered, all of a sudden, what his son had said during their telephone conversation. He was puzzled.

Jinfang shook her head, sighed, and said, "I was really very stubborn in those days. I was already in my teens, but I was so childish."

Jinyuan cleared his throat and said casually, "Hey, doesn't your oldest take after you? I heard that whenever he's upset, he hits himself on the chest."

Jinfang smiled, embarrassed.

Jinyuan looked at his watch and said, "It's late. We'd better let Papa rest. We'll talk some more tomorrow."

"It's all right," he interjected quickly. "I'm not tired."

"Let me keep talking. Some of the things I want to say Brother may not even know about. A long time later, I couldn't help myself, and I tried to read those letters when Grandma wasn't looking. After I read them, I kept trying to figure out a way to write back. In the beginning my mind was full of angry words. Later on, when I couldn't sleep at night, I wrote Papa letters in my head. I told Papa about whatever was bothering me, as if I were putting it down on paper. That is how I would fall asleep, telling Papa all my problems. The funny thing was, Papa seemed to know what had happened to me and what kind of trouble I was in. Papa was always there to guide me."

He gave Jinyuan a penetrating look. Jinyuan just sat there like a statue, looking down.

"During the Cultural Revolution our neighbors to the left and to the right all got raided. I was really scared then. If those letters were discovered, there would surely be trouble. Yet how could I bring myself to part with them? Later, when it couldn't be put off any longer, I had to burn them, except two that I considered the most meaningful. I couldn't bring myself to burn them, so I kept them on me. . . . Papa, I've brought them with me now."

"Ah Fang," Jinyuan stood up and said, gently but firmly, "it's really late. Papa's been traveling by plane for more than ten hours. We should let him rest." Then he turned to his father and said, "Papa, would you like to bathe first? I'll see that Ah Fang goes to bed."

Jinyuan's words were persuasive. Jinfang meekly obeyed. So many things were going through his head now he felt he needed a hot shower to be alone with his thoughts.

He sat on the edge of the bed, staring hard at Ah Fang, who was fast asleep. Now that those two eyes were closed, he finally found the courage to look at her.

Jinyuan came out of the bathroom, wearing striped pajamas. His face was pinkish and he smelled of soap.

"Asleep?" the older brother bent over and asked in a whisper.

"Uh-huh. She's snoring," he said lightly.

As he picked up things scattered around the room, Jinyuan said, "These last few days have exhausted her. Not me; I often travel for business and I'm used to it. But she's never been far from home, hasn't had a good night's sleep for days. You don't smoke, do you, Papa?"

He watched Jinyuan push the ashtray to one corner of the end table. "No. You don't either, do you?"

A bit embarrassed, Jinyuan said, "I used to. Socializing with colleagues makes it hard to refuse them. But a while ago, when I succeeded in contacting you, I gave it up. I figured, Papa is a doctor; he'd most likely be against it. Good thing I wasn't hooked. It was easy to give it up."

He nodded. Suddenly something triggered his memory. "Ah Yuan, you must remember the one time I spanked you when you were young."

Jinyuan's face was a blank. "You spanked me? I have no memory of it at all. Why?"

"After some guests left, I caught you strutting around with cigarette butts." He sighed. "Mostly it was because I was about to leave and you would be going to your uncle's. I was worried; what if you picked up bad habits? I was worried," he muttered. "Good thing you don't remember."

"Uncle was very strict. Otherwise I wouldn't have been able to get into the university. But Papa, I didn't study medicine. Are you disappointed?"

Watching the expression on his son's face, he couldn't help smiling. If Jinyuan's temples weren't already gray, he would have tousled his hair and said fondly, "You silly boy!"

His reaction put Jinyuan at ease; he went on. "It's a good thing I was taken to Fuzhou. They have good high schools. Ah Fang stayed in our hometown and got short-changed."

"Ah Yuan," he began. Now was time to solve the mystery. "What about all those letters Ah Fang thinks I wrote to her?"

Jinyuan swallowed hard and said, "Oh, those. I was young at the time. I didn't know whether it was the right thing to do. We received letters from you regularly after you left Fuzhou, even after you got to Taiwan. Until 1952."

He tried to convert the year to the Taiwanese calendar. He lowered his head, figured for a moment, and said, "I think it was in the forty-second year, 1953, when I asked another friend in Hong Kong to forward letters to you. The previous friend had moved to Taiwan."

Jinyuan nodded and said, "That's right. After that, we had no word from you. By then, I was more or less aware of what was going on, and I felt at home in Uncle's house. So, I took it pretty well. But Grandma was an old woman and Ah Fang was still in elementary school. Those two were—"

Jinyuan looked at him and stopped short. He both wanted to hear and dreaded to hear. Falling silent, they turned at the same time to look at Jinfang. After a while Jinyuan continued in an even lower whisper, "I seldom went back to our hometown in those days. I learned things by listening to conversations between Uncle and Aunt. They talked about Grandma and how her eyes were going bad, probably from crying so much."

He sat there like a stone statue, head bowed, awaiting judgment.

"I heard that Ah Fang wasn't doing well in school, that she was bad-tempered and had an inferiority complex. Grandma couldn't deal with her. I kept thinking that soon you would find a way to send word to us. But ten years passed. I graduated from college and was assigned to work in Beijing. One day it occurred to me that you were probably as anxious to get in touch with us as we were to hear from you, and that the reason you didn't write was because you couldn't. Should I—in that case, should I write to Grandma and Ah Fang on your behalf?"

"So you did, you did."

"So I did. Grandma had given me one of your earlier letters, which I'd saved and carried with me all the time. I tried to imitate your handwriting. Papa, do you think it looks like yours?"

Of course, he had thought so at first glance. He smiled and nodded.

"I made up a story to tell Grandma about an acquaintance in the diplomatic service in Beijing helping me make contact. I didn't dare write too often, or they'd get suspicious. Grandma was close to seventy then, but her mind was still very clear."

He nodded.

"I sent one every few months, mostly around holidays and the new year, so that they could celebrate a bit more."

Jinfang turned in her bed; Jinyuan gently straightened the blanket over her and, after listening for her even breathing, continued in a whisper, "Ah Fang told you that at first she was angry and wouldn't read your letters—I mean my letters." Jinyuan smiled. He couldn't help smiling, too. "Grandma said she did read them later. Not only that, if the next one didn't come for a long time, she would start asking Grandma about it. I began writing more often. I was afraid they might try to write back to you, so I told them it was almost impossible to send you letters. I told them they should tell me what they wanted to say, and I would tell my friends, who would write it down when they were out of the country."

"How long did you do this?"

"Exactly ten years. During the Cultural Revolution, it was total confusion. I thought I should stop before I got them into trouble. But Grandma wasn't well and she counted on those letters."

He closed his eyes, did a little figuring, nodded, and said, "So you stopped after Grandma died."

"Yes. By then Ah Fang was married and had a child of her own. She'd grown up. I said to myself: enough; leave it at that; more may make for complications."

"That's why Ah Fang said there hadn't been any letters for over ten years."

"Lately I don't often think about what I did. It was Ah Fang who reminded me about the letters right before we came. That was why I tried to warn you over the phone. Ah Fang might be very upset if she found out. But I couldn't really explain the whole situation to you then."

True, lots of things could not be explained. His gaze fell on this middle-aged man in front of him who looked just like him. Would he have done the same thing under the same circumstances? Many years ago when he was a new father, he worried that his child might not turn out as expected—that his son might not be like him. Later, after he had gone through life's many ordeals, he only hoped that his son would not take after him. And now, as he faced this oldest of his sons, a sense of awe rose up within him. Was it because the son bore too close a resemblance to the father, or because he was so unlike him in some respects?

> My dear daughter Ah Fang,
>
> I am very happy to learn that you have graduated from high school and are now working. It is truly hard to believe that my daughter has reached adulthood. According to your grandmother, you have always hoped that when you grew up you could follow your mother's footsteps and become a nurse, or be like Brother and study engineering. Therefore, you were upset at being assigned to work in a factory. The truth is there is no such thing in the world as a noble profession or a humble profession. One should be proud of oneself as long as one is supporting oneself and serving the people. Furthermore, the kind of work your mother and brother do may not be suitable for you or interest you. I hope you stay in the factory and devote yourself to mastering a skill. . . .

Shyly Jinfang showed him the letter yellowed with age. "I made a point of saving this one, because this was the first one I told Grandma I wanted to read. I read the others behind her back. I was really foolish, Papa. You won't be angry with me, will you?"

He forced a smile and answered softly, "How could I be? If I were you, I'd be mad at my papa, too. This letter was well written." He glanced at Jinyuan and added, "Did you listen to your . . . eh, to the advice in it?"

"Certainly not." He noticed that in the span of one short day, Jinfang was already beginning to act like a young girl from time to time, very much at odds with her forty years, but extremely touching. "I told myself it was the same old nonsense! But after a few more letters from you, after you repeated it several times, I began to see your point."

Jinfang took out another letter that was falling apart at the creases.

> My dear daughter Ah Fang,
>
> I am happy to learn from your brother that you have a boyfriend. Since he works in the same factory, you must have gotten to know him pretty well. The important things are: a person's character, his health, his ambition to advance himself, and his filial devotion to parents and sincerity in dealing with friends. If he possesses these traits, no other qualifications are necessary. Though Jinyuan is far away in Beijing, you could ask him to come back for a visit at New Year's to meet your friend. He is six years older and your only sibling, and you ought to listen to what he has to say regarding such an important matter as marriage. . . .

At this point he looked up and threw an understanding glance at Jinyuan.

Jinfang blushed and said with a smile, "This letter was . . ."

"This letter was worth saving," Jinyuan butted in. "On the strength of this letter, I went back home and checked out her boyfriend. It was settled very quickly. About two months later Ah Fang and Ah Xin were engaged."

Jinfang patted her brother lightly on the shoulder. "In Papa's absence, of course, I had to listen to Brother. You did approve."

He watched the two of them, overcome with loss. That phase of their lives had passed him by.

"Papa." Becoming very serious, Jinfang turned to face him. He was startled by her gaze, a gaze he recognized from way back. "I've been meaning to tell you that I'm well aware of my temperament. It's not good and it was worse when I was a child. I went to pieces so easily. It's true. If it hadn't been for your letters to show me how to deal with life, to make me feel that I had my father's love, if it hadn't been for those letters, I might—" She covered her face and could not go on.

"Ah Fang." He gently stroked her short, stiff hair. "Listen to me. It was actually your brother—" His eyes met his son's. Jinyuan was shaking his head, gazing at him imploringly. It took great effort to swallow the words that were on the tip of his tongue.

So be it! Since that was Jinyuan's wish, let it rest at that. How else to acknowledge that his son had taken care of a matter that should have been his responsibility?

His children would be taking the train north in the morning, and he would be flying back to Taipei in the afternoon. They all got up before dawn—actually none of them had been able to sleep; each listened to the others toss and turn, but no one dared utter a sound.

All that had to be said was said; every word of advice had been repeated again. The suitcases had been packed the night before. All the travel bags and baskets that seemed to take up so much space had been arranged and tied in neat bundles by Jinyuan.

"Papa, we've said over and over that you shouldn't spend money on us, and here you've bought all these things!" Now Jinfang sounded just like his youngest daughter, Jinmei.

"That's right. Xiaolei told me that the income from the clinic isn't much. And Jinhong is still in graduate school. Plus all the expenses for this trip, the hotel, the food, the shopping. It makes us uncomfortable," Jinyuan added.

"I've told you more than once," he replied, sounding almost impatient, "your traveling expenses were paid by the three older children, Xiaolei, Jinlin, and Jinan, not me." He was close to losing control. "Me, your father—I contributed nothing, nothing at all! I didn't do anything at all!" He felt a pain in his chest.

On the surface he had managed to maintain a semblance of calm and stability over the past five days. Now it was all on the verge of collapse. "This is nothing, nothing! What are a few material goods? Nothing! I'm your father! You're my children! You've gone through so much hardship over all these years. Can a few items compensate for your suffering? These goods are nothing! I am nothing! I—AM—NOTHING!" And he started to pound his chest.

The brother and sister were so taken aback that for several moments they didn't think of stopping him. Then they begged him, "Papa, don't, Papa!" They grabbed his hands.

"You still call me Papa!" he wailed. "What sort of a papa am I—what sort of father . . ."

Sobbing, Jinfang held him in a tight embrace. Jinyuan rested his forehead on his father's shoulder, shaking uncontrollably. All the inevitable emotions that the three had tried to suppress since the night before burst like a dam.

Jinyuan was the first to get hold of himself. He got up, poured a glass of water, and took a tranquilizer from the bottle. He placed it in his father's palm and indicated that he should take it.

When he quieted down, he realized that he was leaning against the headboard, with Jinfang at the side of the bed, staring at him red-eyed. Jinyuan sat on a chair, leaning slightly forward, taking his pulse with a very gentle touch. "Do you feel better, Papa?"

He felt his heartbeat gradually returning to normal; surely Jinyuan was aware of it, too, from his pulse.

He nodded and grasped Jinyuan's hand; his other hand was holding Jinfang's. He looked from one to the other, wordlessly. He could see now that all his wounds had been washed clean. They still hurt deeply, but it was a tangible sort of hurt, as real as these two in front of him, flesh of his flesh and blood of his blood. There was no need to hide the real pain of parting, no need to pretend. He could accept it now with a heavy heart. It was only natural; there was no need to look for an escape.

Here and now, he felt a vague sense of relief.

Jinyuan looked at his watch and realized it was almost time to go.

"I'll go with you. I want to see you off." He stood up.

"Papa, didn't you say you weren't going to see us off, you couldn't go to the station, because you might not be able to stand it?"

"I'll go. I can take it. There's nothing I can't take. If I do it this time, it will be easier next time."

It took Jinfang a few seconds to understand what he was saying. A sweet smile broke across her face, which, in his eyes, was as beautiful as a blossom in spring.

The Vanishing Ball

. . .

by CHANG Chi-jiang

translated by Kathy CHANG

"The ball vanished, vanished. . . ."

While regaining my composure, I repeated that, breathless and panic-stricken, to my other self, the one still lost in the whirlpool. The black hole of time was expanding and splitting apart. The knuckleball of so many years ago was flying straight toward my forehead, no longer simply a footnote to a childhood long past.

My right arm was bruised, my left eye bleeding; my clothes were stained with mud and grass. My lips were clamped tight, fiercely guarding broken teeth.

All my office colleagues stared at me, astonished—this man who, sitting at his desk, now muttered to himself, now yelled, now disappeared, now turned into someone beaten black and blue.

Chen Guoxiong entered through the door and walked quickly toward me, the letter I'd submitted just ten minutes earlier held high in his hand like a sword. His look expressed a mixture of anxiety, incredulity, well-meant anger, and a kind of sympathy approaching scorn.

The early summer sunlight of 1991 streamed in between the two of us, making the field of vision illusory against the brightness.

I

The sun was just beating down on us. Unfortunately, the batter's box was right in its glare.

A flash like a golden snake shot low and cut across the outside corner. My eyes had barely adjusted before I heard the umpire shouting from behind, "Strike three, out!"

"God damn it!" I spit. It was only June, and the summer vacation had not yet begun. Already the weather was hot as fish soup, and we were the fish boiling in the pot.

After me, Tiger and Little Luo also struck out. Three up, three down.

When the name Chen Guoxiong was first posted on the Personnel Announcement Board, I couldn't believe it. A hundred people could have had that name and I hadn't met this person face to face yet, but for some reason, a bolt of thunder cracked in my mind and I was almost certain that this Chen Guoxiong was that Chen Guoxiong.

2

I could feel the fire glowing in my eyes. I'd pitched nine straight fastballs to end the fourth inning. The score was tied zero to zero.

I stuck out my chin, fixing my eyes on the pitcher for the other team—that ugly, dumpy, dark, dirty Shorty. My stare meant, "You stinking TKs! Your filthy feet will never get you to first base." "TKs" was short for Taiwanese kids, what we military kids called the natives.

Chen Guoxiong was almost six feet tall, half a head taller than I, with swarthy skin and shoulders as wide as a fortress. His eyes, eyebrows, nose, and lips curved in a clean and pleasing way; his jet-black pupils shone with intelligence. His round face, even when he wasn't smiling, always seemed to have a touch of a smile about it. He was well-mannered, and he always spoke sensibly and logically. In the office he never gossiped.

Within three months of joining the company, he had received two raises and had been promoted to section head for his eleven colleagues in the second section of the Development Department. His meteoric rise had triggered a flurry of criticism, to his face and behind his back, and barrages of slander were directed at him, including some from me. His private life, the number of personal calls he made each day, the confidence he'd won from the higher-ups, and his trustworthy face all became targets for attack. Even his excellent social and communication skills, dependability, and unrivaled efficiency added to that "camouflage of conspiracy." The old man from my native Shangtung province whose desk was in front of mine even went so far as to whisper under his breath to me that any "grassroots guy" who was not a member of the Kuomintang and thus lacked proof of loyalty to the country wasn't fit to work for this semiofficial trade firm and the country it represented.

But I myself still lacked any real desire to attack or destroy him. If I nurtured any antagonism toward him, it had nothing to do with his obstructing my own limited potential for upward mobility. It was something more vague and intangible. Especially when I checked into his family background and found that his father was a native Taiwanese landowner, with enough property to hold about ten military compounds. High-rise apartments and office buildings now multiplied on that property. That land, extending beyond where my home used to stand, had once held the grass baseball diamond of my childhood, where I ran, sweated, fought, and cried.

3

At the end of the grass field rose a column of twisting green haze.

Beneath that green smoke was the roaring torrent in a large drainage ditch that we called "the river." On both sides of the river grew grass taller than our heads, and from far away it looked like the arch of some green monument. To us, "crossing the river" was the ultimate glory. When the ball streaked like a rocket across that horizon, it escaped the limits of physical strength and imagination as well.

It seemed that this fierce pitcher's battle was going to have to be determined by an act of God. Painfully I raised my aching arm, vaguely realizing that the more brilliantly Shorty and I performed and the calmer we appeared, the greater the terror that grew in us: sooner or later, one of us would collapse on the pitcher's mound in a final agony of sand, tears, and unspeakable defeat.

"Whoever loses will quit the diamond for good." Recalling the devil's pact we had made before the game, I snatched the bottle of ice-cold soda water from Tiger's hand and gulped it down.

Jeers and laughter burst from the TK camp. Cannon had struck out, swinging so hard that he'd thrown himself to the ground. He tossed his bat and walked back to the bench, his downcast face covered with blue, red, and yellow streaks. I put my arm around his shoulder and wiped the sand off his face. Under the sand, his face was dotted with pimples, pus, and blood.

After summer vacation, Cannon would have to report to a noncommissioned officers military academy. Maybe that would give him a bit of dignity, and he would turn into a different person. Cannon's grades were so poor that even the teacher for the slow class gave up on him. His mother, a native Hakka, called him "half monkey" or "good-for-nothing." He spent his days hanging out with his gang, an unlikely heir to the glory his father had won by losing a leg in the Da- and Er-Dan Battle. Cannon certainly lagged far behind those promising children in private schools who lived in the front-row houses of the military compound and always stayed indoors, studying hard, and who, a decade later, would be returning with advanced degrees from abroad. Cannon's "gang of rogues" included me, Tiger, Little Luo, Tony, Horse-eye, Swindler, Swiper, and Stinking Asshole, nine of us all together, just enough to form a baseball team—a team defeated a hundred times in as many games. A year before, we'd pooled our pocket money, usually spent on comic books and pool, and we'd bought nine fake-leather baseball mitts, two cracked bats, and a box of cheap balls. We plunged into battle with all the official and nonofficial TK teams within a three-mile radius. The results were always the same. At sunset, the nine of us would be sitting silently on the cement pipelines along the riverbank, heads hanging, passing around a single cigarette, the wet filter always tasting bitter. Or we would pick a fight with the other team. As it grew dark, a gang of "half monkeys" with aching arms and black eyes would swim across the river and sneak into the compound and back home to endure another barrage of scoldings from our parents. The scoldings might include the Twelve Guidelines for Youth, "counterattack and save Great China," "study hard to go to the United States," and "there is no future at all in playing baseball." And indeed, every self-contradictory sentence our parents reeled off proved true. If I could have foreseen what the next five or ten years had in store for me, I would have given up that damned baseball, which almost tore my father and me apart.

The night before, as usual, my father had given me a sound scolding. "Do you realize you'll be taking the senior high school entrance exam next month? Do you know that every other student in Taiwan is making a last-ditch effort, staying up all night to study? Do you know that if you fail and fool around for three more years, you'll be drafted? And then you won't get another chance to succeed for the rest of your life. I'd rather see you get into a military academy than be drafted. But you haven't got character or courage. Even President Chiang wouldn't want you."

I was still thinking about my losing streak, which mattered more to me than President Chiang. Under my breath I said, "I can play baseball."

"Baseball! Baseball, my boy, is a game for rotten, uncivilized Taiwanese kids. Why do you mess around with them? It only pays off if you can make the national team. You were just a kid when you lost your mother. Last year your grandpa died. Someday I'll be gone, too, and then what will you do? You better set your mind right now on studying hard so you can get some kind of government job. Then maybe someday President Chiang will want to see you."

"Huang Jinghui and Zheng Baisheng, they're TKs, and President Chiang met with them just the same."

"TK? What's a TK? Hey! Hey! Where do you think you're going this time of night?"

I raced to the yard at the front of the military compound. Feeling something throbbing in me, I practiced my pitch all night long, throwing balls against the gray wall. The most important game in my life was coming up, and I didn't want to have any regrets about it. I hurled with all my strength, faster and faster. The white streak the ball made bouncing back off the wall blazed like the rising sun, which soon lit up my dark state of mind, my neglected childhood, and the future I wanted to avoid. I pitched with deadly speed until the ball was stained with blood from my raw hand, until the ball, surpassing the speed of light, hit the wall and vanished into it, never bouncing back.

. . .

"Have you ever experienced something vanish before your eyes? I mean, have you ever discovered suddenly that you've lost something very important, something you can never get back again? Like the house where you grew up in your old hometown, a special childhood toy, a meaningful photograph, a relative or a close friend, a memory, or . . ."

The evening after Chen Guoxiong was promoted to section head, the eleven of us invited him out to celebrate at the Szechwan Fish Restaurant. Our motives were dubious; we really wanted to check him out and to get on his good side. Chen Guoxiong seemed very gracious and comfortable among all of us with our provincial accents. The dozen bottles of Shaoxing wine, twenty rounds of bottoms-up toasts, and endless ingratiating banter did nothing to unsettle him.

Later, as our dinner was winding down and we were still high on wine and laughter, he and I made impromptu plans to go to a nearby pub. I thought we both were looking for some kind of answers to questions we were hesitant to ask.

Leaving the restaurant's noisy atmosphere behind, we climbed onto the bar stools and stared quietly at our drinks.

Through the light-pink liquid, I gazed gloomily at a game that seemed buried within my own blurred reflection.

I must have had too much to drink. I looked up at him, my eyes red, my tongue thick with a flurry of questions about "life," "memory," "vanishing," and some such crap—maybe these were questions I was asking myself. But when I said, "or, did you ever watch a ball fly—," he suddenly spoke up: "You look like a friend of mine." His voice was both distant and clear.

"Friend?" I must have looked baffled.

"A friend from a long time ago, a good pitcher—I never knew his name."

I turned from his gaze. The game inside the glass became a swirl. At that moment, I felt hatred rise in me.

"A friend—are you sure?"

"A friend." His voice was clear and distant.

4

"Who are you calling *friend*?" Tiger pushed Shorty's arm away. But Shorty only moved closer and patted Tiger's angry shoulder. "Calm down, we're, we're friends."

Tiger had struck out all his turns at bat that day. Short and stout, with firm, short legs, he looked like an angry dachshund now. Tiger was the "permanent fourth batter" on our team. Already this summer he had scored seven homers. But that day, probably because his arms weren't long enough, he'd been tricked by an outside change-up and had struck out. He was so angry that he grabbed his bat and smacked it on home plate. On the fourth smack, his bat cracked in two. Just in time, Shorty caught the end of the bat before it bounced up and hit his knee.

When Tiger pushed Shorty, tensions immediately flared between the two teams. Suddenly we were all gathered around home plate, pushing, yelling, shoving, and exchanging insults. A big guy from the other team threw out his chest, and with a "fuck you," stuck his middle finger up the back of Tiger's head. I dashed over, gave him an elbow, and took Tiger aside. "If you want to get pissed off, get pissed off at the ball, not at your own bat."

Well, I struck out three times that day myself. To tell the truth, Shorty's pitch was crooked and unpredictable, making him a top-notch knuckleball pitcher. Given his size—half a head shorter than

I—his pitching skill could only be a natural gift. Little Luo described his pitch as "an open-mouthed snake with an eight-forked tongue." Yes, he always had a calm sneer when he pitched. He never clenched his fist or yelled. When he twisted at the waist and flipped his arm, a swarm of golden snakes rushed over the plate somewhere between your knees and your elbows; it was very difficult to tell which one was real. After the initial shock, you would realize that all but one were illusions, but by then you were out. Facing those venomous snakes he was about to unleash, I always tried to muster all the energy of the universe into my bat, bent on hitting the real one right on the head. I had played twelve games with him, and I'd only managed one one-run homer. That was the only run we'd scored in all twelve games between our two teams. In the other eleven games, I struck out all thirty-three times at bat. Tiger and Little Luo could not even touch his ball at all.

Later I learned that, like us, Shorty's TK team liked to visit all the diamonds. The difference was that his team never lost. Still, we weren't afraid of them, and I never regretted the stakes—"quitting all diamonds"—we had wagered on today's game, even though I knew we would lose.

I never regretted it. When my old man gave me a hard time, I still didn't chicken out or quit practicing in secret. When my teacher held up my report card, pointed at me, and unloaded all those mean words, I returned the stare, if somewhat cowed. Last night, Shorty himself had come to declare war on us. Right then I realized that our two teams, the mainlanders and the TKs, needed a face-off, something symbolic like a duel, to settle things once and for all.

. . .

I've never trusted the saying, "the brave cherish the brave." To me, enmity has always seemed much purer, cleaner, and more enduring than forgiveness or fraternal love. It's easy to maintain and is conducive to being played over in people's angry minds, thus outliving life's many trivialities and stupidities. It can even be passed on, all the older generation's worries and fears that thrived in hearts full of unvented anger and hostility.

I would rather spend my whole life hating Chen Guoxiong, hating all that followed from what had been "settled" fifteen years ago, though now it was coming alive again and putting out shoots.

Ever since Chen Guoxiong had assumed the position of section head, he had deliberately overlooked my tardiness, negligence, procrastination, and sporadic bad temper. A few days ago, someone informed him that I'd taken a kickback from another company. Without looking into the matter, Chen, as head of the second section, defended my innocence. I knew that he trusted me instinctively. He could not have known that moments earlier, playing on my old fellow Shandong province colleague's resentment, I had planted a rumor that he was taking advantage of his position to profiteer for his family's businesses (his old man had a hand in the high-tech electronics industry and owned an office building and seven satellite factories). The more he overlooked—or tolerated—my delinquency, the more he seemed to rekindle in me the old hatred of fifteen years ago and to remind me of the frustrations I'd suffered since. His appearance exposed my true nature and character and made me want to hide away in shame. As my hatred toward him grew, I became actively involved—against my better judgment—in the group that constantly undermined and badmouthed him. I could not forgive myself. I was lost in the whirlpool of memory, staring hard at that hateful, abandoned self, racked with shame at being so loathsome.

Right at this moment, Chen Guoxiong was heading toward me, and he looked as though he was marching to a duel. But what

I saw was the Chen Guoxiong of three months ago, walking into this office for the first time—handsome and disgusting, polite and arrogant, and with a smile in his eyes, a foxy, penetrating look. I could barely recognize that grown-up face, but I was sure it was him. Because of the look in his eyes, as he walked so confidently toward me now, I felt like I was the one rushing headlong toward him, while he just stood waiting there. He had always been waiting there.

5

The night before, when I'd pushed through the crowd and taken angry Tiger aside, I'd caught the glance of a pair of jet-black and shining eyes.

Shorty was surrounded by our gang. His swarthy, small, and ugly face turned to encounter all the poisonous stares of those around him. He stared back, undaunted, his lips set tight in a straight line.

He'd come to declare war. War, he said, because Little Luo of our Fu Lian Military Compound was the ringleader of a band who blocked their school's back door, greeting everyone they met with a round of punches and demanding money after beating them. If a guy had no money, Little Luo and his men would drag him to a garage and gang up on him. Shorty said that his West Bing Gang wanted no underhanded retaliation; they just wanted to have a final baseball game, fair and square, with Fu Lian. "The loser can just hold his dick, kiss his ass, and say good-bye."

"Fuck you, don't you know where you are?" Tiger pointed to the marble plaque inscribed with the characters FU LIAN NEW VILLAGE. "How dare you come shooting your mouth off here!" Tiger raised his fists and was just about to let him have it.

I held Tiger back and shot a warning look at Little Luo, Stinking Asshole, and the others. For one thing, I didn't want to bully Shorty by outnumbering him; for another, I'd already noticed that in the snack shop facing the village stood at least a dozen TKs with their right hands in their schoolbags, and they were all looking in our direction.

At that moment, my old man's scolding of five minutes earlier echoed in my ears: "Even President Chiang wouldn't want you."

I held Tiger back, but I could hardly control myself anymore. I fixed my eyes on Shorty's, which remained calm despite our hostile glares, and I glanced at those shifting heads and flickering knives in the snack shop. I knew we didn't have a chance in hell, and I'd have to live with what happened. The deep hatred inside me surged up to fill every pore in my body.

And suddenly for no reason, I flashed back to that miserable "gang-up" afternoon one year before. It seemed it was the day of the Tomb-Sweeping Festival. Tony, Little Luo, and I had gone to play basketball at Shorty's junior high school. All of a sudden, dozens of sly, ugly rats, armed with screwdrivers and wearing Tiger rings, cornered us. The leader, the shortest of them, slapped me hard in the face. "I've heard about you. Yeeeah, you're a tough mainlander. Isn't that right? You're their leader. Isn't that right?"

"So?" I spit back my answer and stuck my chin in his face. His reply was a punch in the nose, followed by a kick in the shins. I staggered, almost falling to the ground. Then I was hit with a storm of fists, spitting, scratching, and Tiger ring blows.

Little Luo and Tony were already face down on the ground, begging for mercy. So I was left to take the whole beating. As I tried to protect my vital parts and my bleeding nose, waiting in despair for my death, a dim flicker of light shone through the crowd at me. It was part scorn, part sympathy, and something else that penetrated through all those fists, all that hatred, to somehow reach my very core.

Feeling no pain, I dropped my hands to my sides. Something deeper inside was flogging and lashing me. I looked at that short guy. I had never seen him before, but with his silent gaze, he had taken pity on me as I was being beaten black and blue, feeling nothing. That short guy's gaze set my wounds on fire and stabbed to the heart of my fragile dignity.

Now I clenched my teeth and caught the knuckleball glow of his eyes.

"Tell those rats behind you, who say they play fair, tomorrow, 1 P.M., grass diamond. Whoever loses will quit the diamond for good."

. . .

"Don't forget! Tomorrow afternoon, one o'clock sharp. The Russian Tour Delegation predeparture meeting can't get started without you." As business ended the day before, Chen Guoxiong had patted me on the shoulder, speaking solemnly. That whole afternoon, he'd been busy clearing things for me with the higher-ups. I kept my back to him and nodded.

Yes, it had been the day of the Tomb-Sweeping Festival. April 5, 1975. I couldn't be mistaken. I would never forget it. Sixteen years ago, on the morning of the Tomb-Sweeping Festival, all the newspapers, the television, even the sky were blanketed with black and jarring reminders. That was also one of Grandpa's last days. As if oblivious to his own grave condition, Grandpa had clung to Father all morning and cried, "What do we do now? Finished, finished, all of China is finished." To soothe him, Father kept saying in a low voice, "Father, old President Chiang is gone, but we still have Chiang Junior."

"Chiang Junior won't do. He's never served in the army. How can he lead our fight back?"

That afternoon, Grandpa dragged himself into the bathroom just in time to see me, with a broken nose and bent chin, cleaning myself up. He stared at me, a strange and frightened look in his faded, blinking eyes. He reached out and his arms, going all the way through my body, waved in the air. Then he began to sob and cry, as though I did not exist, as though I were the ghost of someone already dead whose eyes hadn't closed in peace.

As Grandpa lay there, about to breathe his last, his eyes suddenly grew round and, as if prophesying, he kept repeating, "They say the military compound will be torn down, and it will, won't it? They say we won't get assigned an apartment, and we'll have to buy one, won't we? How can we afford it, son?"

"Father, don't worry so much. Even if that's been decided, it won't happen for a couple years. And, besides, the party will surely assign us an apartment. It will. It will."

Father was wrong. "The party" did not assign us an apartment. Buildings went up to replace the military compound, but not "a couple years later." It was thirteen years later, in 1988, the year Chiang Junior died. That was also the year after my father, who always believed that President Chiang would lead our return to the mainland, died. My father's last wish was for us to put his ashes on an altar in the new home he'd earned by "sacrificing his whole life for the party and the country."

6

As the night sank into silence, Tiger and my other buddies all crept home, but I stayed outside practicing in front of the military compound. I hurled balls relentlessly into the darkness. The gray, weather-beaten old wall thudded in echo to my heartbeat.

As Shorty had walked away, he'd cast a long, meaningful look in my direction, as if to say, "Whatever kind of game you play against us, you're sure to lose." A moment later, at least three dozen guys shoved out of the snack shop, the bookstore around the corner, and the alley next to it, with their knives, their chains, their long and short clubs, and swaggered off. Tiger's face had turned green and his knees were knocking. The other boys in our gang unclenched their fists and retreated quietly.

I wasn't afraid, only full of despair, because I almost wanted to believe Shorty. In this waxing night, I stood alone by the compound gate, watching the grass diamond half a mile away and the bloody, devastating war to be played out the following day under the vicious sun.

The first pitch I hurled against the old wall bounced back with a snap, and a tear crept down my cheek.

No good, no good. The pitch was crooked, not straight enough, not man enough.

The second pitch returned with my old man's lecture, "Do you know what every other junior high school student is staying up to do now?"

It was not straight enough, not fast enough. I only pitched straight, fast and straight.

The third pitch bounced back and split my tooth in two. I heard my broken tooth speak to my trembling self, "President Chiang won't want you." I murmured to myself, "But that's a strike."

The fourth pitch, fast and straight. I couldn't see, and the ball felt sticky.

The fifth pitch, fast and straight, like a blaze.

The sixth pitch, a blaze.

The seventh, eighth, ninth, and every one that followed, all turning into burning blazes.

The white blaze gradually reddened into a glow like sunshine. The ball was dyed red. When the blazing ball smashed into my mitt, leaped to hit my chest, and released a shower of my sweat and tears, I heard my exhausted body say to my unyielding brain, "It's no use, your whole life is a washout."

. . .

"I'm gonna win. I never pitched so well." As I said this, I suddenly realized it was 1991, and I was staring at a blank letter of resignation. I sat in my tiny rented room, my eyes fixed by the bare fluorescent light and memories flickering before me.

Gradually it dawned on me that to rid myself of that nightmarish battle from that particular year, I had to fight it all over again.

Three months earlier, when I'd read the name Chen Guoxiong on the Personnel Announcement Board, I'd told myself that this battle would be inevitable. A few days before that, Tiger had visited me after completing his military service. Downing sorghum wine and pouring out his troubles, Tiger suddenly asked, "Do you remember Chen Guoxiong?"

"Chen Guoxiong?"

"That dark, disgusting Shorty, who always pitched crooked balls. Damn it, that guy is something now. In reform school, I met a whole bunch of TKs, all his buddies. I heard he graduated from Taiwan U. Fuck it."

I was stunned. The bottle in my hand fell from my senseless grasp, shattering into pieces. For the first time in fifteen years, I was drawn into the tunnel of time, returning to our lost baseball diamond that no longer existed.

I thought that I'd long forgotten that game, as well as how, in the days that followed, I'd failed the entrance exam, been unable to find a decent job, and had to come up with rent for housing after the military compound was demolished.

My current job was the best Father could secure for me before he died, after lobbying all his contacts in the government and the party. With only this much security, I worked as little as possible, lived like a slob, and tried my best to forget about myself.

In the four years since I'd joined this trade organization, I'd had no girlfriends and made no friends, and I didn't pursue promotion or training opportunities. Most of the time I spent boozing with my senior colleague from the Shandong province. Red-eyed and spitting our disgust, we drank a hard liquor called Wujiapi and exchanged belches that stank of alcohol, stomach acid, and vomit—a smell approaching that of a reeking corpse. Or I would listen to him talk:

"That March power struggle, damn it, it was all planned. After Lee Teng-hui, it would be Lin Yang-kang. The second son of the Chiang family would never become the president of 'The Republic of Taiwan.' And this is called localization, do you hear me, boy? Localization. It's all over, even if your name is Chiang."

As I gazed absently at the countless wrinkles and the wine-reddened nose on that old man's face, I was really hearing the last words Father had mumbled before he died four years earlier. "I can't expect anything from you anymore. Work hard, and behave yourself, kid. Understand? Remember, put my ashes in the new home. You know what every other student in Taiwan is doing right now? Don't play baseball. Be good." Back then, I could not say a word or shed a tear. But on one particular evening four years later, due to some strange juxtaposition in time, with my hands trembling too much to write a simple resignation letter and tears in my eyes, I shouted at my father's ghost: "But it was a strike! I never pitched so well!"

7

As the last blaze flashed, striking out the last batter of the opposing team, my mind suddenly went blank. It was just like that last earth-shattering hurl at dawn that day.

It struck me vaguely that in a flash, something of crucial importance was accomplished, and destroyed.

And then the sun's silver rays pierced like spears into my drained body and brain. No sooner had the last blood-stained pitch been hurled than I passed out. Nevertheless, that ball remained steady in the air, spinning by itself against the brightness. No. It would be more accurate to say the ball was advancing on some vague course in another dimension where its speed was imperceivable to human eyes. The sun's blaze stabbed into my pupils. Wait, I could see now that the ball was overtaking the light. In the open space between me and the wall rose a series of barriers: three gates appeared in the inner circle and three in the outer. That ball flew straight through the first screen, which stopped my startled gaze; behind the second I glimpsed the haggard sight of my back several years later; and behind the third appeared the dour face of a man in his thirties, then the blurred silhouette of a man in his forties. Each of my selves was gazing as the ball followed its course, breaking through each barrier and dying away, and the ball's track linked together my life and my destiny as it unfolded. My entire life was coupled to that superfast pitch, frozen in each frame but hurtling relentlessly onward. When the ball reached its target, the old wall collapsed with a deafening crash. Amid the rubble appeared a black hole, into which the disintegrating ball vanished.

I must have fallen face down, my body rigid and straight. From far off came a hushed cry, "The ball vanished!"

Gradually the buzzing grew louder around me. A group of people seemed to have hold of my arms and legs and were lifting me. I didn't even know where my head was. I heard Tiger's voice: "Practicing all night must have worn him out. But I never saw him pitch so good! Fuck! No hits, no walks. Seventeen sons of bitches struck out. Damn! This should be the final game in a world series!"

I struggled to open my eyes, only to be looking up the umpire's nose. He said, "That's seven innings. Zero to zero, a tie. You gonna go into extras?" I tried to raise my arm but I couldn't. I tried to close my fists, but it was like trying to hold mercury.

High-pitched laughter broke out from the TK team. Five or six sons of bitches gave us the finger. Something exploded inside my chest and brain, like the hollow crunch of bones breaking.

"Fuck your whole family and your family's ghosts! Suits us fine! We'll see who's chicken!" That was Tiger shouting back our response to the challenge.

"Stop talking, Tiger."

On that evening three months before when we'd gotten boozed up on the sorghum wine, I'd almost wanted to break his neck. After I'd begged him over and over to stop talking about the past, he just wouldn't shut up.

With the first bottle, he grumbled about all the little things that happened to him in the army and in jail. As he drained one glass, I kept him company by downing one, too. Then he went on about his bad luck and how much he hated society, draining another glass as I drank two. Then, his face beet-red, he switched to the subject of Cannon, who'd been executed, shot to death, the year before, after his court-martial for stealing guns and deserting, which I already knew about. I downed three glasses in a row and said quietly, "Stop talking."

"Damn it, the world is too weird. His old man gets a leg blown off in the Da- and Er-dan Battle, and he eats a bullet from his own people." Tiger seemed deaf to my words.

"Tiger, shut up."

"And now it's those old chickenshits who are making out the best. I heard Little Luo played the real estate market two years ago and made a killing, and he's even got Tony and Stinking Asshole messing around with stocks. Fuck. I get pissed off every time I think of what a chickenshit Little Luo was in a fight. You even tried to cover up for him. And now you should hear how they talk about you."

"Tiger, come on, I'm asking you to stop."

"And look at you. You used to be first for a one-on-one fight, but now you don't even want to talk about it. Stop? Why? Your old man used to win the Best Service Award for Officers in the village. Didn't you used to say he had enough medals to fill a suitcase? And now look! His dear son stuck in this dive. Damn it, you let me finish. You're having drinks with me now, a good-for-nothing, drinking sorghum wine, and if your old man's ghost knew about this . . ."

"Fuck you! Fuck your mother, your sister, your aunt! Shut up! Now shut up!" I grabbed the bottle, ready to hit Tiger over the head.

But I couldn't even raise my arm, and I certainly couldn't hit anyone. I should have just lain down. My anger could no longer rouse a fight in me. This thirty-year-old body, sodden with wine and cigarettes, could no longer pick on anyone.

Tiger's face paled. He stared at me strangely. His dim, unfocused eyes reflected my unconscious trembling.

That bottle remained in my hand, until Tiger uttered a name: Chen Guoxiong.

8

"Go on Guoxiong! Those pigs' pitcher—his arm's shot. Give 'em a 'good-bye home run'!" The jeers were gradually rising in pitch.

My arm still hung limp. Shorty's aluminum bat shone over the batter's box, like a python ready to be released.

In the second half of the eighth inning, my first two pitches gave them two hits, and they were on second and third base already. No one had struck out. Shorty, whose real name was something like "—hsiung," might be the last batter up this game.

I couldn't raise my arm, but I had to. Raise it and hang in there till the end, because our team had no substitute pitcher.

I turned my back to the batter's box and tried to wipe the saliva, snot, and cold sweat from my face.

In all hundred games of the past year, this same feeling had always overcome me at the very end: my arm was as heavy as lead, and every ball they hit seemed to take wing and fly far beyond me to the outer reaches. Our worst score was zero to thirty-six. Today's game could be our closest, but it could entail the worst possible fate for me. I'd pitched all hundred games, since we had no other pitcher.

Taking his position on first base, Tiger shouted encouragement. In the outfield, Tony and Little Luo were either staring blankly at the foul line or taking a nap. I knew they were already exhausted.

The hopelessly limp arm had to be raised. I flipped off the sweat running down my face. Suddenly, more than anything, I wanted the bat shining in the batter's box, the ball in my loose grasp, this grass diamond, the sky overhead, and even my life itself to simply disappear.

The reason I choose to disappear is that I am confused—why couldn't that game simply be a game? Why did that fastball vanish? Maybe my answer lies in the fights we lost before ending up here in Taiwan in 1949, the Sipingjie Street Battle, the incident of 500 martyrs in Taiyuan, or the ordeal at Xubang Battle. I don't have an answer. My life has been filled with cries of "Long live President Chiang." I was brought up on the injunction, "Kill Zhu De and weed out Mao," entirely unrelated to me and yet informing my childhood, these stories about Chinese killing Chinese.

Last night, I wrote down this paragraph as the reason for my resignation, which I would hand in first thing in the morning. Then I would walk out of the office, never looking back.

Most of the night, I argued with my father's ghost and blamed Tiger, who'd had no idea of my situation when he told me about Chen three months ago. Eventually, I got out of bed and deleted this paragraph that, of course, no one would understand.

But in fact, I was afraid that Shorty could read my mind—that damn look of his. I could never get away from that grass diamond.

9

Silently I squatted beside the pitcher's mound. The world around me started spinning, spinning relentlessly as a whirlpool.

As Shorty started around the bases, Tony, deep in center, ran right over to the dike that bordered the field. Angrily, he threw off his mitt. The umpire was making circles with his arm. The TK team was shouting, "Home run! A good-bye home run!" Tiger fell to the ground, crying bitterly. The old sun sank lower as though to chase the home run ball as it flew into a blood-red cloud over the western horizon.

I remained there, squatting in the center of that scarlet swirl.

Game over.

. . .

I remained very calm. All that had followed from that game fifteen years ago and had remained alive and unsettled could be put to rest now, or set back to zero. Like this resignation letter I labored over, with still not a word on it.

In fact, there was absolutely no reason for my resignation. However hard I thought, there was still no reason. Some would say that I fled because my crime was about to be exposed. Others would say that I packed up because I couldn't stand spiteful incriminations. My only worry was that, without enough savings, my cigarette, liquor, and coffee addictions, as well as my insatiable appetite, would do me in.

My meaningless life would continue. The night before handing in my resignation letter, I fumbled through the wine bottles, cigarette butts, broken china, and old dishes before I found the dusty urn with Father's ashes. I could hear him grumbling: "Now I really am gone, just look how you manage on your own!" I pleaded with him to forgive me for messing up the last and best arrangements he'd made for me. I told him that after the military compound was demolished, I forgot so much, even the nightmares about our old house in the village. I forgot about the paint peeling off the red door; the low, broken eaves; the sodden, moldy *tatami* mats; how sunshine and shadow crossed on our east-facing window each dawn, creating ambiguity as well as promise. I forgot my childhood, the legend explaining our past, my lost ancestors and their relationship to me, the collapsed old wall, and a father's hopes for his son, which I continually thwarted. In particular, I could not remember the apparition that came to me in the middle of the night, the senile outpouring of details about another hometown more real than our military compound. . . . Gradually I realized that I had not forgotten. I simply did not exist. I did not belong to my grandfather's past or my father's future for me. The resignation letter was only meant to prove that I did not exist—an undeniable reality.

I told Tiger not to call others fools or bastards. If you have guts, follow the path of those tough guys from Windy Town. Take your chances at robbery, murder, eating bullets. If not, be man enough to drive a taxi or mix cement. Yeah, a cement mixer. Papa, now that the Six-Year National Development Plan and the Taipei Mass Rapid Transit Project are under way, you wouldn't object to me taking a job that "contributes to the country," would you? If worse comes to the worst, I could be a street peddler on the street, playing hide-and-seek with the police. My Taiwanese is good enough to attract buyers, even if I stammer, like a knuckleball.

Game over. Childhood, good-bye.

10

The fight just erupted.

In the infield, both teams threw themselves into the brawl. The ball Shorty had hit to score his homer had plunged into the river. Standing on the dike, Tony shouted, "The ball's disappeared!" It was the only one we had left after a year of very hard-fought games.

Little Luo rushed up to grab Shorty's collar. "Fuck you, cough up that ball! Cough it up!"

"Fuck. Fuck you all. That pig pitcher of yours is useless, and you stand here griping." The whole TK team rushed over and beat Little Luo until he curled up like a shrimp. "We could give you a hundred balls, and you'd still fuck up. Fuck you. Get the hell off our diamond."

Then our pals joined the free-for-all. Behind home plate, the noisy crowd jumped from the bleachers into the fray. Beside me, I watched our men falling one after another. Cries of pain, shoving, pushing, and angry banter engulfed me as I stood rigid beside the pitcher's mound. Just like the time when Grandpa's hands went through my body, no one noticed my existence. I saw Tiger chasing Shorty, bat in hand, all the way to the outfield. Then Shorty swung backward and Tiger was down. Then Tiger was on his knees and some other TKs ran over and threw him to the ground, beating and trampling him. Tossing his bat, Shorty stood to one side, looking both uncomfortable and satisfied, but he was watching another bloody figure by third base.

Then I realized it was my other self fighting near third. When I saw what was happening to Tiger and Shorty's smug expression, I gathered all my strength, broke through the crowd, and rushed at Shorty.

My overwhelming and undirected anger forced me to attack that enemy whose name I didn't even know. Frightened by my hellish look, Shorty ran. I was after him at full speed. I kicked and shoved aside two huge guys who tried to block me before I reached the dike. Through a film of blood dripping from my left eye, I saw the last of the sun casting a thick, red, and clotted net over the water. I focused on Shorty's blurred figure and kept running, no longer knowing whether I was the one chasing or the one running away. . . .

The early summer sunlight of 1991 streamed between me and Chen Guoxiong, our confrontation twisting into flame. He rushed angrily toward me, the resignation letter he brandished in his hand raised like his eyebrow. I, on the other hand, had fled to another world. Chen Guoxiong, if you are smart, please let me go "without a word." Please don't try to retain me. Maybe you understand and maybe you don't. But that's how it is. My friend,

I've already deserted the battlefield and lost my homeland. Please don't force me to go back. Really, trust me. I've never pitched so well in my life.

11

Shorty kept running, and I kept chasing. On the river's surface appeared a white beam, like a ball, racing me in the other lane.

Shorty's figure grew clearer. I was almost out of breath and wanted only to stop now, stop this endless chase. But I couldn't stop. My feet had a mind of their own as they dragged my torso on, and a frightening force was pushing me from behind. A powerful wind blew, and suddenly my body began to inflate. My upper body swelled out of my small clothes, my skin jaundiced and covered with freckles and warts. My legs went limp. My sweat turned into wine, and my burned-out anger stank of cigarettes, bile, and rot. The river reflected back my mustached face, messy hair replacing my crew cut. The reflection kept changing; my face aged five years, ten years, twenty years. Completely drained, I felt like throwing up, but I still couldn't stop running.

At thirty, I was still chasing fifteen-year-old Shorty. Where the river ended stood a scrap metal plant. The river was sucked into a whirlpool there before plunging into a culvert underground. Shorty and I collapsed almost at the same time, and then we jumped at each other, fighting, pummeling, and wrestling toward that black swirl. I crawled on top of him, feeding him my fists; he kicked my belly, shoved me away, and struggled to his feet. I jumped on him again, beating his face, beating him as my tears fell. I was screaming at myself to stop, though no sound came out of my mouth. Shorty and I pounded each other blindly, crying out in pain. Then I grabbed a broken brick to hit him. He grabbed a rusty metal rod, pointed it at my gut, and shouted, "Get lost! Get lost! You can't beat me on my family's land!"

Before I realized what his words meant, I heard a loud cry: "Mainlanders go home! All of you!" The words cracked overhead and struck me like thunder.

I was stunned, my mouth wide open. I forgot the weapon in my hand, forgot I was crying.

By now, the missing ball popped up in the water, leaping about in the whirlpool. Shorty and I watched that ball wash into the culvert, swamp, and sludge. The ball blazed astonishingly white, like a lotus. It passed through our surprised gaze, floating, rolling, blossoming in that forever receding, fast disappearing black hole.

Epilogue: In Remembrance of My Buddies from the Military Compound

. . .

by CHU Tien-hsin

translated by Michelle WU

Before you read this story, please prepare in advance—no, I'm not asking you to fix yourself a cup of boiling jasmine tea and to be careful not to burn your lips, as Eileen Chang asked her readers in "The First Tripod of Incense." As for my request, I apologize because it is more of a hassle—I am asking you to please play the song "Stand by Me." Yes, I am referring to the original soundtrack of the movie, written by Stephen King, bearing the same title. It shouldn't be too difficult to find in the music shops. Anyway, it will be your loss if you choose not to play the song.

All, right, dear reader, thanks for your cooperation. Let's begin.

Even if you haven't seen the movie, I am sure that you would be fascinated by the tone of the little boy narrating the lyrics. On a long, boring afternoon, he tags behind the big boys as they go on an adventure to a faraway place, because rumor has it that there is a corpse of a man who died of unknown reasons there. The little boy is scared and excited and incredulous, yet he hopes to God that he will not piss in his pants the moment he actually sees what he wants to see. Thus he psyches himself up over and over again, and reminds himself vehemently: I'm not afraid, I'm not afraid, I'm not the least bit afraid, as long as you're on my side, I sure as hell will not shed a single tear!

. . . The sound fades into the distance, as a figure gradually becomes clear on the screen. I don't know how to describe her, a big girl in puberty, or a little woman. Undaunted by the onset of her first menstruation, she is holding her breath—totally oblivious to the music of the TV advertisement selling Queen Bee Dark Sugar Soap, intent only on pulling down the shirt tucked into her skirt, to make sure that her chest in the mirror is as flat as it was in elementary school. Feeling assured, she darts out of her house without glancing at the chewing gum commercial on TV, with sixteen-year-old Jenny Tseng[1] wearing a miniskirt, dancing and singing, "My love, my love, Yinglun heart-to-heart chewing gum. . . ."

She runs to the front gate of the compound. It is a sunny Saturday afternoon, and at the riverbank, ten to twenty boys, ranging from first graders to those who have reached the conscription age, have converged like a flock of birds. At the entrance of the compound, between two tall stone poles (nobody knows their exact function), hangs a red banner, with the words NUMBER X CANDIDATE XXX HAS THE FULL SUPPORT OF THIS COMPOUND. Set against the bright blue sky, the banner flaps in the wind. It seems as if a banner would be hung there for a few days once every few years. About twenty years later, she will remember that scene in a flood of emotions, and for the first time in her life, vote for a political party different from that represented on the red banner.

She circles around the boys, like a strange bird from another world, trying to join them, and how she longs to feel and sense the body temperature and sweaty odors from fooling around and wrestling with the boys. She even misses the smell of their burps after a heavy lunch. The burp of Ah Ding, whose family comes

[1] Jenny Tseng (Zhen Ni) was a popular teenage idol who frequently appeared on TV.

from Jiangxi,[2] actually smells hotter and more pungent than Peipei's, whose family comes from Szechwan.[3] The kids from the Wang family, who come from Zhejiang,[4] always give off reeky burps that smell of steamed fermented tofu[5] and fish, and Ya-ya and her brothers, who are Cantonese, always belch with the sour, fermented smell of rice porridge. It's strange, though, they never say "*xi fan*," but prefer to say "*zhou*" instead.[6] And the "Cantonese *gan*" that they love so much are really *liu ding*.[7] Not to mention the Shandong Zhang family's kids, who belch stinky garlic and onion burps. The kids of the Sun family from Beijing have a mother who makes all kinds of desserts from flour, so they wander around always with some kind of food in their hands, and the aroma of these wheaten goodies can really drive one crazy. . . .

But now she circles like a strange bird. These boys have been buddies with her from morning to night for more than ten years. Yes, they really have hung out together day in, day out, like brothers. They would even stay over at her house, when they forgot the time while playing, and sleep side by side with her and her sisters. She even watched Mao-mao come into this world, as she and her buddies crowded to Auntie Mao's bedroom window, watching her scream in the agony of labor. Mao-mao's big brother was so proud then, as he carefully selected only those who were on his side and gave them permission to watch. And there

[2] A province in central China.

[3] A province in southwestern China, noted for its pungent and spicy cuisine.

[4] A coastal province in central China.

[5] This is a Chinese delicacy also known as "stinking tofu." It can be steamed or deep-fried.

[6] "*Xi fan*" is the Mandarin term for rice porridge, and "*zhou*" is the Cantonese term for it.

[7] *Gan* is the Cantonese pronunciation for oranges, and *liu ding*, the Taiwanese name for oranges.

is Ah San, who was one year her senior, whom she has loved on the sly for almost a decade. And there is Da Tou, whom she always ends up quarrelling or fighting with every time they meet, whose ambivalent attitude puzzles her, not knowing whether she is friend or foe to him.

But something has gone wrong in the past six months. She is baffled. She thinks she has done an impeccable job of concealing her womanhood. For example, she believes that menstrual blood gives out an odor, so when her period comes, she takes great pains to stand downwind, to prevent the odor from spreading; for instance, when she discovered she could no longer stop her breasts from swelling, she cried and started to wage a daily battle against them. She stole her mother's scarf to bind them tightly, and wore a vest from elementary school inside her clothes to flatten them. Once, while she was wrestling with the boys, someone punched her in the chest, causing her to burst into tears and almost faint from pain right on the spot. She even stole her father's cigarettes and smoked with them, imitating the way they smoked and hid their cigarettes, thereby becoming recognized as an accomplice to the crimes they committed. She was even reluctant to study hard, because she felt it would be easier for them to accept her if she had lousy grades.

Of course, it was not until about ten years later, after she graduated from college, started to work, and was considering granting her boyfriend her hand in marriage, that she could look at those boys, or, I should say, men, eye to eye. How could they talk about and speculate on the size of her breasts, and exchange information on sex that swelled to disproportionate mysterious dimensions due to ignorance, in her presence? They whispered into each other's ears, as if passing on a confidential business secret, that so-and-so's big brother had returned from military service and had become a member of the mainlander's gang near the airport, and that if anyone got into trouble or got into a squabble with the neighboring compound, he could be called on to settle things; and Da Guo, who was the only person who attended the private junior high in the city, said he saw the Pan family's second daughter glued to the arm of an American GI as they walked down Zhongshan North Road—what a bitch! And everyone would empty out his pent-up dirty curses, howling like an animal, achieving an oral climax as if in *Deep Throat*. There was also Ma Ge, whose sister was about to marry an American soldier. He used to sculpt a Marlon Brando hairstyle from *On the Waterfront* with his mother's facial cream, and teach the big boys new dance steps that he had just learned from his brother-in-law. But their dance steps were often interrupted by the *Tanada Club*[8] television program, featuring the off-key songs sung by the audience, blasting from the Tang family's TV set. And there was the second son of the Ding family, who would pace up and down the square, with his algebra textbook in hand, as he worked out the equations in the air. He would blabber about MIT every time he worked out an equation. Ding's physics teacher loved to talk about the various myths regarding MIT like a Muslim worshipping the holy land of Mecca. Having received second-hand information from the second son of the Ding family, it wasn't until the beginning of the 1970s that she came to realize that the contemporary meaning of MIT was not the "Massachusetts Institute of Technology" that she had come to know so well, but "Made in Taiwan."

Thus, no one would mourn the passing of childhood for many years, as she did. Even when she was attending an all-girls school, and when she and some of her closest friends exchanged views on their Prince Charming during a slumber party, as her

[8] This was a popular television program featuring talent competitions. It was sponsored by Tanada Seiyaku, a Japanese pharmaceutical company.

turn came, she did not draw up a blueprint of her prince defining his educational background, blood type, height, horoscope, and economic status like her peers. Instead, she only said, "He must come from a military compound."

And in the dark, her eyes were illuminated with a strange gleam, like an animal in search of prey in the night.

That year, she moved away from the military compound to a new neighborhood at the edge of the city, where a few mainlanders, a lot of Taiwanese, and people from all walks of life converged. Suddenly, all her ties with the flock she identified with were severed; she was like a river that had merged into the ocean. In the years that were still stifling and closed, she started to strum and sing, "Where have all the flowers gone?" on the guitar. She did not understand then that it was a famous antiwar song that had taken the outside world by storm only five or six years before; she only felt the lyrics touch a chord in her heart. Yes, where have all the boys gone? Where have all the boys from the military compound gone?

She met a big bunch of local Taiwanese boys, and was deeply puzzled by their steadfastness, which differed greatly from her brothers and sisters in the military compound. For some peculiar reason, the brothers and sisters that she knew all thought of leaving this place. Those who did well in school, and whose families were willing to borrow money to support them, would go study abroad; those who did not do well in school would leave this place by becoming sailors; and the girls who were not cut out for school managed to leave the country by marrying American soldiers, thanks to the Vietnam War. Many years later, when she was fed up with being accused, along with the political regime that came from the China mainland, of "not considering this island as a permanent home," she really did ruminate over the reasons they never really regarded this piece of land as a place in which to take root in their lifetime—at least not during those years—

She came to a very simple conclusion, that is, they didn't have any tombstones to sweep during the Tomb-Sweeping Festival.[9]

At the gate of the compound where they lived, there was a graveyard that covered several hillsides. From Youth Day[10] till the beginning of spring vacation, they would wander in the hills and woods, playing and peeking at other people sweeping tombstones. The strangeness of the local rituals and offerings and the sad and solemn expressions on the faces of the locals baffled them.

At that time the tiered rice paddies were already plowed for the spring sowing, so they had to be careful not to step into them. But it was not easy to walk along the ridges of the rice paddies that were covered with puddles of water. Actually, everything was wet during that time of year; even the stalks of freshly picked wildflowers and grass dripped with water, and the air was also moist with water, wetting the hair, plastering strands of it to their faces. The graves that they normally avoided revealed themselves suddenly as though uncovered by receding tides, and they would visit one tombstone after another, emboldened by the presence of people, and read out the tongue-twisting names inscribed on the tombstones as if engaged in a competition. Those who wanted to show off their courage would even steal the incense sticks and fresh flowers from the tombstones. . . .

But this day would always pass by with no special ceremony. When night fell and they went home for dinner, they would find their parents acting strangely. Some would be burning paper

[9] Tomb-Sweeping Festival is observed on April 5. It is a Chinese custom to visit the grave sites of family members on this day in remembrance of one's ancestors.

[10] Youth Day is celebrated on March 29.

money in their backyard, but because they did not know whether or not their relatives back home were alive, they could only state ambiguously that the money was burned for ancestors of the X family. Therefore, their expressions were especially complicated—they dared not express grief; instead, their faces would be marked by memories made all the more lucid and poignant by the passage of time.

So, a land where none of your relatives are buried cannot be called home.

Therefore, the anxiety and instability in the air that she could not understand at that time did not stem from the irrepressible commotion characteristic of adolescence. Rather, it was an anxiety caused by the incomprehensible fear of not being able to take root anywhere.

During the nights of family gatherings before the advent of television, when there wasn't much entertainment, the parents used to tell their children stories about their exodus to Taiwan, and life in their homeland on mainland China. Due to a complex set of emotions and the inflation caused by years of retelling, almost everyone's parents came from families that owned a lot of land or money (Mao-mao's family owned a farm five to six times as large as Taiwan), and every family used to have more than ten maids, a platoon of orderlies, and half a dozen chauffeurs. The nuggets of gold discarded by each family during the flight from mainland China also increased with the passage of time. If added all together, the amount would surpass the amount of gold that Yu Hongjun[11] moved to Taiwan for the Guomindang. . . .

With such experiences and such a past, how could they bring themselves to live out their lives on this little island?

[11] President of the Central Bank of China during the exile of the Nationalist government to Taiwan.

This was the conviction that they clung to until a certain age. A number of years later, people like her would gradually mingle with local Taiwanese classmates who came from farming families. When she was invited to go to their homes to do her homework, she was astonished by the disparity between the standard of living of her local classmates and that of those living on her compound. These Taiwanese did not like to turn on lights, and the rooms in their houses were dark and dim even in the daytime; their toilets were located right next to the pig's barn; and they preferred to fetch water from the well rather than turn on the faucets. They did their homework in the courtyard, with stools as tables. She exclaimed to herself in surprise upon finding out that the classmates who competed with her for the top position in class actually did their homework and prepared for tests in this fashion every day!

After doing their homework, they went to the fruit orchard at the back of the house where a dozen pomelo trees stood, to play house. As she watched her classmate's mother, plainly dressed in farming attire, clucking and feeding the chicken and ducks, and her classmate's father laying out unknown herbs to dry under the sun at sunset, she felt an unfathomable sadness.

Later, her classmates would invite her to go to their house every year for the annual *bai-bai*.[12] She gradually got accustomed to the abundant but unfamiliar dishes, and started to enjoy the open-air opera performances like the other kids, to laugh with them when they laughed, even though she didn't understand the lines. Gradually, she came to understand vaguely why they were always so down to earth.

Like her, all the kids in the compound gradually came to realize this, and as if they had reached an agreement, all ceased to

[12] This is a festival when lots of food and flowers are offered to the gods and spirits. Very often, this gives the people a chance to enjoy scrumptious feasts.

boast about the homeland that they had never seen. Only when an unknowing and naïve little kid bragged about the mountain in his grandfather's backyard being taller than Mt. Ali would they suddenly become quiet, and pretend that they did not hear anything. No one even ventured to expose the lie.

So, they all sought a way out.

The boys had to face this problem earlier. In the sixth grade, before mandatory education was extended to nine years, they were surprised that the local boys could choose not to take exams and continue their education (even though, in private, they wished they could do that too), and instead go home to help with the farming, or become apprentices to carpenters or plumbers. For they had no other choice but to continue their schooling. There were a few exceptions, though, such as Bao Ge, the eldest son of the Chen family. One year, a motion picture company made a Chinese martial arts movie in the woods on the top of the hill, and Bao Ge went to watch; his role changed from that of spectator to that of a volunteer who served as a stuntman for the price of a lunchbox in a scene in which he was kicked over by the male lead, and then to that of an assistant who helped the crew load the props onto the truck. When the cast left, Bao Ge went along with them without even taking a change of clothes.

This somewhat outrageous example circulated around the compound for more than ten years, and everyone thought Bao Ge was dead. It was approximately twenty years later that someone in the group who was accustomed to reading the film and entertainment page in the papers would discover, in an obscure corner of the page, that Bao Ge had died from liver cancer in his early forties, leaving behind a son who was only in kindergarten, and that Brother Bao had been alive all that time, as a martial arts instructor for a television program at a certain station.

"Oh, so that's where you've been all this time," she exclaims as she reads the paper.

At the same time, the other important pages of the paper are filled with news related to power struggles among the second-generation sons of prominent mainlanders. She reads them all in detail, nonchalantly, while her husband, who is also reading the paper, condemns the mainlanders, of whom she is one. (She had actually gone against her word and married a local Taiwanese boy.)

During those years she did think of Brother Bao—only once, on her wedding night.

Her husband was sending off their friends and colleagues who were there to *nao dongfang*.[13] Sapped of energy, she could not muster enough strength to listen to their jokes. So she went back to the bedroom alone, without turning on the lights, because she was afraid of facing the feeling of unfamiliarity and afraid of what was about to happen. This was in part due to the fact that she was still a virgin, but it was also because of the dark and strange new bedroom, which caused her to suddenly lose her identity as a modern metropolitan woman whose knowledge of sex far surpasses necessity, and to find herself in a bedroom as dark and strange as this one—the bedroom at Bao Ge's house. She was in second or third grade, playing with Bao Ge's sister and Bei-bei. They had formed their own *Huangmeidiao*[14] troupe, and they were looking for a towel or blanket with which to dress up in traditional costume. While looking for a hair clip on the floor, she picked up an old booklet without covers. Curiously,

[13] This is a Chinese custom. Friends and relatives of newlyweds like to play jokes on the couple on their wedding night in their bedroom, after the wedding banquet.

[14] A form of folksy Chinese opera, very popular in Taiwan during the 1960s and 1970s.

she leafed through it under the five-watt light bulb. It was a book on sex, written in coarse and vulgar language, and it was all very new to her, so she read it very attentively. It taught men how to arouse virgins, and how to stop the bleeding after the hymen had been ruptured, and she vaguely heard Bei-bei warn her, "That's my brother's, and he won't let anyone read it!"

When she came to the part where it described how one could tell whether or not a woman was a virgin by her lips, breasts, and sitting posture, she suddenly became aware of the silence around her. She looked up, saw a tall shadow in the doorway, and discovered that Bei-bei and the others had disappeared some time ago. She sensed immediately, however, that the man wearing his father's army undershirt was Bao Ge. She threw the book away and mumbled "Bao Ge." Bao Ge did not say anything and approached her slowly, though it seemed as if he came close to her in no time, as he breathed loudly. As he came close to the light, she was terrified by the catlike gleam in his eyes.

Actually, nothing happened at all. She ran nimbly out of the bedroom in a flash, out of Bao Ge's house, into the sunlight. That fragment of memory blanked out like a roll of film that had been exposed to light, and the first rough and vulgar impressions of sex remained locked in that bedroom. Later, seeing Bao Ge in broad daylight gave her no qualms, and she really did not think of him at all until her wedding night. Then she thought: it would never have occurred to Bao Ge, not even in his dreams, that a girl would think of him at the most important moment in her life, even though it was in such a bizarre way.

Actually, there isn't just Bao Ge, there are many, many more men who have caused many girls to think of them on their wedding nights.

They are mostly known as Old Zhang, Old Liu, or Old Wang (depending on what their last name is).

Usually there would be such an Old X in the compound. Because he was single and way past the marrying age with no possibility of starting a family, and most often possessed no special skill as a retired sergeant, the compound sort of supported him by allowing him to build a shack behind the administrative office at the gate. He was given some money and put in charge of answering the phone calls. He was responsible for delivering meeting notices, repairing street lamps, and, when teenage boys from neighboring compounds ganged up to challenge the boys in the compound, for mediating at the right moment. Come wintertime, the children would circle around and watch him roast a wandering little black dog outside the compound, and in summer he would be seen skinning a snake in the pungent, toxic aroma of the oleander tree. This was Old X.

They were usually illiterate, and could not even decipher their own name, or the tattoos saying "Kill Zhu and Remove Mao" or "Fight Communism and the Russians" on their arms. But they were the first teachers for many kids in the compound. He had an inexhaustible supply of stories depicting war against the Communists, scenes from *Romance of the Three Kingdoms*, the *Outlaws of the Marsh*, and other old legends or ghost stories. Despite their very heavy accents, for some unknown reason most children had no trouble understanding them; even though their shacks resembled garbage dumps, the children considered them to be treasure troves, as there were many bullets polished to a sheen with tong oil (if you agreed to run past the hillside graveyard on a night when the power had gone off to buy him a bottle of booze, he would probably give you one), various medallions, processed insect corpses and snakeskins, and rationed soybeans fried into delicious snacks. Also, there definitely would be cards, incomplete sets of Chinese chess or Go, and he would teach you how to play them or tell your fortune for you.

And then, it wouldn't be long until a subtle change took place among the children who showed up there—depending on Old X's sex drive and self-control.

Among the children, there would be one who was especially gluttonous, or one who liked to win the favor of the elders, or one who was obedient and dared not go against the wishes of her elders . . . let's call her Little Ling. When Little Ling arrived at the run-down shack of Old X, all the other children would stay far away, as if obeying their animal instincts that beckoned them to stay away from their sick or wounded companions. . . .

Most children would not realize that danger and uncertainty were hanging in the air; only the bolder boys, finally, would wait for the day to hide and peek behind the window. They could usually find Old X and Little Ling doing strange things together, with either him without his pants on, or Little Ling with her clothes removed. This old man usually did not cause Little Ling to bleed, or leave any mark on her to arouse the suspicion of her mother when she bathed at night, either because of his limited sexual ability or for fear of causing trouble. However, the boys usually ran away before they got to see this part. Due to a sense of guilt, they didn't tell any of their companions what happened, nor did they even warn their own sisters. They even continued to visit Old X's shack, and in between storytelling sessions or chess games they sometimes fell into a trance as they stare at Old X's crotch, remembering his big cock, with no comments except: damn, what a huge monster he is!

As for Little Ling, sooner or later would come the day when she would confide to a girlfriend what Old X did to her and be met with one of two reactions. The other person might burst into tears and suddenly hold on to her hands tightly, and regardless of whether or not they returned to Old X's place they would remain the best of friends throughout their childhood. But the more common reaction would be: the other person would start to look indifferent and quietly turn away, keeping Little Ling at a distance. She might not reveal the secret, but all her companions would immediately get the message, like animals, and without any curiosity stay far away from Little Ling, leaving her alone to live and die.

But the strange thing is that such news could only spread out horizontally, eluding the younger siblings. Therefore every year, unavoidably, there would be a few or a lot of Little Lings. When the old Little Ling found her little sister and her friends displaying mysterious behavior, the bolder, older Little Ling might reprimand her: "Don't go to Old X's place!" "Be careful! You'll get in trouble if Mother finds out."

Later, she would wonder why she never thought of telling her mother. Every Little Ling behaved in the same manner, enabling the Old Xs to live in peace till twenty, thirty years later. When the Little Lings got married, or when they made love to their boyfriends for the very first time, they all remembered Old X in the distant shack, in the distant military compound, from the distant times. The traditional and conservative Little Lings would worry about whether their hymens are still intact, while the healthier and more cheerful Little Lings would shed tears of happiness, feeling very grateful that the hands fondling their bodies are no longer hesitant, greedy, and feeble, but young and forceful, clean and resolved. . . .

These things would be already beyond the imagination of the Old Xs, because at the same moment they would be obsessed with the problem of getting rid of their tattoos so that they could return to the Chinese mainland to visit relatives. Those who were more courageous went to plastic surgeons to scrape off their tattooed skin, so if you came across an old mainlander in his seventies, with white bandages around their arms, between

1987 and 1988, that's right, he was Old X. . . . I'm sure it is quite difficult for you to imagine that he was the man many a young girl would think about on her wedding night. Of course, we don't need to get into the feelings of the young women any more now.

At this point you must be asking, and the mothers? Where had the mothers gone? What had they been doing? Why hadn't they taken good care of their children?

The mothers, like all other mothers who lived in poverty at that time, were busy making ends meet. All day long they wracked their brains thinking of ways to feed the family with their meager salary. If the mother was from the mainland she would have sold her last piece of jewelry by her tenth year in Taiwan, and during Chinese New Year of that year she would have gritted her teeth and pulled out the *cheungsam* or padded jacket from the bottom of the trunk to make new clothes for the children. Without their husbands' explanation of the Lei Zhen[15] incident in September or any disclosure of additional military secrets, the mothers knew before anyone that they, like the political leaders in power, would never return to the mainland.

Except for shopping, the mothers stayed at home. During the radio days they listened to *93 Club* and *Broadcast Novels*; during the television days, they watched *The All-Stars Show* and *Joy to the World*. It was later, when people became immune to fear, that more mothers started to play mahjong, since they no longer had to fear the terrible penalty stamped on their ration cards (on their first offense the penalty had been to cut off so

[15] Lei Zhen was the victim of political persecution. He founded the *Free China Magazine* with many liberal intellectuals. The opinions they expressed were intolerable and offensive to the GMD leaders then.

many months of rationing, and the second time they were caught playing mahjong, so many more months).[16] Usually the regulations were not that strictly enforced. If the sound of mahjong playing leaked out from someone's house, a few days later the wife of the highest-ranking military official would pay the guilty party a courtesy call. Of course, if the family playing mahjong happened to be the family with the highest-ranking officer, the biggest house, the first red brick wall in place of a bamboo fence, and the first television, then nothing would happen at all.

But very often the mothers varied according to their armed service affiliation.

The mothers in the air force compound were the most westernized. They knew how to wear make-up, and it was said they all danced and spoke some English. The mothers from the army compound were conservative and honest; maybe it had to do with the low pay of the army. The playing of mahjong was the most rampant in the navy compound, which had the greatest number of psychotic mothers, possibly because their husbands were away from home most of the time. The military police compound mothers were almost all native Taiwanese, and they were all young, some of them still childless. The children who went to their compound to play would feel alienated and not go anymore because they couldn't understand Taiwanese dialect.

The strangest of all the compounds was the military intelligence compound. The fathers of the compound were away most of the year, and some residents never met each other in their lifetime. Many of them were Cantonese, and all the adults and chil-

[16] In the 1950s, unregistered group gatherings in private were prohibited for political reasons. Mahjong was also a form of gambling considered to be detrimental to society.

dren would talk about Mr. Dai day in and day out, as if Dai Li[17] were still alive, a father figure to them all.

Some of the mothers in the military intelligence compound started to live with a widow's mentality. The strong took over the responsibilities of the family and supported the young and old, and we can deduce the length of the husband's missions by observing the age differences of the children. Other psychotic mothers would let their children run all over the place like wild animals, leaving them to themselves. The children of the compound all dreaded filling out family survey forms at the beginning of the semester. One girl who always got first place in class once broke into tears at her desk, because she was afraid that people would find out that she was different, that she had taken her mother's last name instead of her father's, because he had to work under cover. This embarrassed her to the extent that even when Little Ling told her about Old X in exchange for her top secret, she went back on her word and wouldn't give in.

As for the many who married local boys, they later became dissatisfied with life. For example, a woman's husband failed to share the housework like the mainland boys in her memory, and therefore she came to the conclusion that he must have been influenced by the rampant male chauvinism lingering from the time of the Japanese occupation of Taiwan. For example, come election time, she would feel compelled to speak in defense of the Guomindang and debate with her husband to the verge of bringing about a family conflict. Therefore, to the lonely girls who sometimes wonder where all the boys from the military compound have gone: in addition to deeply sympathizing with you, I must also remind you not to forget how

[17] Dai Li was the founding father of the Chinese military intelligence system, a legendary figure who was killed in a plane crash in 1946.

much you once wanted to leave the compound and this land, in whatever way.

Do you remember the age when you had just begun to contemplate the future? Contemplate it, even though you were in love with some boy from the compound, and on the summer nights when all the parents were busy watching the soap opera on television or enjoying the cool breezes, the hillsides would be filled with lovers (before or after, you would discover almost the same scene in Tennessee Williams's movies, the young boys and girls wandering through the night in the conservative, sweltering hot, patriarchal and repressed small town in the American South, not being able to express what their bodies and souls thirsted for), and among the deafening cries of the cicadas, you would explore each other's bodies feverishly, while bidding your lover a silent farewell in your heart. Naturally, many farewells came when the boys had to serve in the military or go to military school after flunking the joint entrance examinations for college, but most of the time, they were the result of the girls' coldhearted decisions.

Do you remember? You, the girl who missed the opportunity and failed to leave—unlike those who went to the United States in the 1950s by marrying black Americans and American GIs, or those who went abroad to study in the 1960s or became stars or singers, after finding out that this was the only profession in which one could reap rich harvests without much toil, a profession much suited to the resourceless who wanted to get rich overnight in the years of Taiwan's economic takeoff—you gradually got tired of your childhood buddies who had nothing better to do but to gather at the ball court by the gate of the compound to smoke, chat, play ball, and wait for military conscription (even though they werethe people you wanted to hang out with till death intervened at some point in your life). It wasn't because of the profane words flung at you by some boy who'd just reached puberty while you passed by, hinting at your figure or sexual organs, nor was it the fact that some boys had grown to be as strong as wild beasts, and their stares and voices gave you a strange and uneasy feeling. . . .

It was just that you vaguely became aware that the childhood buddies who accompanied you on adventures into the hills and wilds were no longer qualified to accompany you on your adventure into the outside world. You couldn't even admit that you almost looked down on them, and felt that they didn't know anything at all about the future.

Therefore, when you left home to go to college or to start working, you were naturally attracted by the local boys who were quiet, conservative, and down to earth, in comparison to the boys from your compound. Even though some local families were worse off economically than those in the military compound, and the local boys seemed to be far less ambitious than the boys from the compound, who had grandiose visions of China and the world, the sense of stability and the many surprising attitudes of the local boys all opened a new window, bringing in a fresh breeze to your suffocating life. However, many years later, in careful retrospection, you would find out that your sense of suffocation did not come entirely from life in the military compound.

You girls who have left the military compound, and who still think of life in the compound, I can fully sympathize with your pang of nostalgia when you suddenly hear someone swear in a mainland dialect among the crowds. I will not laugh either when I hear of someone wanting to publish an ad in the paper to seek out her childhood companions or to form a "military compound gang," because she does not want to admit that the only "buddies" she had are those whose names constantly appear in the criminal reports in the papers. She could recognize them at a glance, even though the papers scarcely revealed any personal information about them (such as so and so Taisheng,[18] of Shandong descent, residing in Zuoying, Gaoxiong, or Gangshan, or Jiayi City, or Puxin, Yangmei, or Nanshijiao, Zhonghe City, or Liuzhangli, Nanjichang . . . the military compounds from south to north, and east to west). You also dread coming across taxi drivers who speak with a heavy mainland accent, and who start to curse the Guomindang and Democratic Progressive Party as soon as the traffic comes to a halt. You look at the strands of white hair on the back of the driver's head, and you can immediately conclude that he belongs to the group of soldiers who, straight out of military school, proudly chose to serve the country, but who had no means of joining the job market after retirement in their thirties or forties. . . . Otherwise, brothers from the military compound, where have you gone?

Of course, you feel indignant when your local Taiwanese husband diverts toward you the anger he feels after reading in the paper about privileged second-generation mainlanders such as Li Qinghua[19] and James Soong.[20] As you think back on your life, you cannot find a shred of privilege, except for the period of time when Mandarin was promoted and Taiwanese was banned; you were exempt from any form of physical punishment, humiliation, or discrimination (many years later your husband would still fly into a rage at the mention of this), simply because you had no way of offending the taboo. Very soon, in a matter of years, you all had to pay for this policy. A majority of your buddies, who could not make it into government agencies and who didn't go to

[18] Taisheng literally means "born in Taiwan."

[19] The son of Li Huan, the former premier of the R.O.C.

[20] James Soong (Song Chuyu) is the son of a former GMD general, who had good family relations with the Chiang family. He is presently secretary-general of the GMD's central Standing Committee.

military school, would be turned down by the managers of private and small companies because they could not speak or understand Taiwanese.

It would be difficult for someone who didn't live in a military compound, or for those who were born after the 1960s, Taiwanese and mainlanders alike, to understand that many kids from the military compound (especially if their compounds were equipped with markets, restaurants, and schools) had no experience at all with the "Taiwanese" before they left in their twenties to attend college or serve in the military. The only few exceptions were those with Taiwanese mothers, who could go to their grandmas' homes during summer vacation, and those who had Taiwanese friends in school. For the large number of mainland mothers, their only contact with the Taiwanese through the years was with the "civilians" who sold vegetables in the market. Therefore, in the minds of the mainland mothers, the Taiwanese are basically divided into two categories: those who can do business and those who cannot.

So you are indignant at being classified as belonging to the privileged group; you also have a difficult time accepting the injustice of being equated with the Guomindang simply because your father is a mainlander. Rather than saying that you grew up drinking the thin and diluted milk of the Guomindang (which is the way your husband puts it when he jeers at you), you actually feel that your relationship with the party is more like that of an estranged couple who should have gotten a divorce long ago. Sometimes you hate the party more than your husband hates it, because within you are feelings of betrayal and desertion. Even though you were never formally inducted into the party, you cannot help but jump to its defense when you hear people (who do not bear the political burden of the GMD) attack it vehemently. As you seek out loopholes in your opponent's speech, you also wish to God that you could spill your guts and criticize the party without feeling guilty.

It's not that you don't have the chance to do so. Remember the last time you went home to your mother's alone with your kid? Didn't you criticize the Guomindang at the dinner table while watching the evening news? Only because no one (such as your husband) was standing to your left (politically speaking) could you happily play the role of an unburdened oppositionist, resting assured that someone to your right (your father) would always stand up to defend this party that you love and hate, that you should have separated from years ago.

You might not know that in the still of night when the elderly have trouble sleeping, your fathers also cannot help but admit they wish they were in your shoes. How your father wishes that one day he may be able to be like you and to holler at the top of his lungs, "Damn you motherfucker GMD! You tricked us into coming to this island and lied to us for forty years." It was only until the moment we returned to the mainland to visit relatives that we found out that in the eyes of our remaining relatives, we were Taiwan citizens. Taiwanese, though on the island where we have lived for forty years we are constantly referred to as "You mainlanders." Thus, those who are accustomed to reading their children bedtime stories will find out sooner or later, in Aesop's fables, that they resemble the bat who is neither bird nor beast, a being with no identity.

To sum up, you must admit and adjust to the fact that people like you are becoming a rare species.

The truth is, if you compose yourself and rely only on your animal instincts, it will not be difficult to find, among the sea of humanity, the buddies you have either lost track of or deserted. For example, the chief conspirator in the NT$100,000,000 kidnapping case: when he recited the lines, "Proudly I paraded across the city, unperturbed by my imprisonment. I shall relish the slash of the blade across my neck, for my youth has not been forsaken!" before reporters, didn't you blurt out, "Oh, so here you are!" before you could carefully go over the incident, and read about his brief personal background?[21]

In junior high, weren't you bewildered by the new Chinese teacher in his fifties, who spoke with a Hubei accent and was still single, simply because he always strayed from the textbook in his lectures? Once, with tears in his eyes, he recited, in the fashion of Peking Opera, the lines that the young Wang Jingwei[22] composed in prison, after his failed attempt to assassinate the prince regent. You conscientiously copied the verse into the blank space in your textbook, and wondered why this notorious traitor in the history of the Republic could have such an admirable and human side to him as well. Probably because the Chinese teacher kept violating such taboos, he was transferred at the end of the semester.

Now, many years later, you come to assume that he wouldn't have any way of knowing how many young and hot-blooded youths he had inspired, and how he had led them to seek out a just and sacred reason for their cause.

So the boys who used to hang around at the gate of the compound, your gutless buddies—or so you thought because they only dared to challenge the gangs from neighboring compounds instead of venturing into the other world—were among them. Just when you were about to give up on them, some were already

[21] The author is referring to Hu Guanbao, an executed bandit who flunked military school and eventually obtained a master's degree from an American college.

[22] He is a controversial figure in contemporary Chinese history. Originally a revolutionary hero who was the comrade of Chiang Kai-shek, he later took a different stand and lost to Chiang in a GMD power struggle. Therefore, he is remembered as a traitor in modern Chinese history because he had cooperated with the Japanese during the Sino-Japanese War (1937–45).

polishing their knives, joining gangs, robbing banks all over the island, and killing people in cold blood. When they were busted, you didn't even need to read the story in the newspaper explaining that the bandits grew up in a certain military compound on Guangfu Road in Xinzhu to recognize them. One look at the picture of the criminal in handcuffs and shackles and you would be able to address him by his childhood nickname; as for Brother So-and-so, who traveled all the way to the United States, convinced that he was removing a traitor for the good of his country, you have no trouble at all believing that he was just living up to his lifelong motto: "I shall relish the slash across my neck, for my youth has not been forsaken!"[23]

Of course, not all the brothers who gathered at the gate of the compound fall into this category. The eldest son of the Shen family, like many of his buddies, sailed away to the seven seas, and became a successful securities broker.[24] Twenty years later, in a newspaper interview, you can still detect characteristics of the military compound in him. When no one in the entire country believes that the reason he wants to convert the former Tangrong property into land for commercial use is to build a beautiful building like those he has seen in other beautiful countries, and not just to make a huge profit out of the transaction, you are probably the only person to believe that he is telling the truth. On the other hand, you are surprised that a

[23] The author is referring to Che Qili, a mafia leader who went on a special mission to assassinate Henry Lin (Jiang Nan), the author of a controversial biography of former president and son of Chiang Kai-shek, Chiang Ching-kuo. The events surrounding the murder are the subject of *Fires of the Dragon: Politics, Murder, and the Kuomintang* by David E. Kaplan.

[24] The author is referring to Shen Qingjing, a self-made tycoon who started out as a sailor.

successful businessman like him, with billions of dollars worth of assets, would still harbor such an ambiguous, unfathomable, and hopeless love for his country, like the patriotism that you showed a dozen years ago.

And there were others, right? Such as the Wang family's Brother Xuan. They were the first family in block number five, who operated a breakfast stall from their front door. Xuan Ge would help his mother with the washing, fixing, and money-changing. Thirty years later, when you see him, the minister of finance, promoting his policies in newspapers, on television, and through other media, your female instincts tell you not to doubt his integrity, intent, and expertise. Rather, it is the pervasive "my country's future is my responsibility" type of mentality, typical of those who grew up in military compounds, in his speech that makes you feel uneasy.[25] Nevertheless, it gives you every right to exclaim in a flood of emotions, "Oh, so here you are, my buddy from the military compound!"

Well, those brothers, the good, the bad (from the viewpoint of law), the successful, the failed (from the viewpoint of money and power), the existent, the nonexistent, the remembered, the forgotten, and the mere twisted memories . . . please allow me to overlook time and space and consolidate 1949 to 1975 (the year Chiang Kai-shek died and the ideological myth collapsed) into a moment in time. Also, please allow us to convert our eyes into cameras, because I have already laid down the tracks for you, in the back alleys of the military compounds at the edges of cities and towns for the middle- and lower-ranking GMD officers;

[25] The author is referring to Wang Jianxuan, the former finance minister known for his sense of righteousness and his blatantly direct approach. He is now running for a seat in the legislature.

please take your time as you move along these tracks. . . . Music? As you please, but my selection is a popular old Mandarin song, "Take Care of Yourself Tonight"; those of you who have undergone military training on Mt. Chenggong[26] should remember this song, for it is broadcast all over camp every night at bedtime: "The south wind caresses your cheeks, bringing the thick fragrance of flowers; the south wind caresses your cheeks, as the moonlight and starlight dims. . . ."

Let's go—

Don't be surprised, the guy lifting weights in the backyard of the first housing unit is, you got it, Li Liqun.[27] . . . Other than painting, he doesn't make any noise, therefore he does not disturb Gao Xijun,[28] who is studying under the lamp next door, right across from Chen Changwen,[29] Jin Weichun,[30] Zhao Shaokang.[31] . . .

Shh, let's pass by quietly, these two families are more interesting. The girl dressed in a go-go outfit practicing an English song is Ouyang Fei-fei. At sixteen she already has a very nice figure, but she still isn't satisfied with herself and hopes to be as tall as Bai Jiali, who lives next door. Of course you wouldn't be surprised to see Bai Jiali in the fourth housing unit, draped in a bedsheet and pretending that it is a nightgown, with a mock microphone in hand, repeatedly practicing the lines, "Honorable

[26] All the boys in Taiwan have to receive six weeks of mandatory military training in the Mt. Chenggong Camp during the summer before they start college.

[27] A well-known actor in Taiwan.

[28] A renowned economist and opinion leader in Taiwan.

[29] A prominent lawyer who is actively involved in politics as well.

[30] The publisher of *Business Weekly* and a prominent member of the business community.

[31] A renowned politician who once served as a legislator and director of the Environmental Protection Administration.

guests, ladies and gentlemen, today I am going to introduce to you . . ."[32]

Hey, you! Don't start staring! The little girl who is reading a novel (on the sly) under the tiny light bulb in the fifth housing unit is also very cute. She could be Zhang Xiaofeng, or Ai Ya, or Han Han, or Yuan Qiongqiong, or Feng Qing, or Su Weizhen, or Jiang Xiaoyun, or Zhu Tianwen (listed in order of age); anyway, she's so tiny that I cannot tell you who she is.[33]

Of course, not only girls like to read for leisure. We have skipped one house; you may have noticed a little boy reading. What? Can't you tell Cai Shiping from Ku Ling?! You've done both of them wrong, it was Zhang Dachun, so we better move on fast lest he start to abuse us with Shangdong vulgarities. Yes, he's been like this since childhood. . . .[34]

The little girl and little boy next door playing house who have just finished their homework, bet you couldn't tell, are Cai Qin[35] and Li Chuanwei.[36] Of course, they could also be Chief Chao Chuan and Annie Shizuka Inoh Nengjing.[37]

In the ninth housing unit, Little Ling is quietly taking a bath.

The tenth house is pitch dark, because Zheng Di and Zheng Jie, who are still in grade school, have accompanied their mother, who went to ask for the settlement fee their father left behind

[32] Both Ouyang Fei-fei and Bai Jiali are very popular singers and television program hosts.

[33] The names mentioned here are all contemporary women writers who have contributed to Chinese literature in Taiwan.

[34] The names mentioned here are all popular male writers who have dominated the contemporary literary scene in Taiwan.

[35] A famous singer.

[36] A well-known anchorperson for news programs on TV.

[37] Chief (Zhao Chuan) is a popular male vocalist, and Annie Shizuka Ino (Yi Nengjing) is a popular teenage idol, singer, and actress who starred in such films as Hou Hsiao-hsien's *Good Men, Good Women* (Haonan hao hü).

for them. They are from the military intelligence compound that I have mentioned. No one has seen their fathers since the family moved in . . . until thirty years later. . . .

The eleventh. . . .

(Parting is such sweet sorrow, we'll meet again in our dreams.)[38]

Oh!

In remembrance of my buddies from the military compound.

[38] These are lyrics from "Take Care of Yourself Tonight."